# PETRA'S Canvas

## ANN ROBERTS

Bella
BOOKS
2011

First Bella Books Edition 2011

Printed in the United States of America on acid-free paper
First Edition

Editor: Anna Chinappi
Cover Designer: Linda Callaghan

ISBN: 978-1-59493-231-1

*For Susan*

## Acknowledgments

It's tricky to write about well-known places. Too little accurate detail can leave readers shaking their heads and too much information ensures that the descriptions will become antiquated within a few years. I've split the difference and while I hope you recognize the basic landmarks, I've invented several of the locations.

One place that is absolutely real is the Fairbanks Inn. My partner and I were fortunate enough to stay there a few years ago. I'm grateful to Kathleen and Alicia, the very hospitable innkeepers. They manage a wonderful establishment and were gracious enough to let me interview them. If you're going to P-town, check them out! As for some of the historical mentions, I consulted Karen Krahulik's *Provincetown: From Pilgrim Landing to Gay Resort*, an excellent resource.

This book wouldn't have been possible without the help of my wonderful editor, Anna Chinappi, who lives to be cheerleader, critic and questioner. Thanks for making it better. And finally, I am always grateful to Bella Books for their continued support of my writing.

## About the Author

Ann Roberts is the author of *Furthest from the Gate*, *Keeping Up Appearances*, *Brilliant*, *Beach Town*, *Root of Passion*, *Beacon of Love* and the Ari Adams' mystery series that includes *Paid in Full*, *White Offerings*, and *Deadly Intersections*.

She lives in Arizona with her partner of sixteen years, their college-bound son, and two Rhodesian Ridgebacks, Sadie and Duke. Please visit her website at www.annroberts.net.

# Chapter One

Their marriage would be an endless ride on the Tilt-A-Whirl. That was the image that came to Dani O'Grady as she stewed in the front pew of Trinity Cathedral witnessing her only son marrying his ex-stripper girlfriend. Trapped in a swaying and rocking domed car, her poor Liam would eventually scream and throw up—preferably on his superficial and egocentric wife Cassidy—until they both pleaded for it to stop.

She fidgeted on the hard bench and scrunched her nose at the four different perfumes assaulting her olfactory system. *The Obsession is making me want to barf, but I love the smell of Pleasures and whoever is wearing True Star has exquisite taste.* She turned her head slightly to the left and attempted to identify the fashionable guest, but all she got was a good whiff of Uncle Jimmy's Old Spice. *Yuck.*

Attending a church wedding was like swallowing an entire bag of O'Grady Sour Puckerz. It seemed all sweet and sugary at first but eventually it turned tart and bitter—and Liam's nuptials were no exception. In fact, it was worse because she was paying for it. She'd lobbied for a less traditional ceremony, but Cassidy whined until Liam promised her a fairy-tale wedding. Dani had acquiesced on every detail except the horse-drawn carriage.

So she paid for forty minutes of heterosexual religious drivel. As the minister droned on she pictured him in drag. *He's already wearing a long robe, but I wonder how he'd look in Dastardly Pink lipstick?*

"The Bible makes it clear that marriage is the cornerstone of society." *Whose society? Not mine apparently.*

"Marriage is sacred and any man and woman who enter into this union make a commitment to God." *Then God's gotta be pretty pissed about the divorce rate.*

"The Lord has bound your hearts together in the spiritual fellowship of marriage." *Doesn't fellowship imply kindness and inclusivity and not a huge Keep Out sign for ten percent of the population?*

When he finally asked if anyone objected she opened her mouth then quickly clamped it shut when Ray elbowed her a little harder than necessary. She took a deep breath. Thank God her personal assistant was beside her to ensure she maintained an appropriate level of decorum and stayed out of the *New York Post* gossip column.

She'd made her case to Liam several times, but he insisted his motivation for marrying Cassidy was the mutual love in their hearts, not the pea-sized embryo growing in her belly. The fact that he'd knocked her up after a drunken night of passion didn't dissuade him from doing the right thing despite Dani's argument that the right thing wasn't always defined by a puritanical moral compass.

And she saw what he couldn't. She was certain that underneath the pounds of lace, satin and sequins of Cassidy's Dolce and Gabbana wedding dress was her true heart—the one of a greedy predator. And Dani wondered if she'd folded the divorce papers and tucked them inside her garter belt for quick access once she became Mrs. Liam O'Grady, daughter-in-law to Dani O'Grady, CEO and heiress of the O'Grady Candy fortune.

She fished an O'Grady Peanut Cluster from her handbag and one of her ear buds. Her red hair surreptitiously covered the white cord, and soon "Stairway to Heaven" drowned out the arrogant minister while she quietly chomped on the sweet and salty nirvana.

"Shh," Ray whispered.

She quickly dialed down the volume, swallowed the candy and closed her eyes. *Chocolate and music. My favorite drugs.* Clearly her lesbian cynicism was in overdrive and if she was going to endure the next several hours of hugging, smiling, dancing and accepting congratulations during this traditional heterosexual ritual, she needed to locate the small nut of sincerity that lurked in the deep recesses of her brain, dip it into a vat of charming personality and cover it with a chocolate coating of dishonesty that would fool everyone, including Liam, who understood her emotions better than she did.

Why had she ever let him pursue that psychology degree? Why hadn't she forced him into the candy business rather than let him spend his days working with vets suffering from post-traumatic stress at the VA? *Why couldn't I squash that strong altruistic conscience he inherited from his grandfather?*

She'd gladly agreed to an open bar for the 300 guests despite the Plaza's ten thousand dollar price tag, and she'd definitely need a shitload of martinis by six o'clock. She felt a vibration against her hand and slid her phone onto her lap. Ray scowled and she glared. After all, she was the boss.

It was a text from her latest hookup, a woman with fabulous lips and the most annoying laugh she'd ever heard. After one night she'd known the great lips weren't enough, but the woman had snuck Dani's number from her phone while she was in the bathroom. *And if I could only remember her name . . .*

She wanted a real date and Dani didn't do dates, particularly with women who only wanted her money or a trial run at lesbianism. And this one definitely wanted a sugar mama. She rolled her eyes at the message.

*You're so hot. I want to lick your heat.*

She grimaced and noticed Ray was reading over her shoulder. There was more, but she quickly tossed the phone back in her purse and closed it.

They were in the home stretch of the ceremony now, each parroting the vows uttered by the minister. She almost chuckled out loud at the thought of Cassidy promising to love, honor and cherish Liam, her dear son who'd practically grown up with her since she had been barely twenty when he was born, the result of a one-night threesome with two strangers she'd picked up in a bar. *So who am I to judge Cassidy?*

Cassidy's eyes bulged as he slipped the diamond crusted wedding ring onto her finger. It nestled against the impressive two-and-a-half carat rock she'd demanded for an engagement ring. Even after the minister resumed his diatribe she continued to stare at her hand like a child enamored by the shiny object. *No, not a child, a cat. Like a puma or a bobcat, one of those vicious predators sitting under a tree with a victim's leg between its huge paws, chewing until the bone was clean.*

"Smile," Ray growled through clenched teeth and pressed her fingernails into Dani's palm.

She stifled a yelp and forced a smile, picturing little staples securing the corners of her mouth into an upright angle. *I won't think about it anymore. I won't think about how much the ring cost or the five-tier cake Cassidy demanded or that I'm sitting in Trinity Cathedral and God's lightning rod could strike me at any moment if the Christian right is really <u>right</u>.*

She gazed up at the enormous stained glass, imagining a bolt of searing electricity firing from Jesus' eye and striking her dead. Then she glanced at Liam and his tentative smile. If Jesus really was divine he would reduce Cassidy to a pile of diamond shards and burnt lace.

Ray pulled her to her feet, and she automatically applauded as Mr. and Mrs. Liam O'Grady descended the altar, Cassidy's boobs jiggling with every step, threatening to pop out of the low-cut neckline. Dani thought the gown was entirely inappropriate, but it ensured Cassidy would get what she wanted at the reception—complete attention. All the women would talk about her, and the men would ask her to dance just to be inches from that chest.

She followed the procession down the aisle with her frozen smile still in place, regretting every step. The ridiculous silver pumps could've been wooden clogs for as well as they fit. And she was rather certain her slip had crept up amid all the standing and sitting required during the ceremony. It felt like she'd acquired a boil the size of a basketball on her butt. *People will think I'm wearing a bustle, and I've time traveled from the nineteenth century*. Thank God Uncle Jimmy shuffled behind her, lost in his own private world, mumbling about his own wedding fifty years ago at Niagara Falls.

"I need the bathroom," she whispered to Ray as they arrived at the vestibule.

"Hurry," Ray hissed. "I agreed to come with you on the condition that you didn't disappear, remember?"

Like any good assistant, Ray knew all of her tricks including the one where she quietly slipped away from any distasteful large gathering and either left or hid to avoid the air kisses, gossip and sniping that were the inevitable side effects of such events.

"I promise," she whispered.

She nodded at Liam who gave her a questioning look and sidestepped toward the powder room. She rushed inside and locked the door behind her, grateful to separate herself from the awful affair. She glanced about the small space littered with all of the preparatory detritus Cassidy and her attendants had abandoned when the ceremony began. Casual clothing, makeup and garment bags covered every chair and sofa. Instead of shoveling a heap to the floor she leaned against the door and pulled up the folds of the cerulean blue silk dress. As she suspected static cling had plotted against her and her slip had climbed over her ass.

She yanked at it only to have it grip her thighs like a cast. *That's not going to work*. She held her dress up and tiptoed across the mess to the full length mirror and studied her slip. She debated whether she should just remove it and let everyone stare at her French bikini underwear lines, but when she thought of what might show up in the expensive photographs she dismissed the idea.

She turned and took in her profile. At forty-five she sweated daily with her dictatorial trainer to keep her size ten figure although certain designers were bent on humbling women and ran their sizes small, forcing her into a twelve. *At least I have decent boobs and an okay ass except for today.* The long mirror lifted her self-esteem and the afternoon sunlight played on the highlights she'd added to her shoulder-length red hair. It'd been a gamble to wear it down at a formal event and she'd wondered if it was appropriate for church. Most of the female guests had pulled theirs back for a dramatic, elegant look but she'd rebelled against the advice of her stylist and opted for something softer, perhaps because she needed to lighten her mood.

She wrestled with the slip that refused to unclamp from her thighs. No matter how much she pulled at the fabric, it boomeranged against her pantyhose.

"There's an easy way to get rid of that," a voice said.

She jumped and whirled around. A woman in a gray suit leaned against the bathroom doorjamb, an unlit cigarette between her fingers. Long chestnut brown hair framed an oval face and her features were perfectly symmetrical. Her black dress shirt was stylishly untucked and she'd only buttoned it halfway up, revealing a decent amount of bronze skin. She was beautiful and Dani doubted she'd seen her twenty-fifth birthday.

She went to the bathroom sink and turned on the tap. "Water naturally fights static cling," she said.

She approached Dani with dripping hands and dropped to her knees. Dani stepped back, nearly falling over a makeup case left on the floor, and the woman grabbed for her waist and pulled her upright. Dani gazed into her warm brown eyes and heat poured out of her as strong hands stroked the fabric along her thighs until the stubborn wrinkles disappeared and the slip returned to its full length.

*I'm having a hot flash. That's all it is. I'm nearing menopause.*

*I'm old, and I'm stuck in a small confined space with a woman who's made my libido go nuclear.*

Only when her fingers grazed the curve of Dani's buttocks did she question her motives. Until that moment she'd touched her as a sister would. Her eyes widened as the firm hands traveled up and down her backside.

"Who are you and what are you doing in here?" she finally thought to ask.

The woman rose and pointed to the gold nameplate fastened to her jacket—*Cat, Special Moments Photographers.* "I was just hiding out until Cassidy texted me."

She noticed the expensive camera resting on a heap of plastic garment bags. Undoubtedly Cassidy wouldn't want the help to get too close to the guests. *Or maybe Liam. This woman is beautiful and exotic.*

"Well, that should take care of it. Drop your hem and let's see if it worked."

She twirled in front of the mirror and when the slip didn't move she knew the static cling was defeated.

"You look great but you're shaking."

Cat's hands trailed down her arms slowly like a sculptor working with clay. Perhaps she was being reshaped by this strange woman.

"Nerves," she lied.

"Then you need this." She withdrew the cigarette and a lighter from her jacket and lit up. "Here," she offered.

She hadn't smoked in years, but today was a perfect excuse. She took a long drag, the nicotine instantly buzzing her.

"I have a confession to make," Cat said. "When I was fixing your slip, I noticed your tattoo. It's a Petra, right?"

"Yes," she said, realizing that it would have been impossible for Cat to miss the wide band of color that spanned the length of her back. It was a miniature version of a painting by her former lover Petra, who'd made her living as a tattoo artist while she struggled to sell her work.

The piece was called *The Cleansing* and depicted a New

Mexico sunset after a monsoon. When the original finally sold for $50,000 and Petra vaulted to the forefront of the art world, she no longer needed a patron or a partner. Dani came home from a business trip to find half the closet empty and the studio she'd built for her abandoned except for an easel displaying a small pen and ink drawing of a character she assumed was Petra, crying in a corner with a paintbrush in her hand, having literally painted herself into a corner. An undergraduate English major, the symbolism wasn't lost on Dani.

"It's almost exactly like the original. But the contrasts between the dark and the light are a little off."

She chuckled. "That's probably my fault. Old age pigment."

Cat rested her hand on Dani's hip. "You're not old. And I know who you are."

The pronouncement reminded her of *who* she was and *where* she was. She dropped the cigarette butt into a used Coke can and headed for the door.

"I need to get out there, and you should get your equipment ready."

Just as she said the words a chime sounded and Cat checked her phone. "You're right. But I'm not done with you, Dani O'Grady. I want to see the rest of them."

She stopped with her hand on the knob. "The rest of what?"

"I want to see Petra's canvas."

"How did you know?"

She didn't answer. She adjusted her jacket and slung her camera over her shoulder, freeing her long hair from the strap.

The knob twisted in her hand as someone tried to open the door. "Dani? What the hell are you doing? Everyone's waiting. Are you okay?" Ray called from the other side.

"Girlfriend?" Cat asked.

"Personal assistant. I don't believe in girlfriends."

Cat gently pulled at Dani's bodice to expose much of her left breast, which was covered in blue and black ink to honor

*Loose Heart,* the painting Petra completed when she met the *next* woman of her dreams who would later take Dani's place as her lover. Whenever she looked at it she felt a combination of rage and despair.

"This must've hurt like hell," Cat whispered, her fingers massaging the sensitive slope.

Ray's bark and the other voices disintegrated against the power of Cat's touch. She rested her head against the door. *What in the hell am I doing here? This is my son's wedding, but I've got absolutely no desire to leave this room.*

"Mom! Are you okay?"

Her eyes popped open. "Just a sec, son," she called. She pushed Cat's hand away and said, "We've got to go."

"I know," Cat agreed, pulling her into a kiss.

Dani thought of a decadent chocolate truffle she'd had on a trip to San Francisco. When she opened her eyes the door was ajar and Ray's stony expression had replaced Cat. Her eyes were tiny slits and she'd crossed her arms.

"Do I want to know what was going on in here?"

She smoothed her dress and glanced in the mirror. "Nothing. I ran into the photographer when I came in to fix my dress. When the hell are they cleaning up this mess?" she asked in her highly annoyed tone hoping to change the subject.

"I have no idea," she said, grabbing her arm and pulling her through the door. "You're late. Half of the guests are already through the receiving line. I'm going on ahead to check on the reception." She pointed her finger and added, "Don't get lost," before she hurried away.

She assumed her place next to Liam whose face was a mixture of terror and anger, most likely from being sandwiched between his past and his future. *I pushed him out of the nest and demanded he fly. Instead he hooked up with a vulture who will eat him in midair.*

"What's wrong, Mom? You seem totally distracted."

He expertly read her moods, an unintended consequence of growing up while his mother was too young to recognize how the world would affect her on any given day. Life had been a daily science experiment with changing variables that often surprised them. He'd been her support, her comfort and her anchor against a depression that periodically suffocated her, particularly after Petra had left.

She kissed him on the cheek. "I love you, you know?"

He grinned. It was another exchange that had occurred often. He asked if she was okay, and she never answered the question but she always knew he cared. She wouldn't burden him with her worries. *I'm really going to miss having him around.*

Cassidy's saccharine voice amped up a notch as several of Dani's wealthy associates greeted her in the line. She cooed and thanked them for coming, shaking hands and cowering anytime someone wanted to kiss her. All of the dirty old men couldn't lift their eyes above her burgeoning cleavage despite the laser stares of their wives who hid their contempt and jealousy behind Botox smiles. Dani's attorney Harry Eisenberg offered only a nod to Cassidy, well aware of the future financial and legal headaches she could cause after little Thyme was born. *Why in the hell would anyone name a child after a spice used for embalming?*

He gave Liam a strong hug and she smiled. At eighty, Harry had watched her grow up and raise Liam. He'd always been a part of their lives, promising her father on his deathbed that he would look out for Dempsey O'Grady's only daughter and take care of her fortune. Their relationship endured a defining moment when she was a high school senior—the afternoon when he'd come upon her and her first girlfriend making out in the den while they watched *Desert Hearts*. The young woman, a college student who tutored her in French, quickly departed and he stayed rooted in the spot. She'd never forgotten the thoughtful look on his face or what happened next.

He asked simply, "Is that the way it is?"

She'd said, "Yes, that's how it is."

He nodded. "As long as you get a good grade in French then I suppose she can offer whatever incentives will work."

He'd smiled then just as he smiled now, like a man comfortable with all of his secrets. He introduced them to his much younger date and Dani forgot her name as soon as he said it. Harry never dated the same woman twice, and Dani marveled that women in their thirties would date a man who was decades older. Of course, it didn't hurt that he still had a full head of silver hair, a great tan, all his teeth and incredible strength.

He patted Dani's hand and rolled his eyes. She nearly exploded in laughter but coughed instead.

"I need to speak with you today," he whispered.

She caught the edge to his tone and frowned. "What's wrong?"

He shook a finger and stepped away, allowing her to greet the next set of guests, a pair of Cassidy's stripper friends who'd managed to wear nearly an entire outfit between them. The well-to-do New Yorkers who never ventured below Central Park West except to work on Wall Street openly stared at the pair covered in purple and red respectively. After they passed, gushing about how perfect Liam and Cassidy were together, a hand touched her elbow.

"We need some pictures in the church," Cat whispered.

"Of course," she said, tapping Liam on the arm and avoiding another glance at Cat.

She led everyone back inside practically galloping toward the altar. She badly wanted a martini. Cat artfully posed the various groups, starting with the bride and groom. It only felt slightly awkward when she took her place next to Liam while Cassidy's parents, a nice couple from the Midwest, sidled up next to their daughter. Cat shifted slightly to the right to compensate for Dani's lack of a spouse, a partner or a father for Liam. She was alone and had been for much of her life except for the Petra period. She'd found only enough time for Liam, running the company and the occasional meaningless affair, usually while she was on a business trip. If she was an expert at anything it was locating the gay bars—or bar—in every town where she traveled, even those that supposedly didn't have a gay community.

She carefully stepped off the altar and caught a glimpse of Cat staring at her legs and the tattoo that ran the length of her left calf. Their eyes met for a moment and then another stream of encouraging words burst from Cat's lips as the bridesmaids lined up to claim their moment in O'Grady history.

Dani's cell phone vibrated again, and she thought of the hookup. Sure enough it was from her. *Baby, you rocked my world. Let's make some more wet magic.*

She shook her head and was about to reply when another text came through from Valerie, her CFO, who was still at the office crunching numbers for the end of the second quarter. When Cassidy had insisted on a June wedding, Dani had anticipated the event colliding with the end of the quarter, which was always a busy time. She tapped the keys while she stole a few looks at Cat, who flirted with Liam and the groomsmen as she positioned them on the altar.

Valerie texted a more complex question, and realizing Liam wouldn't approve, she hid behind a post and resumed her business. *What did we ever do before cell phones?* They parlayed back and forth several times until Valerie was satisfied. She pocketed the phone and discovered the wedding party had gone. Only Cat remained, repacking her gear. She smiled warmly when she saw Dani.

"I thought you'd left."

She shook her head. "No, I had to answer some texts. Where'd everybody go?"

"To the reception. I think Liam thought you got a ride with your assistant." She slung her bag over her shoulder and grabbed the folded light fixture, struggling to balance them both. Dani quickly took the light from her before it hit the floor.

"Thanks. That's too expensive to break."

They exited the church and she scowled at the vacant parking lot. *I paid for the whole damn thing and they left me behind?*

"Um, if you need a ride, I'd be happy to give you one," Cat said, "but I need to make a quick stop. I forgot a light so I need to hit my apartment in SoHo before I go to the Plaza."

She instantly saw the ramifications and remembered her chocolate-covered kiss. "Your apartment?"

Cat dumped her gear into the back of her old Karmann Ghia and grinned. "I have to have that light. It's a special one for indoors. You wouldn't want your new daughter-in-law's face covered in shadows, would you?"

Dani chuckled. "Was I *that* obvious?"

"No, but I'm an artist and I notice things."

"I thought you were a professional photographer?"

"That's a job. I'm really a sculptress. So do you want a ride or do you want to grab a cab?"

The cab would take less time and judging from the smoky look on Cat's face, it would be far less dangerous than stopping at her apartment. *If I walked around to the front of the church and hopped in a cab, I could be at the Plaza enjoying a martini in twenty minutes. And hugging Cassidy.*

"Fine. I'll take the ride. Thanks."


Cat expertly navigated the blocks between the church and her tiny SoHo apartment, veering down side streets and averting the congestion of the major thoroughfares. Dani pelted her with questions to keep the conversation mundane, learning that she was originally from Massachusetts and attending the NYU grad program in fine arts.

"What will you do with that degree?"

She looked annoyed as if others frequently asked her that question. "I want to work at the Met," she said evenly. She seemed to relax when she noticed Dani's approving nod.

She pulled into an alley and parked the little car in a reserved space behind a walk-up. Dani's mouth went dry as she turned off the engine and faced her.

She hesitated before she said, "I should only be a minute."

She bounded out of the car as Dani let out a slow breath, not realizing she'd been holding it. Her shoulders sagged and she pulled the rearview mirror toward her. All she saw were the flaws—the crow's feet that seemed to quadruple each week, the circles under her eyes that no amount of foundation could hide and the worry lines—rather worry *trenches*—that crossed her forehead.

*Why did I ever think she'd invite me up to her apartment? And what kind of photographer would she be if she showed up an hour late to the reception?*

She flipped the rearview mirror away and sunk deeper into the seat, wishing now that she'd taken the cab. A minute later Cat threw open the door and set the light in the tiny backseat while Dani sat up and attempted a regal, matronly pose, one suitable for her age. She folded her hands in her lap and crossed her legs at the ankles waiting for Cat to shuttle her to the Plaza and complete her gesture as a good samaritan. She was completely resigned to being rebuffed and totally unprepared when Cat leaned over and kissed her passionately.

The chocolate-covered kiss turned into a fountain that showered her until she tingled. Cat's tongue tantalized her mouth, and she kissed her back completely, her ladylike demeanor vanishing. *I'm the elder here. I've had ten times as many lovers as she has. I'll show her who the expert is when it comes to sex.* She pressed against her and was surprised again when Cat gently pushed her away. She shook her head in bewilderment, and Cat reached for a handkerchief in her pocket.

"You need to fix your lips or your son's going to know exactly why you're late."

She pulled the rearview mirror toward her and rearranged her face while Cat drove. She was humiliated and wanted to cry. Only Petra had ever succeeded in making her feel that way—constantly. *That's because she's the only person I've let into my life. One-night stands don't have any power. And Therapist Number Five said I hate sharing power.*

That much was true. She was a control freak who micromanaged everything in her life—her business, Liam and the few relationships she coveted. But she'd allowed Petra to drive their relationship and keep control. She'd given her everything, including her body for an art piece, and Petra had made a fool of her.

She automatically touched her chest and thought of Cat's gentle caress earlier and her comment about how much it hurt. She'd been correct.

When Petra had inked her chest she thought she might pass out. Later she realized that had been the point. They'd been together a year, and she had decided she would double the profits of O'Grady Candy before she turned forty, but Petra had made certain she paid for it. Petra took a lover, which traditionally had refocused Dani on the relationship, and when that didn't work, she took another and another. But Dani remained distant, spending most of her time at the office, fueled by the soaring profit margin that grew each month and the expansion opportunities that burgeoned.

One night she came home and found Petra surrounded by her tattooing equipment. She thrust a martini into her hands and pushed her into a chair. Incredibly thirsty for her favorite drink, she gulped it quickly and, unbeknownst to her at the time, the Percocet tablet Petra had dissolved in the glass. Three doctored drinks later she was swooning.

She said nothing as Petra peeled off her shirt and bra. When the point of the drawing pencil scraped across the flesh over her heart, she mumbled her protest but Petra only snickered. The spiked cocktail dulled the pain of the needle as it pierced the tender flesh, but it also made it impossible for her to think. She needed to form words. Petra had never inked her front, and she'd never wanted a tattoo near her breast. Petra had known this.

"Don't make it too big," she had managed to say.

"You'll just have to be careful with your wardrobe choices," Petra had teased.

Five hours later it was done, the last thirty minutes with her enduring a searing pain after the alcohol and Percocet had worn off. She'd groaned softly and Petra had smiled, perhaps in admiration of her talent or in pleasure of the pain she'd inflicted.

Before Petra covered the fresh creation with a bandage, she led her to the mirror and waited for the reaction. At first Dani saw only a large blue-black blob above her breast and she scowled at the size. She'd have to be quite selective about the open-collared shirts she picked unless she wanted people to stare at her chest.

"It's called *Loose Heart*," Petra had said, wrapping her arms around her waist and gazing into the mirror with her. "I think it appropriately summarizes this moment in our relationship. Don't you agree, darling? Are we not loose hearts?"

She studied the tattoo closely. The heart's lobes were bloated and spider web cracks covered the surface. While she admired the design's intricacy and the unusual use of color, it wasn't pretty. It wasn't loving. She'd been branded. *And against my will, too.*

Petra fondled her breasts and circled her nipples until they stood at attention. She closed her eyes and let the touch smother the aching pain on her chest. She'd thought they might make love until Petra groped her viciously and she cried out.

Her eyes flew open and she stared into the mirror at the dark eyes meeting her own. She still held her breasts in a vise-like grip.

"You need to rethink your priorities, darling," Petra had said cooly. "Spend tonight staring at your new artwork and pondering our life together. You've hurt me deeply. I'm wounded and I need comfort. I'm going to Dominique's. I'll be back in the morning." Then she'd kissed her gently on the cheek and added, "Don't forget to put a bandage on it before you go to bed."

She'd released her and spent the night with the woman who would eventually replace her while Dani had curled up on the bed in a fetal position and sobbed. She'd promised herself she'd stop working so diligently. *And I did work less and for a while she noticed. But only for a while.*

Now the tattoo seemed to burn. It was a common occurrence, one that she'd learned to accept over the years.

She returned the handkerchief to Cat and resumed her professional pose. She could see the Plaza in the distance and was surprisingly relieved. *I never thought I'd be grateful to see Cassidy.*

"Were you disappointed that I didn't ask you up?" Cat asked her eyes glued to the creeping traffic in front of her.

The question disarmed her but she answered quickly, "No, of course not."

Her gaze still focused on the road, Cat took Dani's hand and brought it to her lips. She kissed her knuckles several times and murmured, "Liar."

# Chapter Two

After a quick scolding from Ray about her tardiness, Dani found Romeo, her favorite Plaza bartender. He handed her a martini, and she made the rounds playing the part of the gracious hostess and the proud mother of the groom. She worried for a moment about what she would say if people asked what she thought of Cassidy. Fortunately everyone, particularly those old enough to have marriageable children, worded their comments as statements not questions.

"Cassidy's such a lovely girl."

"Cassidy and Liam seem quite happy."

"It was a beautiful ceremony."

It certainly was. The insane price tag could've fed a country in Africa for a year. She'd already decided that to appease her humanitarian guilt she'd donate $100,000 to a charity as a way to offset her daughter-in-law's hedonistic tendencies. *I can't wait for Cassidy's Christmas list. I'll bet the luxury car catalogs will soon litter their apartment.*

The slew of round tables that dotted the ballroom was a racetrack, and she navigated each turn making pit stops with influential colleagues and closely related family members. She posed for pictures, gave endless hugs that saturated her with ten different perfumes and pretended to listen attentively as two of Liam's former schoolmates vehemently shared their concerns in whispered tones. It shouldn't have surprised her that his fellow Harvard classmates were so perceptive or they just recognized that a shotgun wedding to a stripper was a bad idea. Halfway across the room Romeo found her and replaced her empty martini glass.

By the time she was close to the finish line—a seat next to Uncle Jimmy—she'd made a lunch date with an old friend, secured a meeting with a lucrative distributor and gained a pleasant buzz that would ensure her smile remained plastered on her face. Romeo was indeed the best bartender in the world, lacing her martini with extra gin.

She found Jimmy at a table near the back. All of the chairs were vacant, and she slid next to him certain that no one would join them. Jimmy was facing the wall, engaged in a rambling conversation with her dead father, Dempsey O'Grady, his brother, and business partner for forty years.

She pushed her chair closer to discern his mutterings over the live band and the wedding chatter. He smelled of Old Spice, the only aftershave he'd ever worn, but his liver spots, wrinkles and disappearing hair revealed his age. He was barely hanging on at eighty-seven. She often visited him at his care center to listen to his stories and his piecemeal version of the past, gleaning tidbits of advice that periodically dislodged themselves from the vise-like grip of Alzheimer's.

"Can't make the deadline . . . need more time in development . . . Traynor's an asshole . . . never'll make the shipment."

He was talking about the sixties and the seventies. She'd learned everything she could about the O'Grady employees and Traynor was one of the vice presidents her father had hired and Jimmy later fired. She sipped her martini and listened as his babbling turned to reminiscences of his life—his and Dempsey's mother who'd made the original candy, including Curly Q's, Sour Puckerz and Choco Delite.

"Gotta talk her into it, Dempsey. She's the future," he muttered and Dani smiled. She'd heard this conversation a hundred times. "It doesn't matter that she got an English degree. Dani's bright, and we need to send her to Wharton. She's gotta take over someday. And now that you've got the cancer . . . "

He choked up at that moment as he always did, and she tapped him on the shoulder until he came back to the world.

"It's okay, Uncle Jimmy," she said, suddenly missing her father terribly.

Applause filled the room as Cassidy and Liam made their entrance with Cat following behind snapping pictures.

Her gaze found Harry and when he noticed she was alone with Uncle Jimmy, he disconnected himself from his date's arm and joined her at the table.

"Hiding?"

She looked offended. "Of course not. Someone needs to keep Uncle Jimmy company, and it certainly won't be his good-for-nothing children," she added, throwing a glance at the table full of his offspring, their spouses and bratty kids. She'd bought them out years ago and kept the residual payments flowing into their bank accounts, thus ensuring they stayed far away from the business. It was an arrangement that suited everyone.

"What did you want to talk about?" she asked, finishing her fourth martini and motioning to Romeo, who acknowledged her in a second. *I'd marry that man if I was straight.*

Harry squeezed her arm and stared into her eyes. "I got some news yesterday that's a little shocking."

She chuckled. Once she hit forty very little surprised her. No topic was taboo, and she was open to just about anything. Even Liam's decision to marry Cassidy only threw her for a second. And now that the wedding was over she was working on an empathetic face for when he announced his inevitable divorce.

"Tell me."

Harry set his face in first position like a car getting ready to shift. He always started a serious conversation with the same expression. "Well, I wouldn't even mention it today except I know that you'll eventually check your messages and she may have already called you."

"Who?" she asked absently, noticing the hoots and shouts rising from the dance floor as Liam removed Cassidy's garter with his teeth. She shook her head and looked back at Harry.

"You have a sister, well, a half-sister," he added.

She froze. "Excuse me?"

"You may recall that your father spent a lot of time working the Eastern seaboard gaining distributors."

Uncle Jimmy swiveled his head. "Providence, Boston, Burlington, Augusta."

"While he traveled around," Harry continued, "he made dozens of trips to Provincetown."

Uncle Jimmy laughed and his shoulders bobbed up and down. He was staring at them now as if he was part of the conversation, a huge smile on his face.

"Apparently there was a woman there. Her name was—"

"Cruz."

They turned to Jimmy who seemed completely lucid.

"Cruz," Harry confirmed.

"What was she like, Uncle Jimmy?" she asked.

"She was *magnetico*," he replied and turned back to the wall.

"Like a magnet," she surmised. "Was she Spanish?"

"Portuguese," Harry said. He reached into his jacket pocket for the tiny leather notepad he carried with him and put on his reading glasses. "Her name was Cruz Santos. Her family came from Portugal and landed in Provincetown where they were fishermen for decades. Eventually they bought a part of the pier and opened a restaurant. One night your father walked in and their affair lasted a few years. Apparently she learned she was pregnant right after they broke it off. She had a baby named Olivia. That's your sister or half-sister, I guess."

Her first thought was that it was a joke, but she looked at Jimmy's smiling face and knew it was true. She swirled her drink, remembering that Dempsey was an enigma and never around. He always worked, and she went to boarding school after fifth grade. Their family survived because of the U.S. Postal Service. The fact that he had a second life *shouldn't* surprise her.

"Did Mom know?"

Harry shook his head. "I don't think so. You know how she was, Dani. Your mother was a distant woman. She wanted the money, the house and the social circle, but she never really wanted Dempsey. That's the truth." He waved a hand. "I don't want to get into the particulars right now. This is Liam's day. I just wanted you to know."

"Did you know?" She shot him a sharp glance that demanded honesty.

"No." He pointed a thumb at Jimmy. "I think he's the only one who did."

"Cruz. Cruz," Jimmy twittered. "Let's go down to the Seafarer, Jimmy. I'm feelin' like some chowder."

She imagined that was the name of the restaurant, and her father often *felt like something*. Her mind went into business mode and all of the ramifications. There was too much to process and her brain cells were numb from the alcohol.

Ray hurried over. "Get up here. It's time to cut the cake and for you to appropriately beam at your son and new daughter-in-law no matter how much of a slut she really is." She grinned at Ray whose expression remained deadpan until Ray turned toward Harry and frowned. "Today is not about business. Am I clear?"

Dani ignored her and asked Harry, "What does Olivia want?"

"I don't know. I'm guessing money, but she didn't say on the phone. She just wants to meet you."

Ray pulled her from the chair and she said, "I'll call you on Monday," dismissing the problem as business.

And that's what it was. Olivia wanted money from the company and Dani had no intention of thinking about finances today. *Today's about drinking.* She grabbed another martini as they passed the bar and joined her son by the cake. Cassidy's sister was making a toast, the content and vocabulary of which could've been written by a first-grader. Between the giggles and the tears she managed to convey her heartfelt message of love for her big sister who'd taught her so much. *Like how much grease to put on the pole?*

Once the reception rituals were completed—cake, toasts and the first dance, she stepped outside to the patio. She hated receptions almost as much as the ceremony. And why was that? She liked cake. She enjoyed dancing with Liam. But the other stuff was so *hetero*—throwing the bouquet and that whole garter thing was just macho man. *Too much ritual, that's it.*

Couples passed by, giggling from the booze she'd paid for as she leaned against the railing and stared up at the sky. She couldn't believe she had a sibling. Throughout her life she had often bemoaned the lack of a sister or a brother, but after eavesdropping on a conversation between her parents when she was ten, she knew she'd be an only child. Her mother Margaret insisted that she'd done her wifely duties and produced an heir. She told Dempsey she was done with breeding. It would ruin her figure. At that moment Dani realized how cold and vain her mother really was. No wonder he had sought solace from another woman.

She was almost jealous of him. He'd found love elsewhere but Dani had felt alone through her childhood. While most of the other wealthy mothers on the Upper West Side employed nannies to raise their children, Margaret O'Grady wouldn't stand for it. Therapist Number Three had convinced Dani that her mother couldn't bear being compared to someone else, and Margaret had decided that Dani's subsequent isolation from the world was a small price to pay for her pride. So she'd spent the first six years of her life friendless until she went to school, which proved disastrous. With no social skills she was again isolated until she went to boarding school four years later and escaped her mother's bizarre world.

She drained her martini glass, imagining she was her mother at one of their fancy parties. Margaret had lived for all the frivolity of wealth like expensive wedding receptions, beautiful gowns and a handsome husband. Dani had never been interested in any of those things and when her mother suddenly dropped dead from a heart attack just before her eighteenth birthday, it had been surprising and shocking but her pain floated to the surface and never submerged. And according to Therapist Number Two, that was a linchpin issue for her, one they never explored since she fired her after the sixth session.

The full moon illuminated the rich green lawn surrounding the hotel. Cigarette smoke wafted through the air, and she noticed a dark figure and a burning ember in the corner. She could tell from the outline it was a woman—Cat. She was staring in her direction but Cat said nothing and didn't acknowledge her. She felt incredibly vulnerable standing in the moonlight while Cat hovered in the shadows. She had to know she was there. The patio was empty except for them and a drunken couple making out on the steps. She watched the ember burst each time Cat took a drag. Realizing it was a battle of wills that she wanted to lose, she joined her in the darkness.

"Why are you standing over here? The moonlight's gorgeous tonight."

"I can see it," Cat replied in a voice that floated away into the night. "And I don't have to share it with anyone except you."

"What do you mean by that?"

She passed the cigarette to her and she inhaled deeply. *I could get used to this again.*

"There's an old legend about gazing at the moon. If too many people stare at her she becomes self-conscious and that's why she changes. It's an old explanation for the rotations of the earth. Legend says that if you stole a glance at the moon or hid in the darkness, the moon wouldn't notice and would stay full forever."

"I've never heard that," she said.

Cat molded herself against Dani's back and stroked her hair, pulling it to the side and revealing her neck. When her soft lips touched the exposed flesh, Dani closed her eyes and the imprint of the moon was a curtain dividing her practical, sensible self from the one she hardly knew, the persona that only Petra had seen—a darkness that glimmered whenever they made love.

Cat's touches grew more brazen without her reproof, and she pushed her against the stone wall into submission. She fell deeper into the unknown and felt no desire to scurry back to the safe side of the curtain.

Cat kissed the slope of her breast once again, caressing the angular heart-shaped tattoo, broken in half, as apparently Petra's love had been. Dani was too involved in her work to recognize her growing detachment and what little she noticed she dismissed as Petra's quirky artistic nature. *It was my fault. If I'd paid more attention to what was happening, I might've kept her.*

"I'm really horny," Cat whispered. "I want you naked, and I want to see the rest of them."

She rolled her eyes at the trite line, but Cat was determined to have her way. She unzipped her dress and unfastened her bra before Dani could stop her.

"Wait!" she hissed, pulling away and stepping behind a large potted plant. "We're in public." She re-hooked her bra but couldn't reach the zipper. "Help, please."

She turned, offering her back to the moonlight and Cat gasped. She'd heard that sound many times before from shocked lovers and even a salesclerk who'd accidentally opened the dressing room door when she was half naked. She carried Petra's favorite work on her back titled "At the Edge," a highly detailed and complicated piece featuring two naked women cradling each other during lovemaking. Their expressions were riveting, and Petra had told her she'd copied their faces when they made love. Dani had been so flattered by the compliment she'd readily agreed to endure days of agony on her stomach while Petra etched the ink into her skin.

When Cat made no effort to zip her dress she knew she was studying the amazing design. Eventually she heard the click of her shoes and felt the dress tighten around her, covering Petra's masterpiece again.

Cat rested her chin on her shoulder and circled her middle. "You're a goddess. Your body is a temple."

She chuckled slightly. "If you ask to worship at me, I'm going to puke."

"Too much a hackneyed cliché?"

"Slightly."

Cat took her hand and led her through the shadows that surrounded the enormous patio and down the side stairs where the limos waited in semicircle formation to shuttle the wedding party back to their homes.

"Which one's yours?"

She saw Ernest's unique silhouette leaning against the shiny black stretch limo, his wide frame hunkered over the soft glow of his cell phone. He was doing what he always did while he waited for her—texting his girlfriend who worked nights as a health aide.

She pointed toward him and Cat said, "That's perfect for what I want."

"Are you ready to go, Miss O'Grady?" he asked, snapping his phone shut and reaching for the door.

She knew she should go back inside and at least hug her son and new daughter-in-law, but they were probably out on the dance floor with all of the younger, serious partiers. Much of the older crowd had left after the cake was devoured, and only the diehards remained doing the Macarena and Electric Slide. They wouldn't notice she'd gone until much later, but then Liam would be hurt, certain that her abrupt departure was a symbol of her dislike for Cassidy. *Damn that kid. He's always psychoanalyzing everything, and he's usually right when it comes to me.*

Cat sensed her hesitation and rubbed her back. "Why don't you send him a text? Tell him that you're exhausted, and you'll call him tomorrow."

"That's a terrible excuse," she said already reaching for her phone.

"Or you could tell him that you're hooking up with the photographer for hot sex."

She ignored her and sent a message that simply said *I had to go. Love you. I'll explain later, Mom.* He'd think it was work.

They climbed into the limo and directed Ernest to circle the park a few times. Cat wasted no time unzipping her dress again and unclasping her bra but when Dani reached for her shirt, she pushed her hand away.

"No, you first. I'll catch up later."

She disagreed. "That doesn't work for me. We either enjoy this together or it doesn't happen."

Cat looked alarmed but she meant it. Too often she'd paraded around the house naked or nearly naked while Petra remained clothed. She'd claimed her body was inspirational to her work, but it was always Dani who felt vulnerable and powerless. Their relationship was an unbalanced scale where everything worked in Petra's favor, according to Therapist Number Seven. Such a situation would never happen in her business, a fact *all* of her therapists had thrown in her face. She was a gamesman and while she prided herself on fairness, she could be ruthless when necessary.

Cat conceded the point and stripped off her clothing. She stretched across the seat flexing her muscles so Dani could study her toned body. *That's the body I used to have ten years ago. That's what Petra saw when she fell in love with me.*

"Happy?" she asked seductively.

They both heard her phone vibrating again.

"Don't answer it," Cat said sharply.

"It could be work," she said, reaching into her purse. She saw the text from the hookup who was quickly moving to stalker status and groaned.

"What is it?" Cat asked, moving against her.

*C'mon, baby, light my fire* stared at them from the screen.

"Who the hell is that?"

"A woman I met last week who won't leave me alone."

Cat grabbed the phone and expertly tapped the keys. "Let

me help you. I know how to make people go away." She showed her the text before she hit send. *Stop texting my girlfriend, you fucking bitch!* "That ought to work."

She handed the phone back and resumed an erotic pose against the seat. "Now, where were we? Ah, yes. It's your turn to strip."

Dani suddenly felt incredibly inferior. But Cat had agreed to her terms, and she was a woman of her word. Discarding her clothing was like unveiling paintings and Cat gasped at each discovery. There were nine different pieces of various sizes and brilliant colors that had caused her proportional amounts of physical pain in the name of love. *At least that's what I thought.* Each chronicled a time during her relationship with Petra and when she stood in front of a mirror, she relived the high and low points.

Cat caressed her right shoulder and Petra's self-portrait, aptly titled *Epiphany*, which depicted the moment when Petra had realized she loved Dani. She'd captured her warm, vibrant eyes, and Dani always smiled when she stared into the mirror for the key to Petra's love had been her eyes. *And I knew it was over when I looked in her eyes, too.*

After Cat studied the tattoos on her front, *Loose Heart* and *The Flowering*, a blooming pink orchid that rode her panty line, and *Clinging Vine*, a gorgeous symmetrical study of nature that ran the length of her left calf and thigh, she gently turned her over and massaged her back. Dani knew from past experience that lovers were most impressed by *The Cleansing* and *At the Edge*, but her personal favorites were abstract pieces of intense color—*Kismet* on her left shoulder and *Birds of Freedom*, a colorful symbolic design of two birds that adorned her left upper arm.

The most simplistic one was the first and Petra had never liked it, telling her it was merely to acquaint her with the feel of the needle. Using only black ink, she had created an Arabic design on her right upper arm of several swirling lines that reminded Dani of the sun, its rays stretching out like leaves. While it wasn't nearly as complicated or as artistic as the others, she still stared at it the most because it was the first, and the memory of the needle touching her virgin flesh was imprinted on her mind. She'd thought of a cow being branded—the pain was unlike anything she'd experienced except childbirth. And by the time Petra had covered it with a bandage and kissed her gently, she'd decided that Petra would lie to get whatever she wanted.

It had taken nearly two months of coaxing before she allowed Petra to mar her lily-white skin. They'd fought several times over the issue, Petra proclaiming her body would be beautiful with body art and Dani retorting that tattoos were for prisoners and bikers. Petra had stormed out of the condo, leaving her alone with a knot of anxiety in her stomach that grew to a large mass by the time she returned three days later. Dani had barely been able to breathe let alone work. She discovered how much she loved Petra. It was much deeper than the puncture of a tattoo needle.

When Petra had called and said she'd come over, she greeted her wearing only a short robe which she quickly discarded after a deep kiss. She motioned to the dining room table where she'd displayed Petra's tools and planted herself in a straight back chair.

"This won't hurt too much, will it?" she asked.

"No," Petra had assured her as she prepared the machine.

That had been the lie. It had hurt like hell.

"You're amazing," Cat whispered in her ear, pulling her into a sitting position and kissing her fiercely.

Apparently the novelty of her body had worn off, and Cat saw her as a woman, not a sideshow attraction. They kissed and fondled, the gentle vibrations of the traveling limo adding to the pleasure.

"Go down on me," Cat said, leaning back. Her luscious center glistened, and Dani teased her thighs until she rocked her hips begging for satisfaction. She savored the sweet juices she could never market since women were the tastiest candy of all.

When Cat came her whole body shook, dislodging Dani's tongue and nearly breaking her jaw. It was probably her imagination, but she thought her gyrations caused the limo to fishtail across Central Park West.

"Are you okay?" Cat panted. "I didn't hurt you, did I?" She threw her head back and laughed. "It's just that there's nothing more satisfying than sex. Don't you agree?"

She shifted her jaw back and forth without any pain. "Well, an exceptional French chocolate truffle comes close."

Cat stroked her hair. "I've never had one. How is it that you can love candy so much and not weigh three hundred pounds?" She gently pushed her over and stroked her back. "Your body is gorgeous."

She closed her eyes and focused on Cat's caress and the hum of the limo while she imagined skating across the ice at Rockefeller Center. She made one revolution and then another, pumping her legs and feet into a rhythm. She propelled herself ahead, picking up speed as the sharp blades tore through the glassy surface. The other skaters vanished like melted snow and she leaned forward in an arabesque, extending her left leg behind her. It was almost like flying.

She twisted to the left and gained momentum, smiling as her speed increased. She edged the ice harder, scissoring her legs and preparing for the leap. When she vaulted into the air for the double-axle, she moaned and came hard.

The vision disappeared immediately as it always did, and she had no idea if she finished the difficult jump or fell flat on her ass. Therapist Number Five had suggested that the ice rink image occurred because she didn't fully connect with her partner during lovemaking. She'd fired her at the end of that session for her inability to see past the obvious.

She huddled against Cat, whose fingers were still deep inside her causing a small earthquake with each slight movement. Eventually it was too much and she pulled away.

"Had enough?" she gloated, lighting another cigarette.

She could only offer a slight chuckle. *I haven't had an orgasm like that in years. Make a note. More sex in large moving automobiles. To hell with saving the environment.*

Cat put the cigarette between Dani's lips, clearly determined to reintroduce her to nicotine. They shared the smoke and stared out the window at the tall buildings along Broadway. Ernest was obviously just driving around waiting for another instruction.

"I love New York," Cat said.

"Me too."

Cat faced her. "What do you love the most? You've lived here your whole life so you must be an expert."

She loved the city and everything about it, but the best parts of New York were intangible. It was an energy that some people couldn't stand. She'd worked with many customers who'd heard nightmarish tales of the Big Apple and when they came to visit they either fell in love with the raucous environment or demanded that she travel to them for any future business.

Cat nudged her shoulder. "Tell me," she said sweetly.

"I can't explain it. When I was little I thought the buildings could touch the clouds. They were so powerful and magnificent. And as I got older I felt safer being surrounded by so many people. I was never alone when I walked down the streets. And when I was home from boarding school I saw everything—theater, museums, Central Park." She looked at her and sighed. "It's home."

Cat seemed satisfied with her answer for she grew quiet and studied the vine along her leg, clearly marveling at the detail. Petra had been as good with a tattoo needle as she was with a paintbrush. *Clinging Vine* had happened during their first trip together when Petra tagged along to Las Vegas while she conducted business.

She'd caught her half-naked with one of the hotel bartenders in the suite's hot tub. She'd always tolerated the advances and flirtations of other women, somewhat proud that Petra was coveted by others. But she'd gone ballistic watching her fondle the woman's large breasts in the foamy jets. She'd practically thrown the woman out of the suite, focusing on the flowing pictures that covered her arms and back.

"Is that what you like?" she asked. "Is that what you find attractive?"

"Yes," Petra had answered easily, her hands caressing Dani's arms and neck.

She had touched the single tattoo on her arm and knew she couldn't compare to the buxom bartender. "What else do you want to do to me?"

Petra had seen a beautiful trellis that morning as she strolled along the hotel's ground. She described the balloon vine, its creamy white flowers in full bloom and assured her it would look marvelous climbing her leg. Dani had acquiesced out of love or fear, but she wasn't sure which.

She'd lain still for three different sessions while burning needles seared her flesh. It was excruciating but the absolute joy that it brought Petra, who giggled while she worked, made the experience worth the pain. Only when it was over and Petra titled the art *Clinging Vine*, did she once again feel belittled and betrayed, recognizing she'd allowed her vulnerability to be displayed on her body.

When she vented her anger, Petra's only response had been, "My love, it only represents you if you allow it to."

The logic made sense and when so many coworkers and friends commented on its beauty, she stopped thinking about its origin and ignored Petra's later indiscretions, always glancing at her leg when she needed a reminder of what she didn't want to be.

"I'll bet there's a story to each of these," Cat murmured, wondering if she'd spoken her thoughts.

She nodded and extended her leg for Cat to caress. "Yes, but they're very personal."

Cat's fingers traced the tendrils up and down her thigh. "I have a confession to make. Our meeting today isn't coincidental. I pushed for this job the minute I found out it was your son's wedding."

"Why?" she shrugged, nonplussed. As a wealthy woman she was used to people stalking her for favors.

Cat nervously fidgeted on the bench, her sexy confidence entirely depleted. She lit the last cigarette and tossed the package into her purse.

"It's just that we're kinda related," she blurted suddenly.

"What?"

"Not biologically," she added quickly. "But the woman who's like a mother to me is your half-sister, Olivia. It's more like we're connected by someone."

Lying naked in a limo on her son's wedding day, she wasn't at the top of her game. It took her longer than usual to connect all of the day's conversations. Harry had mentioned Cruz Santos, the woman from Provincetown who'd had an affair with her father. Olivia was the product of that relationship.

The mood shifted from pleasure to business in three seconds, and she reached for her bra. It wasn't uncommon for women to come on to her once they knew she had money, but usually she could spot the gold-diggers. She really appreciated the women who just said up front that they wanted a good meal, great drinks and hot sex. She'd misjudged Cat. *Maybe I'm losing my touch.*

"What are you doing here?"

"Are you furious?" Cat asked timidly.

She shook her head. "No, I'm not mad. I just wish you'd been honest about your intentions. If you're here to get something for your godmother, or your pseudo-mother or whatever you call her, I'd rather you talk to me not fuck me. I keep my personal and professional lives separate."

She gestured for the cigarette. Her lungs weren't used to such abuse but it felt good. She adjusted her dress and turned so Cat could zip her up and they could go back to the reception. Maybe Liam was still there.

Cat obliged but pulled her into a hug. "I didn't plan to sleep with you. I was just going to meet you and see what you were like. I'm protective of Olivia, and I don't want her to get hurt. I know she's been talking to your lawyer and wants to meet you." The words tumbled from her mouth and then she paused. "And I've heard the story of Petra's Canvas. It's one of those legends that's been passed around the art world but nobody knows who it is—"

"Thank God for small favors," she sighed.

"Then I saw you in the dressing room. And when I saw that tattoo I knew who you were and I wanted you for myself." Cat kissed the nape of her neck and Dani's spine turned to jelly and her head lolled to the side. "I don't want anything from you. Olivia's talked about you forever and she's always wanted to meet you but Cruz, that's her mother, begged her not to contact you. She said you didn't know."

"I didn't," she murmured.

Thanks to Romeo the world's greatest bartender, her brain had cannonballed into a vodka swimming pool and she refused to surface. Her coherency was drowning.

"Do you want to talk about this now?" Cat asked gently, already tugging at her zipper again. "I could tell you all about Olivia and what she wants."

She scowled and leaned back as Cat cupped her breasts lovingly. She wouldn't concern herself with the questions she should ask or the reasons she should grow indignant about Cat's continued sexual advances. She didn't protest as she nibbled her ear and once again stripped off her dress. Clad only in her bra, thong, nylons and garters, she watched Cat's fingers outline Petra's name above her panty line, which she had tastelessly included as part of *The Flowering* as revenge on Dani for her one and only affair.

"I fucked you because I wanted to fuck you. And I want to do it again and again."

Her voice slowed and softened, lost against the city noise outside and the purring engine. The silky dark hair that smelled like oranges tickled Dani's cheeks as she kissed her neck.

She sighed and pressed the intercom button. "Ernest?"

"Yes, ma'am?"

"I need you to make a stop, please."

"Of course, Miss O'Grady. Where are we stoppin'?"

"At the first liquor store you see. I need two bottles of Stoli and a carton of Marlboros."

# Chapter Three

The sidewalks were still empty when Ernest dropped Dani in front of the O'Grady building on Monday morning at six a.m. Dwarfed by the customary granite skyscrapers that dotted Lower Manhattan, the outrageous five-story pink building with blue awnings and white trim was a New York favorite and featured on several tour bus routes. The storefront looked like a cottage from *Alice in Wonderland* with slanted sides and uneven windows. When the O'Gradys had built the strange façade during the seventies some neighbors had complained to the city until their own businesses saw the financial benefit of the tourists. Even on her worst days, gazing at the building made her chuckle and reminded her that her life was a fairy tale—or rather a cartoon.

Ernest pulled away while she steadied herself against the building. She took a deep breath, ignoring the smell and taste of exhaust that hung in the air. She listened to the early morning traffic already littered with taxi horns and the hum of the city. New York was talking her favorite conversation.

It had been a "ten" weekend as Petra used to say, two days of nothing but insane hedonistic pleasure. The twelve hours of hot sex had easily balanced the torture of Liam's ridiculous wedding.

After Ernest had stopped and purchased the vodka and cigarettes, they'd significantly contributed to New York's air pollution problem by driving through three of the boroughs and all the way out to Islip before her 45-year-old body demanded she replace the limo's lumbar-unfriendly seat with her expensive Kluft mattress if they were to continue their tryst—and Cat had no interest in stopping.

By the time Ernest returned Cat to her car at the Plaza on Sunday afternoon, Dani's condo reeked of cigarettes, empty liquor and wine bottles dotted the expensive furniture and every sex toy she owned was strewn about the place.

In Cat's defense, she'd asked her several times if she wanted to talk about Olivia, but Dani was easily distracted by Cat's cute ass in a pair of edible underwear and her prowess with a dildo.

Only after Cat was gone and she'd sobered up by soaking in the tub for an hour, did her thoughts return to the idea of a sister and a cheating father. After she climbed out of the tub she sorted through old photo albums until she fell asleep three hours later.

*And I'd like to sleep now.*

As she passed through the candy shop all of the smells assaulted her at once and she inhaled deeply. Her critical gaze swept the small store which was clean, bright and functional. Done in greens and yellows decades before, she'd debated whether to remodel, but she couldn't bring herself to rewrite history. The candy sold itself and she could paint the store black and people would still wait in lines that stretched down the sidewalk at the height of tourist season. A display of Butter Swirl drops was slightly askew and she stopped to fix the array before heading to the back.

A small doorway separated the shop from the original, tiny factory her father and Uncle Jimmy had built. When O'Grady expanded they'd opened a plant in New Jersey, but she couldn't bring herself to close the twenty-thousand-square-foot factory that sat behind the shop despite the high operating cost. It was home. It was her best memory of childhood.

She found Gustav organizing the copper kettles used in the caramel room and chocolate kitchen. He arrived two hours before she did because he enjoyed the quiet that would eventually unravel when the other workers joined him and later when the tours came through, full of squealing children being shushed by their tired teachers or elderly people wanting to ask a million questions.

The kids called him "The Candy Man" and his unusual appearance added to the show. A throwback from the flower power era he wore his gray hair in a ponytail and preferred tie-dyed T-shirts and jeans instead of a customary apron. He often colored the ponytail an interesting shade such as mauve or St. Patrick's Day green. He walked with a limp, a gift from his tour in Vietnam, but he was the strongest man she knew with ripped muscles and shoulders.

She enjoyed watching the morning prep—cooking the corn syrup for caramel, steaming the sugar for the cream centers and mixing the chocolate. She plopped onto the stool he'd planted against the wall for her and sipped her coffee while she savored the wonderful smells as they collided together. She could almost taste the Choco Delites, but she frowned, realizing the nicotine she'd reintroduced to her body was interfering with what was usually an orgasmic experience. *Stop it. I certainly don't need to think about orgasms anytime soon.*

Gustav saw her and smiled. "Good morning," he said. The Eastern European accent he inherited from his parents was still thick despite spending almost his entire life in the States. "That was a very nice wedding. Thank you for inviting me and Rose."

Rose was his wife of forty years and an absolute crack-up. She managed the candy store and the tourists adored her. She was as sweet as the candy she sold.

"We wouldn't have had it any other way."

He looked like he might cry and he gave her a quick hug.

When he stepped back he was frowning. "Bah. You're smoking again."

"Don't give me a hard time, okay? It was a stressful weekend."

They exchanged knowing glances, and he returned to his work and she to her copy of the *Daily News*. Gustav, Rose and Harry were their family. They knew all the O'Grady secrets, and she shuddered whenever she thought of Gustav and Rose leaving the pink factory. He'd threatened retirement a few times, but he couldn't bring himself to step away from the refrigerated tables, melting machine or chilling room that he'd designed.

But she knew he wouldn't last forever. After his birthday each year she vowed to find someone to be his apprentice, but the one time she'd managed to cajole him into hiring an assistant, the poor woman had been so nervous she'd spilled an entire kettle of chocolate on the shiny floor before she ran out the back door and never returned.

"What did you think of the ceremony?" he asked.

"Exactly what you think I thought of it," she said, turning to the society page. Plastered above the center fold was a small article about the marriage of Liam O'Grady. *The ceremony was flawless, the flowers beautiful . . . blah, blah, blah.*

They wouldn't dare say anything negative about the O'Gradys since she generously contributed to three of the newspaper's pet charities and sent enormous Christmas candy baskets to all of the departments. If her father had taught her anything it was the power of good press.

She finished her first cup of coffee and felt the strong urge for a cigarette. She hurried up the stairs to her office passing the brightly colored doors at each landing. The three floors separating the shop from the executive suites housed important divisions of O'Grady Candy—shipping, customer service and finance. Each was its own little world designed by the people who worked there, most of whom had more than ten years of service. If she prided herself on anything it was maintaining employee loyalty.

She reached the top floor barely noticing the effort. *At least the cigarettes haven't ruined my lung capacity yet.* The executive offices of O'Grady Candy were unlike any other she'd ever seen. The entire floor was surrounded by glass that provided natural lighting and there were no walls, just brightly colored moveable panels that randomly divided the square footage. Most of them were covered with thank-you notes from New York City school students who'd taken a free tour of the O'Grady Candy factory. It wasn't uncommon to see the entire floor reconfigured throughout the day as people rearranged the panels to create conference areas or private work spaces.

She threw her briefcase on her father's old wooden desk and took her purse out to the fire escape. She wouldn't dare smoke inside. In fact, hardly anyone smoked and if they did it wasn't at work. She couldn't imagine what the staff would think if they saw her now, leaning over the railing and savoring the little magic stick. *It's all Cat's fault. But she's incredibly hot and a good lover.*

She dug in her purse for a small black-and-white photo she'd found in one of the old albums. It was an ancient picture of Uncle Jimmy and her father standing near a bay. In the background was a restaurant called the Seafarer. She imagined it was the chowder place Jimmy had mentioned at the reception and wondered if the photographer was Cruz. Both men looked exceptionally jovial, their arms thrown around each other in camaraderie.

She rubbed her temples and thought about what she'd learned from her investigation into the past. She'd spread the albums out in chronological order across her dining room table and a disturbing fact was easily revealed. While there were ten albums in total, she realized she was only included in the last two. The first six heavily chronicled the childhood of Dempsey and Uncle Jimmy, the upsurge of O'Grady Candy and their respective marriages. At album seven their lives split, and she'd noted the last few albums featured her parents' courtship, marriage, pregnancy and her youth.

The sepia images gave way to bad color as Dempsey and Margaret began their life together—their first home, a visit to

O'Grady Candy and a few pictures of baby Danielle, a name her father had insisted upon and her mother hated.

Dani thought photos served two purposes: they documented history and they revealed the personality of the photographers. Clearly someone in her father's youth had loved to take pictures because any occasion was a reason to break out the Brownie camera—picnics, car rides, even lazy afternoons were preserved for her to see. Throughout the first six albums she had felt a strong kinship to her relatives like gooey taffy that could never be removed. She *knew* them.

Such was not the case when she had flipped through the slim volumes her parents had created. Whereas the old photos were secured to the pages with corner holders or glue in a clear chronological order, the newest ones that featured her were haphazardly placed into cheap plastic sleeves or shoved between the pages randomly. And most of them were school pictures or what seemed to be duplicate copies of event photos that a friend's caring parent thought to have made for her mother. Clearly her father was too busy for such frivolity, and her mother couldn't be bothered except at the milestone events like birthdays with the traditional child-blowing-out-the-candles shot or at Christmas when her mother loved being photographed with her friends.

There had been many pictures of Christmas, mostly of her parents at their annual holiday party. Her mother was gorgeous and lived for the significant social season that surrounded Christmas. In every photo she wore a stunning dress, a drink and cigarette fashionably in her hands while she manufactured a smile, for her mother rarely smiled, posing with friends and her father's business associates. By the time Dani had perused all of the albums, she'd only counted five pictures that featured her with her parents. At that point she'd opened her best bottle of wine and consumed it in less than an hour.

Staring at her dining room table she'd understood how miserable her father had been. She felt duped and betrayed and for some reason she'd connected the experience with the single time she'd cheated on Petra.

They'd had a terrible fight, and Petra had used her greatest weapon against her—absence. She disappeared for two weeks, refusing to return her calls, which sent Dani into a jealous rage and into the arms of a flirtatious neighbor who'd suggested a threesome at their Halloween party a few months before. She had balked and Petra had snickered at her cowardice.

"Where's your sense of sexual adventure?" she'd teased.

She remembered staring at her with hurt eyes. "I'm adventurous but I only want to be with you."

Petra had patted her cheek like a child. "You're so naïve."

She'd never forgotten that exchange and when Petra stormed out, she seized the opportunity and knocked on her neighbor's door. Eventually Petra had walked in on them riding each other, sweating and moaning. She'd thrown the neighbor—whose name she couldn't remember—out of the condo and pushed her down on the bed.

"Stay here," she'd ordered.

She'd returned with her tools and burned a beautiful orchid into Dani's hip. When she had seen the finished product, she knew exactly what Petra had done—claimed her. The orchid was ornate and beautiful and all of her subsequent lovers had commented on its unique petals and the long, flowing stem that traveled to her navel and spelled *Petra*.

Suddenly the window flew open. "Why are you out here?" Ray demanded.

Her small round glasses reflected the morning sunlight, hiding her disapproving eyes, but Dani saw the frown and her discomfort from contorting her five-foot-nine frame through the open window.

She stubbed out the butt and climbed back inside. Ray stared at her, a stack of file folders in her hand. It was Monday and time to review the week before the staff meeting.

"Okay, what've we got?" she said, plopping down in her oversized office chair.

"The Perry account needs your attention. This is the third month they've been late with their payment. Second, Gary would like you to review the Maine delivery routes because we've added three more suppliers." With each summation Ray planted a colorful folder on her desk, covered with wild designs like polka dots or checks. Like everything else at O'Grady Candy even the files were outlandish. Plain manila folders didn't exist.

"And there's one more issue. A problem child." Ray planted a black folder in front of her. "The driver for the Cape Cod region reports that this shop continues to violate the non-compete clause."

Dani opened the file and perused the correspondence and background info while Ray spoke. "As you can see, Valerie's sent several memos and made a few calls but nothing changes."

She shook her head. The conclusion seemed obvious to her. O'Grady retailers couldn't sell any other similar candy types.

"Why haven't we pulled her? Just stop the deliveries. If she's unwilling to follow our rules then we don't supply her. Isn't it that simple?" She picked through the info and scanned some of Valerie's notes from the driver's observations. "Who else is she selling besides us?"

She looked up at Ray who seemed nonplussed by her irritation. "You've asked three questions. In what order would you like me to answer them?"

From nearly four years of togetherness she knew Ray wasn't mocking her. "Let's go in order."

"The shop is called Doces, which means candy in Portuguese, and it's located in Provincetown, not to be confused with Providence, Rhode Island."

"Don't worry," she interjected, "I wouldn't make that mistake."

A memory of running down Commercial Street, an insane blonde chasing her while the tourists watched, instantly filled her mind. She'd visited P-town a few times with Petra and again for several singles weekends just to pick up women for casual sex. She was also forbidden from ever returning by proclamation from the town selectmen. *And isn't that where my half-sister lives? Two times in three days. How coincidental is this?*

"Fine," Ray said through gritted teeth and Dani grinned. She hated to be interrupted. "The owner is Rafaela Tores Verdes and the reason Valerie hasn't halted her supply is because she sells more O'Grady Candy than anyone in the region despite the presence of competing products." She pulled a graph from the folders and handed it to her. "This shows the overall sales for the region and, as you can see, Doces is the highest even in the winter months which traditionally produces abysmal revenue. Valerie wonders if dropping her would be a mistake."

She saw the predicament. The shop was a performer and its location, the center of Commercial Street in the heart of P-town, guaranteed constant sales throughout the tourist season and the fact that she could sell so much in the dead of winter suggested she was a woman with an incredible marketing system. But she still wasn't following the contract which specifically stated that O'Grady Candy wouldn't share shelf space with similar candies from competitors. It was the only way she could stay in business.

She flipped through the folder once again. "So who else is she selling?"

A small smile crept across Ray's face. She rarely thought anything was funny, and there were a *lot* of funny incidences that happened at the O'Grady Candy Company. It was barely seven o'clock and already the four enormous plasma TVs that adorned each wall were projecting different cartoons and "Jumpin' Jack Flash" blared through the speakers of the main office space.

"From what we can tell, she's selling her own stuff."

"What?"

"She's a candymaker and according to the driver, her confections are primo—and that's a direct quote."

She massaged her temples to ward off the impending headache. It was an odd situation, one she wasn't prepared to rule on just yet. Ray deposited the rest of the folders in her inbox and left. Their relationship was one where words weren't often needed. Dani appreciated her talent despite her lack of a personality. On the surface she didn't seem to fit in with the fun-lovin' candy employees, but she knew Ray was a chocolate-covered cherry—hard and dark on the outside but sweet and soft inside.

A loud bark got her attention and Valerie's large golden retriever Sanford bounded into her office space followed by his best friend Spike the Smiling Office Cat. A somewhat homely looking Russian Blue, he'd wandered in one day and adopted the office and its staff. Everyone had fallen in love with his charming personality and his smile. And Spike could really smile, which he demonstrated after he effortlessly jumped into her inbox and turned up the corners of his mouth. She naturally smiled back while Sanford placed his paw on her knee and panted. He had tremendous karma and was the sweetest dog she'd ever met. She rubbed him behind the ears and nodded at Spike. The greeting was good enough for both and they rushed away, scooting between the partitions looking for someone else. It was their morning routine, welcoming every O'Grady employee to work.

She leaned back in her chair and took a deep breath. There were too many things on her plate—this new half-sister, Cat, and even Liam who hadn't called her yet from his honeymoon. She imagined Cassidy had him pinned down on the hotel bed, and Dani doubted he was very upset about it.

She scratched her arms. The tattoos burned against her flesh, a common occurrence any time her personal life interfered with work. She had no trouble managing twenty different issues as long as she could do it from behind her dad's old oak desk and the decisions involved candy. Therapist Number Seven had said that anything outside the realm of the pink cottage was "enemy territory." She rolled her eyes just remembering the ridiculous little man.

She glanced at the huge Rosie the Riveter clock on the wall. The office meeting would start in less than half an hour and she still wasn't ready. Normally her Sunday night was a mental prep time for her Monday meeting, but she'd allowed her personal life to actually consume *personal* time which rarely happened.

She sifted through the files and in minutes she'd pushed aside the bizarre happenings of the weekend and the itching stopped.

By the time Rosie's arms extended to eight o'clock she was ready. She gathered her materials and portfolio and headed to the great room, noticing that some of her colleagues were rearranging the display panels to form a makeshift conference room.

Ray suddenly appeared next to her. "Dani?"

"What?" she asked absently. Her mind was calculating the agenda items and the time needed to address each issue.

Ray pointed to her desk. "That woman over there says you know her—intimately."

She whipped her head toward Ray's alcove. Cat leaned against the wall wearing tight jeans and a tailored blouse. *She looks good enough to eat. But thank goodness I'm not hungry anymore.*

"I'll take care of this," she said.

As she approached, Cat smiled warmly. "Hey."

"Hi. What are you doing here now? I thought you were coming in later this afternoon."

Cat noticed her annoyed tone and stood up straight, towering over her in motorcycle boots. "A job came up. Can we talk now?"

She glanced at her team assembling around the large conference table. The Monday meeting was her baby, and no one else could run it. She wasn't a power freak about anything else except for *the meeting.* They would have to wait or she'd have to cancel it.

"Can we grab lunch later?" she offered.

"Tempting," Cat replied in a husky voice. "But I picked up a job in an hour, and I have a class at one." She noticed the employees and added, "I can summarize this whole situation in five minutes."

She nodded and quickly led her to her desk. Cat glanced about the office space and said, "Interesting," before sitting in a plush chair. "You probably already guessed this, but Olivia's going to ask you for money."

She nodded. *A lot* of people asked her for money, and she gave away a good amount of it.

"She's not a money-grubber or anything," she continued.

"She's done okay running her B and B but she's determined that I have something I don't want."

"And what's that?"

"A husband."

"What?"

She struggled for the words before she blurted, "There's this guy named Nathaniel who's been after me for a year—"

"Your mother doesn't know you're gay? How's that possible?"

She held up a hand. "I'm not really into labels but I guess for the sake of conversation, I'm bi. I've had a few boyfriends along the way but as you know," she said with a wicked grin, "I'm very attracted to women. She's only met the boyfriends."

Dani realized they had an audience. Twenty feet away her office staff made faces, tapped their feet, twiddled their thumbs and Valerie pointed at her watch.

*I work with oversized children. Clearly the downside of the candy industry.*

"So your mother thinks you're straight, and she's set you up with a man. You've obviously given her the impression that this could be serious." She took a breath and asked, "How does this involve me?"

"Have you ever heard of a dowry?"

She glanced at her employees who were all mooning her.

"C'mon," she said, opening the window. Cat followed her onto the fire escape and they lit up. "Your mother wants you to have a *dowry*? Does she realize this is the twenty-first century?"

"Dowry's not her word, it's mine. There's this art gallery for sale in the East End and she thinks that if she could buy it for me, I'd move back to P-town and manage it. Then I'd be involved in the art world and I'd be closer to Nathaniel . . . "

She connected the dots easily. All mothers knew that opportunity forged decisions. If Cat was close to Nathaniel she might marry him. It was a long shot especially given the fact that they would live in a land populated by lesbians. It would be like asking a diabetic to live downstairs in the candy factory. Nathaniel would have his work cut out for him.

"Olivia's totally old school even though she's younger than you," she explained. "I don't expect you to understand how she thinks."

She chuckled and remembered that Cat was only twenty-four. *And I'm sleeping with her.* "Of course I understand. I'm a mother. I tried six different tactics to get Liam *not* to marry Cassidy."

"Yeah, but she's a gold-digger. At least Nathaniel's an okay guy. If I get stuck with him it won't be so bad."

The thought mortified her. No one should be *stuck* with anyone, ever. "How did you wind up in Olivia's life?"

Cat stared at the tall buildings that surrounded them, and Dani sensed the story was rooted in painful memories. She hated to ask, but if Cat wanted her help she needed to know everything.

"It's really not a big deal. My mother grew up in a little town in Rhode Island. She was bored and ran with the wrong crowd, a total wild child. She dropped out of high school and jumped in a van with a guy, and they drove until they ran out of highway."

"You mean they wound up in P-town?"

She smiled wryly. "Land's End. They were young and stupid. The first place they walked into was the Seafarer. They were hungry and young and Cruz took pity on them. She gave them jobs, but a few months later the boyfriend disappeared. Mom found some more friends and the really short version of the story is that Mom got hooked on coke, got pregnant and spent the next few years trying to raise me and battle her addictions. She disappeared when I was four. Left me sitting on a bench outside the Seafarer one morning holding a note for Cruz."

"Jesus," she whispered.

She waved off the pity. "It wasn't a big deal. I was only four. Cruz took care of me and Olivia came back after she graduated from college. They were my family—*are* my family. I wouldn't want to hurt Olivia, but I don't want to get married."

"What was your mother's name?"

"Karen."

"Have you ever wanted to find her?"

Cat took a deep breath and Dani could see the tears in her eyes. "Not necessary. She's dead. Died of an overdose in some flophouse here in New York."

Her motherly side emerged and she touched her arm. "I'm sorry. So how can I help you?" she offered.

A look of relief crossed her face. "When she calls you need to tell her that you won't give her the money."

"That's easy. It's not her money. But do you think that's really going to make a difference? Won't she still want you to get married?"

"Yeah, but it'll buy me some time to think of something else."

"How about the truth? Why don't you just tell her you're gay?"

Cat smiled wanly. "You make it sound so simple but it's not. Olivia's family has been in P-town for generations. On the outside it seems like a progressive and carefree place but that's only to the tourists. P-town is just as rich in heritage and tradition as any other New England town. Olivia is a traditionalist, and she assumed I'd take over the B and B after I went to college and got a business degree like she did. She wasn't happy that I pursued art, but she still paid for it—on one condition."

"You agreed to move back after you were done," she concluded.

Cat nodded, clearly a little surprised at her intuition. "Yeah, I thought that during my undergrad program I'd come up with a plan, a way to cancel the bargain. But every time I came home for Christmas or a summer break she'd have two or three guys lined up for me to meet, usually fishermen. It was awful. I can't tell you how many women dumped me because I returned in the fall smelling like bass."

She could imagine. Although she'd never hidden, she'd known dozens of colleagues, college friends and clients who'd spent a lifetime living in fiction. She kept picturing Cat opening the front door to Fisherman Ted or Fisherman Frank, wearing a rubber jacket, hat and boots, his pole at his side with an enormous mackerel wiggling on the hook.

"So how did she agree to pay for grad school?"

She chuckled slightly and scratched her head. "I needed something a little more concrete."

She shook her head. "You met Nathaniel and made it look promising."

She nodded sheepishly. "Yeah, that got her to open her pocketbook. But now she's pushing for a happy ending." She glanced at her watch and said, "I need to get going."

There was still much more that she wanted to know—*needed* to know. "Do you want to get married? Do you see yourself with a man? With Nathaniel?"

She looked remorseful. "Nathaniel's a great guy and he deserves better."

"And?" she offered, hoping Cat would admit her selfishness was costing him a real relationship.

But she just shrugged. "And . . . I don't know. I've met great guys since I've been at NYU and some fabulous women too. I'm not sure who I want to spend my life with, but I know I don't want to decide right now."

She saw Ray standing on the other side of the window, her arms folded. She looked pissed. The meeting should've ended by now and Ray had things to do.

"So what's the timeline?"

"She's got it all mapped out. I'll earn my master's, move back to P-town, marry Nathaniel and manage the gallery. End of story until she refuels and starts the talk about grandchildren. I think she hatched this idea the day I left for grad school."

She blinked in surprise. "How long has your mother known I was her sister?"

"All her life. Cruz told Olivia the truth when she was old enough to hear it. She said her father was a rich and powerful man, but his life was in New York and he couldn't see her very often."

"So she left out the fact that he was already married and had a kid?"

"Do you blame her? The truth was cruel and it wasn't Olivia's fault."

"No, of course not," she said quickly.

She scratched her arm absently and felt a burning sensation crawl across *At the Edge* on her back. She took a long drag, envisioning the box of Christmas ornaments the handyman brought up from the basement each year. Once the freshly cut pine tree was erected in the huge living room, her mother would stand before the box and remove the lid with a flourish, giddy with excitement over the treasure that was revealed. And as each oddly shaped ornament was unwrapped her mother would narrate its biography while Dani or her father placed it on the tree. The collection supposedly represented their life together as a family—the ceramic figurine they'd bought for her first birthday, the glass globe her mother had found in a Paris shop and the ornate cross from Rome. Suddenly the ornament box seemed trivial, her father's exploits mocking their Christmas tradition.

"Dani? Are you listening? I need your help, and I've got to go."

She glanced up at Cat, leaning against the railing with an impatient scowl on her face.

"My mom's going to call you today. She's going to plead her case and ask to meet you. I need to know what you're going to say."

"I'll probably say hello."

She let out a cry of disgust. "This isn't a joke. You know my secret. Can you keep it from her?"

Of course she could. Secrets provided more leverage than a crowbar. She'd learned the art of leverage from her father who claimed it was more powerful than money. And apparently he was a master of secrets.

She studied Cat who shuffled her feet, unable to stand still on the small fire escape, her nerves electric and palatable. She believed Cat when she said she'd never intended to seduce her.

It had just happened and now Dani had control. She closed her eyes and saw a map of Cape Cod with two small arteries converging into Highway Six, the one road that led to Provincetown. Perhaps they could help each other.

"Hey!" She pulled Dani against her and caressed her face. "Please?"

Her brown eyes were a storm, cloudy with doubt and a hint of desire. She offered a desperate kiss that nearly consumed Dani. When their lips finally parted, Cat's eyes fluttered open, calm and cool, and she instantly realized the dreadful itching had ceased. *Okay, maybe I'm still a little hungry.*

"I'm sorry, but I couldn't help myself. You're completely sexy. Maybe you're what I need."

"Highly doubtful." She stepped away determined to stay in business mode. "I have a proposition for you."

She licked her lips. "I like propositions."

# Chapter Four

Dani immediately clarified. "This is a business proposition, but you'll have to call someone else to take your job today. I'll pay you twice what you would've made."

She raised an eyebrow. "And what do you need me to do?"

"You want me to convince your mother that you don't need a dowry, and I need someone to help me with one of my sellers in Provincetown. Have you ever heard of Doces, the candy store on Commercial Street?"

Her face brightened. "Oh, yeah. That's a great place and Rafi's the coolest."

"So you know her personally?"

"Sure. It's P-town. All the locals know each other. Rafi moved in about three years ago and bought this little store she painted fire engine red." She paused and then said, "Wait. She sells your candy? I thought she only sold her own stuff. Why would she sell somebody else's candy?"

She frowned at her genuine perplexity. She'd definitely want to visit Doces.

"She's one of those people who do stuff for everyone and she's incredibly hot," she added, her voice dripping like liquid sugar.

"Have you slept with her?" she asked, the weight of jealousy settling on her shoulders.

"I only wish. Rafi is one of the most sought after women on Cape Cod. She's rich, beautiful, compassionate and totally unavailable it seems. There was a girlfriend once but she's out of the picture. I think there was a tragedy. But she never hooks up."

She was intrigued. Hooking up was the weekend pastime for P-town. The choice of women was fantastic and opportunities for sex were as convenient as breakfast, lunch or dinner. *If I lived there I'd never get out of bed. And I like good sex anytime.*

She glanced at Cat who still wore her seductive smile, and a tingle traveled down her body. She coughed and headed inside with her following behind.

"And after we complete our business let's go back to your place," she whispered, her hands lingering on Dani's ass.

She ignored the advance and led her by the arm to Valerie's office. When Cat saw Sanford sitting in Valerie's chair she cooed at him and the sexual tension evaporated. He was a great distraction for anything.

"Write down everything you know about Doces and Rafaela Tores Verdes," she instructed as Sanford licked her face. "Come back after your class is over."

Cat nodded and wrote with one hand while she petted Sanford with the other. Dani left her alone and went to gather her staff. She tried not to think about the details as she slogged through her day of meetings, reports, phone calls and her most favorite activity—a trip down to the candy factory to talk to the school children who wanted to know how the candy was made.

She'd don her special candy hat that was shaped like an O'Grady Fluffy Peek-a-Boo, a distinct chocolate with a cream filling that came through the center of the candy. Gustav referred to it as the volcano candy since it looked like white lava spilling over the top of the chocolate. Everyone recognized the hat and the kids loved it.

She tried to spend at least a few hours a week leading the tours, proudly explaining the history of O'Grady Candy and answering the questions from kids who wanted to know if she employed Oompa Loompas, ate the candy for dinner or made chocolate-covered bugs. By the time the tour group left and she climbed the stairs back to the executive offices she always felt invigorated. Going down to the floor was the best reminder about why she loved the candy business.

As usual her work was the ultimate distraction and days dissolved like O'Grady Lemon Droplets in her mouth, something she savored and missed when they were gone. This was a sharp contrast to the sliver of personal time she allowed herself with casual friends and the occasional sexual liaison, which only provided momentary gratification and added little value to the scope of her life, at least that was what Therapist Number Eight had deduced.

It hadn't always been that way, not when Liam was younger and really needed her or when she was with Petra, who had made her cry rivers and laugh until her sides hurt because she lived on the fringe of extremes. She'd always been good to Liam who was at the height of adolescence when they met. And while Petra cared for him, he was incredibly sensitive about their relationship, recognizing they needed time alone, which he willingly provided once he could drive.

Petra's ability to connect with him had been a key part of the relationship, and he was devastated when she'd left. He'd thought the tattoos were cool particularly since he never watched Dani being inked so he didn't know about the pain or the tears she cried.

And sometimes they had enjoyed family activities. Dani remembered a weekend one spring when it had rained endlessly, ruining Petra's plans of painting outdoors. Instead, the three of them had played every board game they owned. Petra and

Liam had stolen money from the Monopoly bank, yelled *Sorry!* at the top of their lungs and howled whenever the Jenga tower collapsed.

Dani had made delicious hot chocolate with O'Grady Milk Chocolate Bars, and they'd sat in front of the window sipping the treat and watching the rain pelt Washington Park. The memory warmed her as she unconsciously hugged herself.

"Olivia Santos is on line one," Ray said through the intercom.

She automatically picked up, then quickly wished she'd taken a moment to gather her thoughts.

"Ms. Santos, this is Dani O'Grady. I understand you want to speak to me."

"Uh, yes, Ms. O'Grady, it's very nice of you to accept my call since I'm sure you're very busy. And please call me Olivia."

Dani heard the pleasant sincerity borne from years in the customer service industry. She imagined owning a bed-and-breakfast was the apex of ass-kissing since vacationers expected the ultimate pampering and the breakfast aspect required the innkeeper to actually interact with the guests over waffles and coffee.

"It's my pleasure, Olivia. I'll admit that I was a little surprised when my attorney told me about my father's . . . other life," she said, cringing at her word choice.

"I feel bad about that, I certainly do, especially since I've known all along. I guess you're still processing the information."

She sighed heavily. "I'll be thinking about this for a very long time."

"I'm sure. I know you're very busy, but I have something important to ask you."

"Certainly," she said. She braced for the request that was coming. Her hands needed something to do so she squeezed the little plastic troll she kept on her desk.

"As you know my mother and your father had a relationship and I was the result, although my mother broke it off after she realized she was pregnant."

"*She* broke it off?"

"Yes. She was Catholic and her priest insisted. He claimed if she didn't he'd see to it that she was excommunicated from the church."

"Could he do that?"

"I don't know but she thought he could. Your father was very upset but he understood. He thought it was simply the end of an affair. He didn't realize it was the beginning of a life. My mother always said that if he'd known about me, he would have honored his commitment and provided support."

"I think you're right," she agreed.

"And that's why I'm calling you now. Before my mother died she called him and revealed her secret. I met our father when I was twenty, two days before my mother died."

Just listening to Olivia utter the words *our father* in reference to *her* father caused her to drop the troll. She suddenly felt ill and thought she might throw up.

"How did he react when he saw you?"

"It was . . . well, it was disconcerting for him. He was sad because she was dying, but he was angry that she hadn't called sooner. I think he was devastated on two entirely different levels."

"I see," she said, but she didn't. There was nothing she could understand. She set her head down on the edge of the desk. *I don't want to understand. I want to hang up. I want to scream at Dad.*

"This is the hard part, Dani. Um, it's okay if I call you Dani, isn't it? Seeing as we're related?"

"Sure," she croaked.

"My mother never took a dime from your father. The day I met him he insisted on writing a huge check, but my mother ordered me to burn it. She told me I needed to make my own way and I listened to her. He tried to call a few more times but I never spoke to him. I made my own way," she said again, and Dani heard the pride in her voice. *And she should be proud.*

Dani's childhood encompassed boarding school, horseback

riding lessons and an Ivy League education, all of which was Olivia's birthright as well. Keeping her end of the bargain with Cat suddenly seemed much more difficult.

"And while I've managed," she continued, "running a B and B hasn't been incredibly lucrative. Many years I just get by, and my tax guy wants to shoot me for keeping the place. He thought I should've sold it years ago but I can't. I love it too much. You know what it's like to love your business, don't you, Dani?"

She smiled faintly. Olivia was good. She understood that persuasion required common ground and alliances. "Very much so. O'Grady Candy is my life."

"I *knew* you'd understand. I have two loves, the B and B and Catarina, who I think of as my own daughter. She's the most important thing in my life. I can't tell you how much she means to me. You have a child, don't you?"

"Yes."

She noticed that Olivia made no explanation about how Cat came to live with her. She was her *daughter*. She grabbed a pencil and wacked it against her head repeatedly. *She'd kill me if she knew what I'd done with her daughter.*

"I'm sorry. I'm totally digressing. That tends to happen when I talk about Catarina. And she's the reason I'm calling. I've made my way, but I'm not certain Catarina can do the same. She has these grandiose notions of working in the art world and while it's wonderful that she has a passion, most artists starve and that certainly won't attract a husband."

She scowled. How could such a sweet and sensible sounding woman like Olivia be so closed-minded and prudish? She bit her tongue and resisted the urge to suggest Cat might not want a husband. Instead, she grabbed a handful of O'Grady Jelly Jams, which she kept conveniently in a crystal dish on her desk.

"So you want to help your daughter," she summarized while she chewed, trying to move the conversation along.

"Actually, I'm hoping we can help her together. There's a man who's got his eye on her. I think he'd propose if he thought she had something to bring to the marriage. Now before you judge me too harshly for my old-fashioned attitude," she added quickly, "please know that my daughter likes him. She thinks he's quite a catch."

She grabbed her head. *She likes him like a good turkey panini sandwich.* "I see," she said. "So you're hoping we can create that opportunity for her."

Olivia gave a sound of relief. "Thank you for explaining it so succinctly. Yes, I'd appreciate it if you could help make this dream come true."

Her teeth sat on edge at Olivia's choice of words. "Olivia, is this her dream or your dream?"

"Well, it's our dream," she sputtered. "Catarina wants this too."

"She wants to get married?"

"Of course or why would I be asking you?"

She heard the shift in her tone. She'd wandered into personal territory that she had no right to question.

"I think it's admirable that you care for your daughter, but I can't give you the money."

"Um, I don't understand. It's an entirely reasonable request given the circumstances."

"Well, I don't agree. You've never done anything for the company so I don't think you're owed anything from O'Grady Candy."

There was a long pause, a dangerous pause that made her nervous, as if she were walking along a jungle path and about to fall into a trap.

"Please reconsider, Dani." Olivia's voice was compassionate, almost sad.

"I'm sorry. You seem like such a nice person. I wish I could help you."

"Oh, Dani, I'm sorry, too. You *are* going to help me. I just wish you *wanted* to help me. I'd hoped we could be friends."

She felt her legs give way as she fell into the trap. "What are you talking about?"

"I have your father's will."

She shook her head. She remembered the carefully crafted will Harry had drawn up for her father many years ago. Harry had proclaimed it a legal masterpiece and considered framing it.

"I've seen the will, Olivia. I don't believe you're mentioned."

"What's the date on the will to which you refer?"

She closed her eyes and tried to remember. "Um, four or five years before he died."

"He wrote this one just three months before he passed."

She heard the crinkling of paper, and she imagined that Olivia was looking at the will while they spoke. "He wrote it out longhand and dated it. I'm not a lawyer, but I think that means mine trumps yours. Isn't that right? Sorta like poker? You've got the full house, but I've got the royal flush."

She winced when Olivia chuckled at her own joke. "So what are the terms? How much did he leave you?" She reached for her legal pad and a pen, estimating she'd be cutting a check for six or seven figures.

"Half."

Her pen froze over the paper. "Excuse me?"

"I know what you're thinking, and I hate to play my ace in the hole but Daddy figured we were sisters and I was entitled to half. I just never thought I deserved it."

*Daddy.* The lines on the legal pad seemed to form jagged peaks like a heart monitor and her blood pressure spiked in just a few seconds. Cat appeared in the doorway and instead of plopping down in one of the chairs, she came behind the desk. Dani suddenly felt trapped between her sister and her lover.

Cat barely whispered, "Olivia?" and she nodded.

She scribbled *She has my father's will. I'm stuck.* Cat looked away nervously and threw up her hands.

"I need to see that will, Olivia," she insisted, "before I agree to anything. Could I interest you in a few days in New York? Maybe come by and visit your daughter?"

When Olivia gasped and Cat looked shocked, she closed her eyes and immediately realized her mistake.

"Why, Dani, you must be psychic. How did you know Cat lived in New York?"

*Think. Think. How would I know this?* "Well, actually—"

"Oh, I know. Your attorney told you, right?"

She leaned back in her chair. "Yes, Harry mentioned her but I haven't met her . . . or anything."

Cat practically crawled onto her lap so she could hear Olivia's part of the conversation.

"She's an amazing girl, but it's time for her to steer her life in a certain direction. She's gone to college, but that wasn't enough. Now she's in graduate school earning another useless degree. I've been extremely patient, but she needs to find a meaningful purpose for herself."

Cat opened her mouth, but Dani put a finger to her lips and she went out to the fire escape.

"And that's why I need your help," Olivia continued. "I really *don't want* half of your company. Cat loves art and there's a gallery for sale. She could run the gallery and sculpt on the side. It could be a wonderful life for her and Nathaniel. But I can't come to the city, not right now. We're getting ready for tourist season here and I've got plenty to do. Would you drive up to P-town? I'm not sure it's your kind of place—"

"I could come up," she said quickly.

"That's perfect! I can't wait to meet you."

Her warmth and sincerity had returned and there was a click on the line. Olivia said, "Oh, can you hang on for one minute, Dani? I've got another call and it could be a reservation."

"Sure."

She glanced at Cat, leaning over the railing, smoking and talking on her cell phone. While she was on hold she checked her calendar. She couldn't afford the time away from the office, but the possibility of losing half the company was far worse. She motioned for Ray to join her.

"Clear my calendar through the end of the week. Reschedule everything and get Harry on the phone."

Ray studied the calendar and then glanced over her shoulder

before her gaze returned to Dani. "This is clearly some sort of cruel joke, and I'd like to know who put you up to it. My family has a history of heart attacks. You're aware of this fact, are you not? Didn't you read my medical history when you hired me?"

"It's not a joke, Ray. I've got an emergency that needs my attention immediately. I've got to get up to P-town."

At the mention of Provincetown Ray narrowed her eyes. "You're not cutting out now because of a *woman* are you?"

"It's not a woman."

"Why else do you ever go to P-town?"

She folded her hands in front of her. "It's complicated and it's business, mostly."

"Business in P-town that's more important than wrapping up the quarterlies? You *really* expect me to believe that after your little rendezvous on the fire escape with that baby dyke?" She followed Ray's gaze to the fire escape and Cat's fine physique. "Wasn't she the one you left with after the wedding?"

"You're far too observant, Ray."

"And do I even want to know what she was doing behind your desk a few minutes ago?"

"Do I need to remind you that you're *my* employee? It's not the other way around," she spat.

Ray grabbed the calendar and murmured, "Gotta be bad if you're playing the power card," as she headed back to her desk.

She heard a click and Olivia said, "I'm sorry that took so long, but I've got some great news. That was Catarina."

Her throat went dry as Cat crawled back inside.

"So what's your great news?" she thought to ask.

"I told Cat that you were coming to visit, and she volunteered to drive you up. Isn't that wonderful?"

# Chapter Five

From her West Greenwich Village loft Dani had an unobstructed view of the Hudson River, and in the evening she'd sit on her sofa with a glass of wine and watch the moonlight patter across the water. It was incredibly soothing after a long day at work.

She loved the Village. It was welcoming to gays but not obvious, a truly enlightened community that didn't need to wave rainbow flags above every doorway proclaiming its open-mindedness. The celebration of diversity in Greenwich Village was palpable but not overstated.

Petra had been the one who wanted to live in the heart of an artists' community and they'd both been sold on the area after a walk through Washington Square Park. Many of the buildings were owned by New York University, and students had been clustered around the fountain area, enjoying the spring weather and studying for the upcoming finals. A fiddler had played for donations under the arch while professional chess players hustled games at the small tables near the entrance. It had been clear the area catered to all types of people—exactly the type of place they'd wanted to call home.

And even after Petra moved out she kept the loft, refusing to accept that she needed to abandon her home simply because her relationship had failed. Dani believed she could make new memories and dull the pain. And until she had all nine tattoos removed there was no way she could ever totally extricate Petra from her life. *And why haven't I done that? Am I hoping she'll come back? Do I believe we'll ever get back together?* All good questions that Therapist Number Six had asked.

And she'd asked herself *why* at least a thousand times since they'd broken up. She'd answered that question a few dozen times when her casual affairs inquired. Her reasoning was simple—she loved the artwork. She knew it was odd and most women would make a different choice. Tattoos were usually the first casualty of a broken relationship, and she'd thought about having them removed but she dismissed the idea as too costly and completely unnecessary for her to feel fulfilled just like abandoning her expensive home. She didn't need to erase Petra's existence to continue with her own. *At least that's my story.* And according to Therapist Number Nine, who'd only lasted one session, she lived in a world of rationalization. She'd fired her after she compared Dani's sense of reality to the rabbit hole in *Alice in Wonderland.*

Standing naked in front of her full-length mirror, she admired Petra's canvas, believing that the artwork added to her beauty. The tats impressed her lovers, but none of them had the background in art to know what they were seeing—until Cat. She usually made a point of hooking up with women who didn't like art or weren't couth enough in her estimation to know a Petra when she saw it.

The colors were so vibrant and the lines so clear, not like so much of the body art she'd seen where the drawings jockeyed for attention against the skin, creating a cartoonish mess that wasn't visually appealing. But despite their beauty she knew the business world had another standard, and she'd insisted that all of them be placed in such a way that would allow her to cover the pieces with her suit pants and jackets. Most corporate executives or candy store owners didn't want to see a sinewy dragon's tail protruding from her blouse, and she respected their conservatism.

But during her personal time she made no such concessions. If the pizza delivery guy or someone at the park got an eyeful, she didn't care if they openly stared. Her tats were a part of her and when she came home in the evening and shed corporate America into her dry cleaning bag, she felt a sense of freedom as though part of her had been suffocating throughout the day. The tattoos were her connection to the world outside of O'Grady Candy and she realized that they might be the *only* connection. She closed her eyes and absorbed the silence in the loft. There was no barking dog, no live-in lover to whine about her miserable day and not even any messages on her voice mail from friends wanting to get together.

She glanced at Cat, asleep under the covers, and threw on some running shorts and a tank top before heading for the kitchen. The remains of Cat's cooking flurry were piled in the sink—pots, pans and knives—from the marvelous chicken risotto dinner she'd made for them before they tumbled into bed. She was certainly a wonderful cook. *I like her moves in the kitchen almost as much as the bedroom.*

She opened a bottle of Malbec and curled up on the sofa. It was extraordinary and buffered the sharp-edged emotions that continually knocked against each other, vying for her attention. She was confused by her behavior with Cat, frustrated by Olivia's narrow-mindedness and angry with her father for leaving O'Grady Candy in such a vulnerable state.

She'd spoken with Harry an hour ago. He ordered her to fax him a copy of the will once she saw it. He'd know immediately if it was Dempsey's handwriting.

"I can't imagine this is a hoax," she'd said, staring at the picture of Uncle Jimmy and her father outside the Seafarer restaurant.

"A simple paternity test will tell us if she's really your sister.

But you'll have to decide how far you want to push this, Dani. I've got everyone in my firm on the alert. All you have to do is say the word and we'll bury this problem for a long time. I've always said that every dollar is worth five pieces of paper to a lawyer, and O'Grady is worth millions. That's a lot of trees, but we could keep it in litigation for years."

Dani shook her head. It didn't seem right to deny Olivia what might rightfully be hers. This wasn't a case of a gold-digger making a false claim against her company. She'd faced several frivolous lawsuits over the years and knew when she was being played. That didn't sound like Olivia. This was someone who could be family. A *sister*.

"I'll think about it," she'd said. "Let me get a look at her, and I'll know what to do."

If the will was real, she was cornered. She'd promised Cat she'd deny Olivia the money but if she did, Olivia would enforce the will and take far more than what she was asking. She tried to imagine what it would mean to give her half of the company. It was more than her mind could process this late at night. More of the Malbec left the bottle and filled her glass.

"Why are you up?"

Cat joined her on the couch and took a serious swig from the bottle. She hadn't bothered to dress and her lovely bronze skin shone against the romantic lighting that Petra had demanded in the loft.

"I'm just thinking. There's a lot at stake here."

Cat cuddled against her and kissed her cheek. "I'm not worried. You're an astute businesswoman. You'll convince Olivia to stay away from your company, and you'll persuade Rafi to do whatever the hell it is that you need her to do."

She smiled at her naïve optimism. *I was that way when I was young. Now I'm old and cynical—like Olivia. I know Cassidy isn't right for Liam as much as Olivia believes Nathaniel is exactly right for Cat.*

"Have you ever thought about telling Olivia that you're bi?"

She sat up straight. "No, I can't. It would kill her."

Dani was touched by her concern. She wanted her life, but she wouldn't hurt Olivia. Unfortunately she couldn't have both.

"Cat, I may not have a choice about what I do. I can't let Olivia take half of my company. I'll help you, but if it comes down to giving her the money for the art gallery or half of my company, there's no choice. You understand that, right?"

"That's assuming the will is valid. Do you think it is?"

"Do you?" she replied. "Is Olivia deceitful, greedy and sinister?"

"No, of course not."

She caressed her face and kissed her forehead. "Then it's probably real. You know Olivia and I know my father. When I really think about it, I'm not surprised."

Her father lived for fun and adventure and had married her mother strictly for her looks. But underneath a stunning exterior was a dour homebody who failed to see that each day was a series of brilliant colors waiting to be unfurled—her father's favorite lesson that he often imparted to her.

"I think you should tell her," Dani said.

Cat scowled and a belligerent sound came from her mouth as she pulled away and went into the bedroom. Dani knew she was upset when she slammed the door. She sighed. It would take time for her to accept the inevitable.

In her opinion, dealing with Rafi would be the easier task. She always approached interpersonal issues like a science experiment that required study before action. Otherwise the financial repercussion could be monumental if she failed to properly manipulate the human elements. Everyone had needs even if they couldn't articulate them appropriately. Over the years she'd recognized those deal-breaking core issues and saved her company millions and added to the O'Grady coffers significantly. As she finished the glass of Malbec she rationalized that handling Rafi was no different. To neutralize the problem she had to discover what she really wanted.

Her cell phone chimed, and she smiled when she saw Liam's

face on the display. "Hey, honey. How's Jamaica?"

She heard loud techno music in the background and he started to talk but she quickly cut him off. "Honey, stop. I can't hear you."

He said something else that she didn't understand, but the music started to fade away. She heard a door click and he sighed deeply. "Is it normal to spend your honeymoon dancing with strangers? Because that's what Cassidy's doing."

"You haven't spent any time alone?"

"Well, a little, but we got here and I found out that she'd made all these plans like a cruise excursion and a Jeep tour. We're out and about most of the day, then she wants to go clubbing at night."

She heard the sadness in his voice and frowned. She wasn't surprised. Cassidy was all about herself and he would spend his marriage like a servant to Cleopatra. *But I'm going to serve as her twenty-first century version of an Egyptian bank. Lucky me.*

"I'm sorry, babe. Maybe you could talk to her? Tell her how you feel. I'm certainly no expert, but I've seen enough *Oprah* to know that most women would love to be told that their man only wants to spend time with them."

"I told her that and she got all gushy and took me to bed and *then* she dragged me out to the club. It's not that I don't like to dance," he quickly added, "I'd planned on us going out. Just not every night."

She blinked hoping to erase the image of them in bed together. She imagined him sulking in a corner of the club nursing a beer while his wife did the bump and grind with a bevy of hot Jamaican men. She felt helpless thousands of miles away, and she hated Cassidy more for ruining his honeymoon. An image of a huge disco ball crashing onto her head made Dani feel a little better.

"Is there anything I can do?"

"No. I guess compromise is a part of marriage, huh?"

That was her Liam, the psychologist, always trying to make the best of a situation. He was the poster child for inspirational sayings because he made lemons from lemonade, saw every glass as half full and believed that a group of people could change the world. *God I love him. I'm so proud of him.*

"Mom, are you still there?"

"Yeah, son, and you're right. Relationships are about compromise."

The music echoed in the background again, and she guessed he'd returned to the club's dance area. "Then I guess this is my turn. I love you, Mom."

"I love you, son. You're an amazing man," she added, hoping that her voice was loud enough to be heard.


Cat offered to drive but she readily acquiesced when Dani told her they could take the company plane to fly from JFK to the tiny Provincetown Municipal Airport. Time was money and she needed to resolve this nonsense quickly and return to her quarterly reports.

As the plane took off Cat caressed the fine leather seats and proclaimed, "I love knowing rich people."

"It doesn't suck," she agreed as she sipped her martini and watched Cat gaze out the window like a little kid until they were high in the clouds. "Now," she said, "you need to tell me everything you can about Olivia." She pulled out her Mont Blanc pen and portfolio and wrote her customary heading for notes.

Cat finished her mimosa and motioned the flight attendant for another. "Actually, you'll really like her. Everyone does. She's a member of the Board of Selectmen, their version of a town council. She's been on a lot of committees over the years, studying the environment, the population and she helps plan the Portuguese festival."

She couldn't believe it. "I don't understand how your mother can live in one of the gayest cities in America, sit on their governing body, plan events and be upset about having a gay daughter. She's living in P-town, for God's sake!"

She turned toward her. She'd worn a slinky blue silk blouse

and black capris that reminded Dani exactly why she'd thrown away her common sense for a woman half her age.

"Look, my family lived in P-town long before the gays came. The Portuguese have inhabited the docks since the eighteen-eighties. That town was built on our backs," she added acidly.

She realized she'd hit on a sore spot. She'd always equated P-town with gay society and realized that for the locals, P-town was a much richer culture.

"And while my mother would die if she heard me tell you this, she wasn't thrilled when all the *happy people* as she calls them invaded our home."

"But she owns a B and B. I can't imagine she'd survive without the gay and lesbian community."

"True," she conceded. "And for the most part the guests have all been respectable. She's only had a few dozen problems and called the cops two or three times. Not a bad average. I think she just wishes Jews or hetero families were the ones renting her rooms."

"It's definitely ironic," she said. "If she was so traditional why didn't she get married?"

"She is married."

"What?"

She tasted her fresh mimosa and said, "About a year after I arrived she met a man and was determined to have the happy family life. That's what she wanted, but he met someone else and wanted out. She wouldn't grant him a divorce so he just left instead of dealing with the lawyers and paying the money. As far as I know they're still married."

"Why wouldn't she give him the divorce?"

She leaned forward and spoke very slowly. "Dani, she's a traditionalist, the fifties version of the happy homemaker."

She shook her head and offered Cat a cigarette. "So what was it like growing up there?"

She shrugged. "Easy. It's a little town where four months out of the year nothing happens because of the snow and then summer comes and so do the crowds. I particularly enjoyed it after I realized I was bi," she chuckled.

"I'll bet. You must've had a great time."

"Oh, I did. There's nothing like working in a B and B when you're a horny teenager. All of those beds. All of those rooms. My first lover was ten years older than me. I came out when I was fifteen, but I looked twenty-two. She was a guest staying there for singles' weekend. I came by to bring her another pillow, and we wound up talking for a long time. Then she asked me to test the pillow for her."

She laughed. "You actually fell for that line?"

"I was fifteen."

"And now you're twenty-four," she said, shaking her head.

She moved closer and rubbed her arm. "Yes, now I'm of age." She licked her earlobe and showered her neck with kisses. "I want you again."

She pulled away. "We can't."

"Oh, yes we can." She unfastened three more buttons of her shirt, exposing her black bra. "We're not related. I'm not even officially adopted. Our familial relationship is practically nonexistent."

"According to whom?"

"Wikipedia." She grinned, well aware that she was driving her crazy.

She unhooked the bra's front clasp and parted the fabric slowly. Technically she was still dressed and wearing all of her clothing, but her nipples played peek-a-boo and Dani suddenly felt very warm.

She tried not to stare at the perfect breasts and focus on her martini. She'd need at least three more. The flight attendant was familiar with her drinking habits and came by and set the pitcher next to her without a second glance at Cat. He also knew her affinity for naked women and that it was common for her and her current lover to be mostly undressed. Sometimes they'd spend the entire flight lounging in the sleeping compartment having sex.

"So if Wikipedia says it's true," she said, returning to the conversation, "then it must be."

"There's a lot of good stuff on Wikipedia," Cat replied, stroking Dani's neck with her fingernails. "How do you think I found out about Petra's canvas?"

She took a deep breath. She'd surfed through many of the websites and seen hundreds of pictures of the tattoos but never her face—except on the O'Grady website as a prominent CEO. All anyone wanted to see was the body art. Cat pulled up Wikipedia on Dani's BlackBerry and confirmed her suspicions. Much of the small screen displayed her backside and "Ecstasy."

She remembered the day Petra had taken all of the pictures. She'd borrowed several lights, a backdrop and a Pentax from a woman Dani assumed was her latest conquest. For two hours Dani had posed in various positions while she took a few hundred photos of the tats—and a few dozen shots of her in compromising positions.

"These are just for me," Petra had growled as Dani spread her legs and threw her head back as requested.

Cat scanned the article which focused on Petra's biography and her creativity. No doubt many of her fans had added to the site, crediting her with such a wonderful idea as modeling her work on her lover, who was only described as "an influential businesswoman."

Several of Dani's other tattoos were shown but never her face or her private parts. When Petra had initially convinced her to sit for the pictures, she'd lied and said they'd only be a part of her professional portfolio and only art scholars would see them. So Dani had been totally shocked the first time someone mentioned they'd seen Petra's tattoos on the Internet. She realized she'd been totally naïve and had called Petra in anger. She'd only laughed and promised to keep her identity a secret, which she'd done since their breakup.

"Let's see what else I can learn about you," Cat said, typing O'Grady Candy onto the Google search line.

She noticed there were now 26,000 references. *That's up five hundred since the last time I checked.* Cat scrolled through a few pages until she found something interesting, an article written about O'Grady Candy when Dani took the helm. She remembered it well and appreciated the fair-mindedness of the journalist and her gorgeous ass.

"So do you really believe it's nearly impossible for a woman to become a CEO?" Cat asked, reading from the article.

"Yeah. There aren't very many of us, and I doubt I'd be one if the business wasn't family owned. The board room is still for men and women don't appear to have the stomachs for it."

Cat scowled. "You don't think women are as strong as men?"

She shook her head. "It's against our nature. Much of the bullshit that men have said about women is true. Most women don't have the brass balls to do what needs to be done."

"You included?"

She shrugged. "I'd like to think I've got what it takes, but sometimes I question my decisions. I wonder if I'd make a different decision if I were a man."

"Really?"

Cat added Petra's canvas to Dani's name on the search line and no hits came up.

"Thank God," she sighed.

Cat set the BlackBerry down and stood. She leaned over Dani's chair, her breasts dangling in her face.

"So what would a man do in this situation?" she teased. "Would a male CEO push me away?" She straddled Dani's legs and lowered herself into her lap.

"This isn't the same kind of situation," she argued feebly, certain that the potent Gold Flakes Supreme Vodka in her martini would be her undoing. It was like a white flag waving in the wind announcing surrender. The vodka and Cat's perfect breasts, which were now fully exposed since she'd stripped off her top and bra, were definitely to blame. She tipped Dani's chin and kissed her deeply while she unbuttoned her blouse.

"We don't have a lot of time," she murmured. "This is a short flight."

"Then I'll need to be fast," Cat said, practically jumping out of the chair and landing on the floor like a grasshopper. She pulled up Dani's black skirt, exposing her pink thong.

"Too easy." Cat laughed and burrowed her head between Dani's thighs.

Dani moaned. *She's obviously licked a lot of lollipops, and I really respect that.*

"Sometimes the best way to go fast is to go slow."

Dani never heard the pilot instruct them to return to their seats and fasten their seat belts—which they didn't. If her ears popped as they descended, she didn't realize it. And she had no recollection of the landing. All she remembered were her loud moans as Cat made her come over and over. And like a magician, by the time they reached the gate and she'd opened her eyes, her skirt was back in place and Cat was offering her a drag on a cigarette, which she gratefully accepted.

# Chapter Six

"Your body is a total fucking turn on," Cat exclaimed when they climbed into the chauffeured car and headed into Provincetown. "I'll ask Olivia to put you in the Penthouse. It could be deliciously romantic."

"We need to slow down in front of Olivia."

She tried to sound insistent. She moved to the other side of the car and pointed to a fold in the seat fabric. "I think you should stay over there." She imagined the Berlin Wall and decided she'd be shot if she tried to cross over to the wonderful land of Cat.

Cat pouted once again reminding Dani nearly two decades separated them.

"Are you mad at me?"

She sighed. "No, I'm angry with myself. I don't want to be attracted to you. I've got issues with it. It's not because you're young. I've dated women in their twenties. It fizzles out pretty quickly," she added, remembering none of her nubile conquests could stay focused through a dinner conversation. "By being involved we're complicating this situation for both of us," she said. "Do you get that?"

Cat nodded slowly. "I agree. We need to set aside our unbelievable chemistry for the greater good."

"Exactly." She opened her briefcase and withdrew Valerie's file on Rafaela Tores Verdes. "Now, let's talk about how you're going to help me. I take it you've met Rafi?"

Cat lit a cigarette and nodded. "Yeah, a few times. Her candy's great and she's cool. The store's cool, too. It's hard to miss." She laughed and added, "It reminds me of yours. It's like one of those telephone boxes in London and considering a lot of the other places on Commercial Street need a paint job, it stands out."

Commercial Street was the appropriately named avenue in Provincetown where everyone shopped. A bright red front would be highly visible and she certainly would have ventured into a candy store if she'd seen one during her many weekends there. Dani flipped through Valerie's files and realized Doces had operated for only three years. She hadn't been back to P-town in four years, not since *the incident*.

She stared out the window at the huge thickets of trees as they wound their way down Race Point Road toward Route 6, the thoroughfare that paralleled the distinctive curl at the tail of Massachusetts and ended at P-town which was also known as Land's End. She marveled at the expanse of green, a foreign color in New York City.

Once they came to the main stoplight on Conwell Street, her inherent GPS kicked in and she knew where she was. They headed south toward Bradford Street and the surrounding forest gave way to civilization and centuries-old housing.

She thought Provincetown looked like many of the other small New England towns balancing the past and the present. The dog park, skate park and strip malls sat on the edges of the community while the history of P-town was preserved at its heart. Many of the spacious, older homes had been converted to B and B's to accommodate the massive tourist trade that converged on the tiny hamlet each June.

They motored slowly down Bradford Street toward the Fairbanks Inn, the B and B owned by Olivia Santos. The famed Pilgrim Monument loomed in the distance, P-town's dedication to the first landing place of white settlers. She'd climbed the series of steps and ramps with more than a few women, and while it was a benign first date, it was also a chance to ogle their fine rear ends. Arriving at the top on a warm summer night was always romantic, and she'd taken advantage of the mood on several occasions.

Showing no respect for boundaries, Cat slipped into her lap and cradled her face. "Just once more."

"No," she said, adamantly. "We're not doing it in the car—again."

They passed several couples, but no one noticed Cat using every weapon in her arsenal—lips, hands and teeth—to get her to change her mind. *Either no one can see us through the tinted windows or they just don't care. This is Provincetown after all.*

She gently pushed her away. "Stop," she said simply.

For the first time her mind was fully focused on the tasks at hand—meeting a woman who professed to be her half-sister and confronting a difficult distributor. Anxiety gripped her like a wrench tightening a nut. She realized she hadn't eaten all day and grabbed two Peanut Clusters from her bag and offered one to Cat who apparently was also famished.

After she'd devoured the chewy candy, she pressed a button and said, "Tom, we're going to the Fairbanks Inn at Ninety Bradford Street. It'll be on your left."

"You know the inn?"

"You knew I'd do my homework, right? And I've seen it. I haven't stayed there but it seems nice."

"It is. Olivia's put her life into it. She gets a lot of great reviews on different websites and blogs."

They pulled up next to a stately red brick colonial mansion from the 1800s with yellow siding and green shutters. She noticed two other buildings, one to her right and one peeking out from behind the trees in the back. She followed Cat through the front door and into the living room, the wide plank floors creaking slightly with each footfall. The room was tastefully done in comfortable oak furniture, and an enormous built-in bookcase covered an entire wall.

"Catarina, is that you?" a voice called.

Before she could answer a woman wearing a red Polo shirt, jeans and sneakers appeared in the doorway her arms open in greeting. They hugged tightly and Cat kissed her on the cheek.

"Olivia, this is Dani."

She wasn't sure what she expected, but Olivia Santos looked nothing like her father. Whereas Dempsey O'Grady's features were typically Irish, Olivia possessed a thin nose and small eyes. Her shoulder-length dark hair was pulled back into a bun and several strands hung loose as if she'd been working. Dani imagined managing an inn was a full-time job. But she knew Olivia, who was striking in her grungy clothes, would be stunning after a day with a New York stylist.

After an awkward beat Olivia threw her arms open and locked Dani in an embrace that she felt obliged to return. She said a few words in Portuguese and although Dani couldn't understand them, the tone was welcoming and friendly. Olivia Santos was clearly glad to see her. Dani glanced at Cat who was chewing her nail.

Olivia stepped away and instantly became the caring innkeeper. She looked about and said, "Where are your bags?"

"They're out in the car," she said. "The driver's getting them."

Olivia turned back to Cat with a huge smile. "I have a surprise for you."

She gave a little whistle and a handsome blond man emerged from the office wearing a button-down Oxford cloth shirt and chinos. An ID badge was affixed to his belt, and Dani could see that he worked for the city of Provincetown. He looked slightly embarrassed as if he was pleasing Olivia by staging this little scene.

"Hey, Cat," he said.

He was rugged and wore an easy smile. Dani instantly guessed he was truly a good guy who would make an excellent husband for a nice *heterosexual* woman, which Cat was not. However, she quickly ran into his arms and while she ignored his pursed lips, she gave him a big hug.

"Hi," she said before pulling away. "How are you?"

"I'm good," he said.

Dani could tell by the way he looked at Cat that he was smitten with her, but he quickly put his hands back into his pockets as if he sensed that any sudden moves might scare her away like a paranoid feral cat. He acted gallant, but she imagined they'd had sex since Cat wasn't above such sacrifices to keep Olivia in the dark.

"Uh, Nathaniel this is Dani," she said with a quick motion.

They nodded and smiled and she was certain he was clueless about Cat's tendencies based on the polite but nonprotective look that he gave her. He didn't see her as a threat. *And I'm not a threat. Cat's fun but she's not the future.*

"I need to get to work," he said in an even voice, "but I'm hoping we can get together sometime for dinner?"

"Of course," she answered politely.

He kissed both her and Olivia on the cheek before disappearing out the door. The scene was both quaint and painful, but she could tell from Olivia's expression that she only saw it as quaint.

"He's such a fine young man, Cat," she said proudly.

"I'll get the bags from the driver," she replied, ignoring her comment.

They watched her hurry out the door and Olivia said, "She's such a wonderful girl, just misguided. Nathaniel is absolutely perfect for her. I hope she didn't bother you with all kinds of inappropriate questions during your flight down here."

Dani's face felt flush and she rubbed her neck, remembering that Olivia assumed they'd just met. "No, she was delightful." She glanced around the room. "This is a wonderful place. How long have you owned it?"

"Thank you for the compliment. It's been in our family for nearly thirty years."

"And I thought Cat said something about you owning a restaurant?"

Olivia nodded. "Yes, my family has owned the Seafarer on the West End for nearly fifty years. It's one of the oldest restaurants in Provincetown."

Cat returned pulling Dani's suitcase and carrying her own tote bag. "Can Dani stay in the Penthouse?" she asked, not bothering to set the luggage down.

Olivia's face brightened at the suggestion. "That's a wonderful idea, Catarina."

They followed Cat past the kitchen and through the sun porch, where she assumed breakfast was served each morning. Outside, several metal tables and chairs dotted a red brick patio, which was surrounded by lush green landscape. She took a deep breath and let the clean air veiled with just a hint of sea salt fill her lungs. She loved New York, but she needed a periodic fix of foliage and trees to offset the smog and skyscrapers that she encountered on a daily basis.

"The main building is the Captain's House," Olivia said, "and over there is the Carriage House."

She glanced at the structure that sat directly behind the Captain's House—a two-story gray clapboard building bordered by shrubs and sculpted hedges. Undoubtedly the many windows allowed the guests a gorgeous view of the trees at the back of the property while the location provided a wonderful sense of romantic intimacy.

Cat was already headed up a steep flight of stairs attached to the third building that completed the Fairbanks Inn.

Olivia paused and threw a glance at Cat, who carried Dani's luggage effortlessly. "To be that young again."

She nodded. *I hope my face isn't the color of an O'Grady Candied Apple.*

"This is the Garden House," Olivia explained. "It has three

levels with guest rooms, a suite and the penthouse where you'll be staying. It's a heck of a climb but it's worth it for the view."

"I'm sure it's lovely," she said. When she reached the top, she felt slightly winded. She was used to stairs but not ones so steep. *And those damn cigarettes I'm smoking certainly aren't helping.*

And the room inside was indeed charming built along the angular contours of the pointed roof, complete with two skylights. A fireplace sat across from the bed and two couches formed a sitting area underneath the bank of windows. It was light and airy and she suddenly wished she were staying for more than a few days.

She glanced at Olivia who tried to smile but kneaded her hands nervously. She imagined this meeting was even more difficult for her because she'd known Dani existed and had filled her head with scenarios of what it would be like.

"I know you want to see the will and we've got a lot to talk about but you should get settled first," Olivia said lightly. "Come down when you're ready."

She nodded and went to the door. There was deference in the way she walked and moved as though each step could bring chastisement. She held the doorknob and looked back at Cat obviously waiting for her.

Cat remained against a wall and made no effort to hoist her duffel onto her shoulder. "You go ahead, Mom. I'll make sure Dani has everything she needs then I'll head down to number nine, right?"

Olivia paused for a second and left.

As soon as the door clicked shut, Cat pulled Dani into her arms. "I know you're going to say no, but I want to give you a really good reason to say yes."

"What's that?"

"It could be our last time. Now that I'm back my mother will put me to work, and I'll have to hang out with Nathaniel. You'll be deprived."

She hugged her tightly, and Dani's common sense was smothered by the desire she felt whenever Cat touched her.

They'd known each other for three days, and already she anticipated where Cat would rest her hands or put her lips—where she wanted to be touched. In seconds their clothes were shed, and they were snuggling under the layers of blankets and sheets finding a rhythm that was becoming quite natural.

Once their pulses had stopped racing, bodies slick with perspiration, Cat propped herself up on an elbow and caressed the broken heart over Dani's breast. She wore a familiar expression and it only took Dani a few seconds to remember it—when an idea lingered at the corner of an artist's mind, taunting her to pull it forward. She remained very still, curious as to what Cat would do. Petra could sit for hours, staring at a canvas or out a window, patiently waiting for the idea to germinate. She doubted Cat would have such tenacity. And she didn't. It only took a minute before she blinked and kissed her.

"I want to know why," Cat whispered.

"Why what?"

"You've half-heartedly resisted me several times but you keep giving in. If I thought for a second you were serious, I would've stepped back. But I know you're not. I know you don't mean *no*."

She laughed and ran a hand through her hair. Cat was completely right. When it came to sex, she rarely said no. "I guess I'm easy," she concluded.

"That's fucking great." Cat fell against the mattress and stared at the ceiling. "My self-esteem thanks you."

"It's not you—"

"Clearly," she said acidly. "Apparently it could be anyone."

Dani sat up against the headboard and hovered over her. "It's just that sex is a pure act to me. It's natural and beautiful and since I find women to be beautiful, I'm easily aroused."

"Are you trying to say that you're attracted to *all* women?"

"No, of course not. Everyone has their types, but I like a lot of different women. And to answer your question, I haven't really wanted to say no because I enjoy having sex with you."

"But it's just sex," she clarified. "It's easy for you because there's nothing else to it."

She shifted uncomfortably, displeased with her word choice. Therapist Number Four, the only smart one she'd ever hired, had suggested that she was uncomfortable with loneliness and used random hookups to quell the overwhelming loneliness she felt. She needed to *be* with someone without the emotional attachment.

She said simply, "Sex is natural and multicolored and sensory driven. Sex is every great candy in the world mixed together."

Cat turned away, shaking her head. "You're just talking about the physical act, not what goes on in the mind."

"Nothing does."

"Excuse me?"

"I try not to let my mind get in the way. It's been more challenging with you because of our complicated relationship. But if I'd just met you in a bar or at a party, I'd have no resistance."

She kissed the top of her head, but Cat wriggled away and got out of bed to get dressed. "Are you telling me there's no room for love in your heart? Sex is basically about lust?"

"It can be," she said. "And now that I've met Olivia, who thinks of herself as your *mother*, that really was our last time. And I mean it."

Cat buttoned her blouse and pulled on her pants. She could tell her anger was smoldering like a hot campfire.

"I think sex can be about lust, too," Cat said. "But that's not what you're saying. You sleep with women *just* to have sex, not because you want anything else out of it. Right?"

She'd summarized Dani's philosophy with a biting judgment behind it like a milk chaser after a great glass of wine and she felt compelled to explain.

"I don't expect anything else from a liaison, that's true. Look Cat, I'm a lot older than you. I've been in different relationships and I've raised a son—alone. I've got different priorities."

She was clearly annoyed. "Stop patronizing me. Ah, the naïveté of youth," she mocked. "You lose a lot when you get older, too."

"That's true," she conceded. When Cat stared at the floor she realized the conversation wasn't about youth or age. She pulled her into an embrace and caressed her cheek. "You're amazing, okay? I mean that."

She worked up a little smile. "Thanks. Dani, it's just that I—"

She cut her off with a quick kiss, not wanting to know the end of the sentence. Then she headed for the bathroom while Cat followed, clearly in a better mood.

"So you don't have any intent of ever finding a partner? Do you care if gays can ever get married?"

"What I want for myself and for everyone else is different. I think everybody should have the right to love or *not love* anyone."

She got into the shower while Cat remained in the doorway. "Is it because you're incredibly rich?"

She pulled the shower curtain back and shook her head. "What?"

"Do you think that women would only want you for your money? Is that why you avoid falling in love?"

She chuckled and focused on the steaming jets. Cat was too young to understand her views of sex and intimacy. And when she was her age she'd had a much narrower understanding of the world too. Relationships were rooms with one door, one exit. Twenty-something women loved to talk a good game about fantasy role-playing, threesomes and sexual freedom, but those were diversions until Ms. Right showed up and justified their subscription to *Modern Lesbian Wedding*.

When she emerged from the shower ten minutes later, her hair tangled over her face, she assumed Cat had left in a huff until she heard, "Don't move."

Worried that there might be a Cape Cod rodent or insect nearby she did as instructed and stood still, the wet towel halfway down her torso.

"Just give me a second," Cat murmured. "Swivel your upper body a few inches to the right."

"What?"

"Just do it and don't raise your head. The rest of you is perfect."

She sighed. The memory of Petra uttering the same direction in practically the same tone told her that she was being studied like a model. Another minute passed, and she thought she heard the soft swipes of pencil strokes racing across a paper. She tried to sneak a peek but was quickly reprimanded.

"Hold still. Don't ruin this."

"You're lucky I lived with an artist," she said sarcastically.

"Was that just lust?" Cat asked. "Or do you let any lover turn your body into her own personal ego trip?"

She smirked. She had no intention of explaining her relationship with Petra to anyone. Even after so many years she still wasn't sure she understood it.

"Okay, you can move now," Cat said, disappearing out of the bathroom.

She dried off and unpacked her suitcase while Cat perched on a chair next to a window, her sketchpad on her lap, savoring the best light in the room. Once in a while her hand would freeze, and she'd glance at Dani before it resumed its frantic motion.

She turned away and smiled at her fierce and naïve determination, so different from Petra who approached drawing as a lazy ride on a curvy road. She drew with the ease and confidence of an expert, someone who knew that the vision would eventually fill the page and wasn't worried that it would swirl down the drain if it wasn't produced quickly. Perhaps she'd been like Cat when she was young, too, but they'd met at an art exhibit in Boston when Petra was thirty and a blip in the art world. Dani was thirty-five.

She'd been dragged there by a friend and was looking to leave early until Petra crossed the room and took her arm. She was exceptionally tall with a Rubenesque figure, and Dani was dwarfed by her commanding presence. She led her to the one piece she'd displayed, a watercolor titled *Ornate*.

Dani had looked sexy that night wearing a sheer sleeveless

blouse over a tank top. Petra would later tell her that she'd been drawn to her lily-white Irish skin, which was perfect and unblemished.

"Do you like my painting?" Petra had finally asked.

"Yes," she said, meeting her fierce gaze.

Her hand had lingered around her waist, just high enough on her hip to be respectable but she felt her long fingers caressing the curve of her buttock.

"What if I asked you to pose nude for me?"

She'd stared into the deep blue eyes. "I'd say yes."

That had been the beginning.


Dani and Olivia faced each other on the couch in mirrored poses. Just as she sat on the edge of the sofa, her knees together and back straight, so did Olivia, who also held two worn pages of yellow notebook paper carefully between her hands. She passed them to her without a word.

She put on her reading glasses and instantly recognized her father's loopy script that most people couldn't decipher. It was almost childlike, and a single sentence could consume nearly two lines. She found it appropriate for a candymaker.

The first paragraph was her father's attempt at legalese, making sure everyone knew he was of sound mind, and that this will superseded all of his other wills. By the second paragraph he made his wishes clear. He acknowledged that Cruz was his lover and Olivia his daughter. She was entitled to half of everything. *And there it is.*

The majority of the second page was a listing of his holdings, all of which she knew by heart—her childhood home in Westchester that she'd sold years ago, the original candy factory, the plant in New Jersey and a summer home in Miami on the beach, which she rarely visited but couldn't stand to part with because her mother had loved it so much. It also made for a great sublet whenever she wanted to schmooze clients and offer them a free vacation spot.

As she read, she heard his voice through the words he'd chosen, the way he put together sentences the same way he talked. She bit her lip, knowing that the will was real. He mentioned things that only her family knew and she imagined that Olivia would soon offer up photographs and other evidence to support her claim.

At the bottom he'd signed and dated it, indicating it was written just a few months before he died. She flipped the pages over but there was nothing else. When she looked up, Olivia was kneading her hands again.

"Well, what do you think? Should I call an attorney?"

She shrugged. "That's up to you."

She pictured a conference room of lawyers facing off, potentially for years. She thought of the bad press and how her father's affair could ruin the company—a company whose main clients were children. She'd made her decision.

She handed the papers back to her. "I don't question that my father wrote it or that you're telling the truth. I believe you but I would like to fax a copy to my attorney."

"Of course, I'll be happy to help you fax it."

Olivia shrunk against the couch. Dani sensed she'd been ready for a battle and wasn't prepared for her acquiescence.

"So are you ready to help me?" Olivia finally asked.

That was a good question. She'd acknowledged it was her father's will because it was. To fight its authenticity in court would be foolish and incredibly expensive, but only force would persuade her to give Olivia fifty percent of the business her family had built. She needed to find a solution quickly and return to New York even if Cat didn't like it.

She went to the front window and gazed out at Bradford Street. At the top of the hill sat the Crowne Pointe Historic Inn and Spa where part of *the incident* had occurred. It was unlikely Olivia remembered the story or knew of Dani's involvement, although her exploits had certainly made the rounds over the years.

"You want security for Cat, right?"

Olivia nodded. "Yes, she and Nathaniel will have a wonderful life together, but she needs to bring something to the marriage."

"Forgive me, Olivia, but what has Nathaniel got? From what I could tell he's a city employee, a civil servant."

"Yes, but he has a good job. Cat's not trained to do much."

"She's a wonderful photographer." Dani stopped herself from discussing Liam's wedding. "At least, that's what she told me."

Olivia set her gaze on a portrait that hung near the fireplace. It was an oil painting of a woman who looked like an extraordinary version of herself. Dani was certain the woman was Cruz and she understood immediately why her father would be attracted to such an exotic person, someone completely the opposite of her mother.

Olivia noticed her fascination with the portrait. "Her beauty was her second best feature. It was her personality that drew everyone to her, including our father."

"How did they meet?" she asked automatically. She really didn't *want* to know their story but she needed to understand.

"He was a regular at the Seafarer. Every six weeks or so he'd come into town and show up to eat the chowder. At first they were just friends, but after a year of talking and flirting he offered to walk her home one night after closing."

An image of the Coney Island boardwalk filled her head—the twinkling lights, the shrill organ music and the clashing food smells. Meeting Cruz must have been like a trip to Coney Island for her father.

"Mom always knew she couldn't have him. His life was in New York, and he loved you very much."

She felt Olivia's gaze on her and worked to control the tears spilling down her cheeks. "Maybe we should stick to business."

Olivia wiped away a few of her own tears. "Absolutely."

She looked at her seriously. "I know that we share the same father, but I don't think of you as a part of O'Grady Candy. And the issue at hand is money derived from my company, the company you've never even seen."

"That's not true," Olivia disagreed. "My mother and I went to the factory one summer when we were visiting New York. I was about fourteen and I didn't want to go. It was far too childish for me but my mother was insistent. I didn't understand why it was so important to her to visit a candy factory, but I agreed and we took the tour inside the funny little pink cottage."

"What did you think of it?"

"I don't remember much. Like any typical teenager who's forced to go somewhere they don't want to be, I just walked around scowling with my arms folded." She paused and sighed. "But years later after our father visited and Mom died, I remembered how oddly she'd behaved that day, looking around like she was waiting to see something or someone. At one point I asked her what was wrong because she acted like a shoplifter."

They both chuckled slightly at the image and the conversation faded until only the mantel clock was heard.

"Can I show you something?" Olivia asked timidly.

"Of course," she said hesitantly, wondering what memory Olivia might reveal.

She disappeared into the office and returned with a red hatbox. When she removed the lid, Dani's jaw dropped. The box was filled with sealed wrappers from every O'Grady candy ever made. Sitting on top and sealed in a protective sleeve was an original Choco Delite wrapper, circa 1942. It was a dark brown skin with playful white writing. The name was framed in a decorative rectangular border and the price—five cents—was posted at every corner. She marveled at the simplicity and the freedom her father enjoyed. She was forced to comply with endless regulations about nutritional information, product weight and the placement of the bar code. And she wouldn't consider stamping a price on the label in fear that she'd never be able to raise the price without customer backlash.

She carefully withdrew each one and set it on the coffee table, grouping like candies together in a label version of solitaire. When they were all dispersed she marveled at her family history. She'd forgotten that Moon Munchies had been available once in three different flavors, and she couldn't believe her father had changed the Wedgie Chocolate wrapper which seemed nearly identical to the original.

"Why did he do that?" she murmured, holding the two tinfoil labels in her hands. Wedgie Chocolate was an oversized dark square of chocolate shaped like a piece of pie designed specifically for chocoholics.

"I once asked my mom that question and she said that it was because he didn't like the way the *e* on Wedgie disappeared over the edge. The lettering was too big."

She compared the wrappers and indeed the later version had smaller letters that ensured the name was perfectly centered on the wrapper.

"Do you have every wrapper we produced?"

Olivia nodded proudly. "My interest in O'Grady Candy is more than superficial as you can see."

Dani picked up a few of the wrappers again, focusing on those she remembered specifically from her childhood. One candy in particular—Winkles—was actually named by her. She'd sampled the first bag of chewy jelly candies on her tenth birthday, the day before they were distributed to the rest of the world. Winkles were still going strong thirty-five years later.

"This is incredible. I'm not even sure the company has all the original wrappers. I know I don't."

"Well, I'd be happy to put them on display if you ever want to do that."

"Thanks," she said, touched by the gesture.

They carefully returned all the wrappers to the hatbox, and she periodically stopped to study a detail she hadn't noticed before.

"I also have a scrapbook of my mom with your dad. Would you like to see that?"

"No," she said quickly. "I mean, I just don't think I can. This was different."

"I understand," Olivia said quietly. She rose with the box

and headed toward the office door. "It's probably best if we don't compare too many memories. Our lives are joined together like the two bulbs of an hourglass. To fill one with sand means the other is equally depleted. I think that's how our lives are."

When she returned she picked up the will again. Dani followed her gaze outside to the courtyard area where Cat hurriedly withdrew her sculpting tools. Olivia watched her for a moment before she faced Dani, her mouth a thin line.

"I guess it's time to put our cards on the table. I want enough money to buy the art gallery for Catarina. Otherwise I'd like my half of the O'Grady Candy Company, regardless of whether or not I've earned it."

# Chapter Seven

After Olivia helped her fax a copy of the will to Harry, she rushed off to her chores. Dani imagined Harry would want to fight since so much was at stake, but she couldn't fathom the bad press. Her arms began to itch and she scratched them violently. She stared out the window at Cat, watching her pound the clay while she processed the dilemma. Whenever she faced a difficult situation and was tempted to make a rash decision, she was reminded of Cosmic Cotton Candy, one of O'Grady's greatest failures that happened during her first year as CEO. The premise of a solid rectangular bar that tasted as delightful as the billowy pink confection seemed to be financial gold. People loved cotton candy, and it was difficult to access unless you were at a fair or carnival.

It should have made a fortune, but it bombed during taste tests even though testers couldn't tell the difference. It was as sugary and light as the real thing—but it wasn't the real thing. Testers divulged that eating cotton candy was as much about the experience as the taste. The stringy goo sticking to a chin was as important as the sensation of the candy dissolving in the mouth. They'd shelved the idea, but she learned a valuable lesson and that was the importance of studying all facets to a situation before choosing a course of action.

She joined Cat on the patio and dropped into a chair. Cat threw her a lurid smile, one that suggested she could be distracted from her work if it involved a return to the Penthouse.

"Your mother is adamant about buying you the gallery. I doubt I can talk her out of it."

She shook her head and continued to work the clay. "Of course you will. She just needs time."

"Cat, I don't have a lot of time for this. I need to get back to work."

She stabbed a tool into the block of clay and crossed her arms.

"What would be the worst thing that would happen if she knew you were bi? And I'm talking about Olivia, not just anyone," Dani added. She didn't need a laundry list recounting all the reasons people hid in the closet from their families.

"She might disown me."

She didn't buy it. "Really? She took you in when no one else would."

"Yes, and I've lied to her about the most important part of my life. She'd resent that more than my sexuality."

"But don't you think she'd get over her anger?"

Cat shook her head and plopped into a chair. "I don't know, and I don't want to find out. There has to be another way."

Dani took her hand and admired the strong fingers caked in clay. She loved artists' hands and appreciated the talent that emanated from them. *I like the beauty and the pleasure they create.* Cat leaned toward her for a kiss but she pulled back.

"That would be a hell of a way for your mother to learn the truth," she said.

She slumped back in the chair and pulled her smokes from her apron. Dani could tell she was scared and worried. *She thinks this is simple. I'm the big CEO and I'll save the day.* She'd obviously been counting on her since she took Liam's wedding gig.

"I think you should tell her the truth," Dani pressed. "Now that I've met her I can see she's a strong woman. She's been through a lot and she runs an inn. And I'm not so sure she doesn't suspect," she added, thinking about the odd look on Olivia's face when Cat offered to help Dani unpack.

"There's no way," she disagreed. "I've always been very discreet."

"I'm not saying she knows, but I think she's wondering why you're not head-over-heels in love with Nathaniel."

She was adamant when she said, "No way. She's clueless."

Dani shook her head and stood. The conversation was going in circles. "Well, you need to help her get a clue. Maybe you'll come up with some sort of a miracle plan, but otherwise I'm writing your mother a check for whatever amount she needs. Maybe you can talk her out of using the money for the gallery."

She headed for the gate and Cat asked, "Where are you going?"

"To deal with my other problem."


She wandered down Commercial Street looking for Doces Candy Shop and trying to forget about Cat. Hopefully she'd come to her senses and realize there was only one choice if she wanted her happiness.

Commercial Street was the center of all activity, a three-mile east-to-west stretch of connected buildings that were an eclectic throwback to a time when unique architecture was the norm and not the exception. Their different shapes and sizes were complemented by varying levels of upkeep. Some were freshly painted while others were dilapidated, the exteriors suffering from the wind, rain and snow that pummeled P-town. Most were shops that catered to the tourists, selling everything from original artwork to homemade fudge and interspersed were some of the most amazing restaurants and cafés. All were specialty shops and only a few were part of a chain. There wasn't a McDonald's or a Starbucks to be found.

Standing in the middle of Commercial Street, she could envision the turn of the century when only the buildings and the streets existed—no power lines or sidewalks, which had been included as necessary afterthoughts. She glanced up at the black strings that crisscrossed in haphazard fashion, providing electricity and phone service but clearly detracting from the aesthetics. And as she crossed the street the sidewalk disappeared, another common sight in P-town.

Ten feet away was a rack of earthenware outside an Italian pottery store. She knew that rack well since she'd crashed into it while she was being chased by a madwoman. *Hell hath no fury . . . What was her name?*

She could trace her path of destruction from the famed Lobster Pot restaurant where *the incident* originated all the way to the parking lot of the Crown and Anchor Inn, the place where she'd stayed and where her Mercedes had been located for her quick getaway. In between the two places there had been much destruction, and she could still hear the crashing and banging sounds every time she thought of that day.

A pedal cart whipped past her and nearly ran into a motorist who didn't understand that Commercial Street had been claimed long ago by the pedestrians. Automobiles were taboo except for trucks delivering the essentials like food and booze to the restaurants. The motorist waved an apology and turned at the next street almost hitting a gay couple too enamored with each other's lips to notice that it wasn't the right time to cross.

A new blue and white café called the Brew sat across from Id, one of her favorite shops, and she decided to grab a cup of coffee to go with the cigarette she was craving. Although the issues of Rafaela Tores Verdes and Olivia Santos swarmed her brain, she easily pushed them aside for an outside table where she could people watch. High season was still a few weeks away, but the tourists who hated crowds or didn't care about the summer event calendar were already there. She stretched her legs across another chair and enjoyed her coffee and cig—and being ogled by some of the tourists.

It was warm enough for shorts and a tank top, meaning that women and some straight men stared at her tattoos. Once in a while someone would stop and commend Petra's work, asking about the artist. The conversation was a memorized script, one in which she mentioned a friend who didn't do commercial work. Inevitably they would walk away disappointed but not before they offered one more compliment or asked her for a date. Sometimes she'd said yes and sometimes no. Therapist Number Six had suggested that the pickup potential was another reason she'd never removed the tattoos. She'd thought a bit more about that explanation before she fired him.

"Would you like anything else?" a waitress asked as she passed by carrying a tray loaded with dirty dishes. She was a thirty-something butch wearing tight leather pants and a CBGB T-shirt. Her short, straggly blond hair hung around her face, and Dani imagined she was constantly pushing it away.

"No, I'm fine," Dani said absently.

"Are you sure?"

She spoke slowly and her emphasis on the word *sure* made Dani look up—into light blue eyes that reminded her of Baby Blue Suckers, the rich raspberry candy that was an O'Grady favorite. She asked the question as if Dani had answered incorrectly the first time and was getting a second chance. She leaned back and said nothing. Propositions were expected in P-town, anytime and anywhere. For many it was an enormous cruising spot, and it wasn't uncommon to turn a corner down a side street and interrupt a hookup happening in broad daylight.

The blonde easily balanced the tray on her shoulder, and Dani could see her bulging biceps from the constant exercise of hefting glasses and plates.

"What does that say?" she asked, pointing to the Chinese symbol on her belt buckle.

"Opportunity," the waitress said with a hard stare.

"I'm really busy," she said.

"And I'm really efficient."

She turned and went back into the café while Dani watched her perfect ass sway in the sunlight. She could easily avoid her by exiting through the white picket fence that bordered the patio and continue down the street toward Doces. *I need to just get going.* She pulled herself up and stubbed out her cigarette debating her choice. *C'mon. I've already had some fabulous sex today with Cat. Am I that horny?*

She headed inside and saw the blonde talking to a guy behind the counter. When their eyes met, she whispered something to him and went through a doorway to the back. Dani followed, already feeling her heart pound. It'd been a long time since she'd hooked up in a public place. The door to the women's room was slightly ajar, and her skin tingled as she stepped into the darkness. She was grateful. This wouldn't be about her tattoos.

The door smacked shut and she heard the latch click. The blonde pulled them against the door and pressed her large breasts into Dani's back. She stroked her arms and intertwined their fingers.

"Guide me," she whispered. "Put my hands wherever you want to be touched. Make yourself feel good."

"What's your name?" she asked practically panting.

"Hope. Now shut up."

She closed her eyes and sunk into Hope's warm embrace. It was like dropping into a pile of soft leaves. She brought her hands to her belly and sighed when warm fingers burrowed underneath the flimsy tank top and popped her breasts out of the brassiere's lacy cups.

Hope chuckled slightly when her nipples hardened after only a moment of teasing. "Now where?"

Hope's right leg parted her thighs, and Dani guided her southward to her zipper. Her shorts fell to the floor and Hope's hands stroked her thong's waistband. A slit of daylight washed over the bathroom courtesy of a small window above the stalls. She could see her silhouette in the shadows but not her face, and it was just enough to be erotic. Her breasts jiggled over the top of her mangled bra and the V of her pink thong seemed to glow in the hazy daylight. She was hot and wet and the minute Hope touched her she'd come. She was certain of it. But like a chocolate with a wonderful cream center, she didn't want to reach the best part yet.

She led her to her buttocks and enjoyed the pinching and squeezing that followed. She even laughed when she threw her forward and spanked her hard.

"I thought you were in a hurry," she growled. "I've got customers."

She slid down against the door until Dani was practically sitting in her lap, straddling her leg. Dani moaned when she entered her. She watched in the mirror as she rode Hope, her hips rocking back and forth against her powerful right leg. She closed her eyes and was back on the ice at Rockefeller Center. She pumped her legs and leaped into the air for the double-axle. She lost count of the orgasms and eventually begged her to stop. When they eventually released the sexual connection, Dani retreated into one of the stalls. When she emerged Hope was leaning against the wall, smiling.

"Well, I should be going," Dani said, reaching for the doorknob.

Hope caught her hand and pulled her into an embrace. She decided the woman kissed as well as she fucked. When they left the restroom together, she noticed more patrons had gathered in the café. At the sight of Hope, her arm wrapped around Dani's shoulder, they applauded wildly. She was too stunned to react until Hope took a bow and went behind the counter to a chalkboard that listed all of the coffee offerings. A corner of the board was labeled Hope's Chest and bundles of hash marks filled the space. Hope looked over at her and drew a horizontal line to complete another bundle of five and the crowd applauded again.

She continued toward Doces, passing Adams' store, established in 1875. It had originally been a pharmacy but when word got out that the family didn't support gay marriage, all of the gays moved their prescriptions elsewhere and cut off the main revenue stream. Not a smart business move she thought as she passed the quaint little white building. She crossed the street and ducked into the Marine Supply, a huge shop that couldn't decide on a specialty so it carried everything, including men's underwear, ceramic dishes and Japanese swords. She loved roaming the aisles and hunting for the oddest items which became her contribution each year to the company's white elephant exchange at Christmas.

She strolled past a table of hula skirts where a cute brunette rearranged an umbrella display. Before she could duck behind a rack of cowboy boots, the woman saw her and went wide-eyed. She thought about running away but threw a hand up in greeting instead. The woman dropped the rest of the umbrellas and pulled her into a corner behind a giant cardboard cutout of Bella from *Twilight*.

"What are you doing here?"

She glanced at her nametag. Joelle. *How could I forget? Was it really that meaningless?*

"I'm just in town for a day," she said reassuringly.

"You vowed never to come back, remember?"

She nodded. She had.

"Does anyone else know you're here?"

She thought of her hookup with Hope and the knowing looks from the entire patronage at the Brew—she shook her head. Obviously none of them recognized her from four years before. Those were the folks Joelle was concerned about.

She chewed her lip and looked beyond a large knife display. "Didn't you get the letter?"

"Of course I did."

"Then?"

It was a fair question. After *the incident* a special meeting of the tourist commission had been called and Dani O'Grady was forever banned from Provincetown. As she'd packed for this trip she dismissed the contents of the letter certain that she wouldn't be there long enough to be noticed.

"I'm not *vacationing*," she argued. "I'm here on business visiting one of my suppliers." *And my half-sister and her sort-of daughter that I screwed. And did I mention I just had a quickie with a hot waitress? All in the name of corporate America!*

Joelle narrowed her eyes. "If Shaylalynn knew . . . "

She smacked her forehead. "That was her name. I've been trying to remember it for the last twenty-four hours."

It was one of the worst names she'd ever heard, a redneck name that completely fit. Shaylalynn was a walking hairdo, a beehive gone wrong that consumed her entire head. The rest of her tried to live up to her hair which was impossible. She was flat-chested and wore scarves to cover up her giraffe-like neck.

"How could you forget her?" Joelle cried.

"It was four years ago. I've had a lot going on."

"Well, she hasn't forgotten."

She shook her head. "Don't tell me you two are still together?"

Joelle's cheeks reddened, and she played with the hula skirts. "She's good to me, you know?" When Dani didn't respond she spat, "It's not like you were ever gonna take me back to New York!"

"Shh," she scolded. "Don't make a scene."

"Well, you weren't."

She shrugged. She'd come to Provincetown that summer to hookup and enjoy the singles scene. Unfortunately Joelle had caught her eye and she wasn't single.

"Look, I've got to get back to work, but you need to get out of P-town fast."

She walked away, and Dani watched her shapely little butt swish past the scuba diving section. It was hard to believe Shaylalynn was still around. She'd thought for sure that she would eventually combust from her explosive temper or she'd wind up in jail for killing someone. *And that could've been me.* But she remembered Shaylalynn was an adopted P-town native whose lesbian bar in the east end brought thousands into the town coffers. Even though Shaylalynn was fifty percent responsible for *the incident* it was a local versus a tourist and Dani became the target.

She left the store without purchasing anything and continued down the street looking for Doces. Painted fire engine red it was easy to spot, the most unique place among unique places. The name Doces in tubular lights arched across the façade. She guessed the sign was eye-catching at night. A small porch with two tables and chairs sat in front of a wide picture window. A few patrons armed with bundles of shopping bags draped themselves across the chairs enjoying their newly bought candy and taking a short breather from their excursion down Commercial Street.

The shop was packed with customers. She scanned the interior painted powder blue with red and white piping. Candy displays filled the walls and several carousel racks created aisles, cueing shoppers to walk in a certain direction. As she made her way through the first aisle she noticed interesting candies sharing shelf space with O'Grady. Upon inspection of the Taffy Twirls, Chocolate Heaven and Bitsy Bites, she determined that they were similar to some of hers and Rafaela Tores Verdes was indeed violating the non-compete clause.

She strolled through the other aisles and realized that Doces carried a multitude of items including novelty gifts like key chains and Rubik's Cubes, as well as hard-to-find candies from the sixties and seventies that she'd forgotten existed.

Dance music played and some patrons bopped to the beat. Three different TV screens were mounted on the walls showing a surreal video of dancing lollipops. It was incredibly bizarre but mesmerizing and like some of the other people, she found herself momentarily entranced by its creativity.

She scanned the crowd and noticed the bulk of the patrons were clustered around a case in the far corner. They were laughing and asking questions, for whoever was behind the counter was quite entertaining.

A lilting voice with a thick Spanish accent rose above the hum of the video and announced, "Madame Nougat insists that you sample this morsel. This confection will awaken your taste buds and make you glad to be alive."

She chuckled at the sales pitch as she inched closer toward the case and the voice. Once she jostled past a straight couple she understood the attraction. Standing behind the counter was a woman in heavy makeup wearing an orange bobbed wig and a toffee-colored dress with puffy white sleeves and a hoop skirt. She held up the candy between two three-inch long fingernails painted banana yellow and showed it to a slight gay man and his burly boyfriend.

"I call this Pirate Booty because of its shape."

Dani studied the amazing candy—a chocolate shaped like a gem. She thought of the ramifications to creating such a unique item. Certainly it would be incredibly time consuming to make such an intricate shell.

"Inside is the sweetest center imaginable," Madame Nougat continued. "A raspberry filling that when combined with the chocolate on your tongue causes a cataclysmic event in your mouth." The men looked at each other skeptically and she said, "Go on and try it if you don't believe me."

She produced a second candy and each man took a sample. Their pleasure was simultaneous.

"Oh my God," one said. "This is fabulous."

The other man nodded his head furiously and soon many in the crowd wanted samples.

She stepped out of the mob and continued her tour of the store. She was impressed with the layout that grouped items such as huge jars of open stock together against one wall and the tiered shelving that displayed all of the candy bars and old-fashioned treats. Everything was clean and freshly painted and when she glanced up at the lighting, she saw a blend of old-fashioned green hanging lamps that added ambience with some excellent track lighting interspersed over the candy displays, ensuring that the entire store was brightly lit. And the sparkling white tile floor added to the appeal.

She scanned the dozens of happy customers who had

multiple items to purchase including many O'Grady candies. She smiled. Knowing that millions of people loved her family's product made her happy. Several Doces employees dressed in light blue bowling shirts and black pants assisted customers. *I'm really impressed. Valerie was right about this place. It's a gold mine.*

As she approached the bank of cash registers she noticed an employee monitoring a red velvet curtain. She realized the group of people standing nearby was actually a line waiting to gain admittance behind the curtain. She sidled up next to a baby dyke texting on her phone.

"Hey, what's behind the curtain? I'm new here and curious."

The girl glanced up and her lips curled into a smile. "Well, if you're new to P-town, you definitely want to visit Purple."

Dani cocked her head to the side. "Purple? What's purple? The curtain's red."

"Once you go inside you'll see why," she said absently, clearly uninterested in a conversation.

Dani joined the line behind a young straight couple who continually groped each other as they slowly moved forward. She noticed no one exited through the curtain—they only entered. And entry occurred when the employee got a message over his Bluetooth.

Madame Nougat's laughter overpowered the dance music again as she introduced another candy to the crowd. From her vantage point, Dani could see behind the counter and the amazing array of chocolates, toffees and cream-filled candies waiting to be purchased.

Madame Nougat held out a tray of yellow spheres the size of gumballs. "Ladies and gentlemen, our next featured candy of the day are the Lemon Balls. They're tart and tangy and oh-so chewy. Who would like one?"

At least eight hands went up and the yellow spheres disappeared. In another five minutes her inventory of Lemon Balls was gone, and it was Dani's turn to go behind the red curtain. The employee motioned to her, and she entered a small hallway illuminated only by black light. Twenty feet ahead smooth jazz wafted through a doorway of purple beads.

She parted the beads and found herself in an entirely different kind of candy shop—one for adults. One side was labeled *Men* and the other *Women*, but every shelf and display was a different shade of purple with black trim. Gone were the bright lights of the kid's candy store. Purple was low-lit and passionate.

She turned to the women's section and strolled past the hard candy area filled with shelves of candy nipples, boob suckers, booby mints, gummy boobs and tit tarts. She almost laughed out loud at the clit ring candy and tried to imagine anyone wearing a giant cherry clit on her finger.

The chocolate display case contained pussies with cherry clitorises, as well as peppermint and boob chocolate sandwich cookies. She found the display of naked chocolate women interesting, especially since there was a variety of breast sizes from which to pick.

"Would you like a sample?" a woman wearing a purple bikini asked. "Perhaps an after-dinner nipple?"

She felt her face flush and couldn't believe it. "Um, that's okay, I'm good."

"No, really," the salesclerk insisted, presenting her with a tray full of nipples. "You'll love it."

She took a bite and was surprised by the taste—a blend of mint and milk chocolate that was perfect. "These are exceptional."

"Would you like me to wrap a box up for you?"

She shook her head and felt her cheeks warm. "Unfortunately I don't have anyone to share them with."

"That's so sad," the saleswoman answered. She fed Dani another candy letting her fingers trace the outline of her lips. "You really need to meet someone." She walked away and left the sweet smell of her perfume.

Dani climbed some stairs to a loft decorated with balloons, party hats and streamer covered in sexual images. Blow-up dolls sat in chairs around the cake table wearing edible underwear. She fingered a pair of fuzzy handcuffs and thought of Petra, who always liked to play games. She'd spent almost as much time being tied up, covered in whipped cream and eating Petra's edible strawberry thong as she had being inked.

She stared out into the crowd amassed in Purple. It was a small space, but at least a hundred customers were sampling the goddess chocolates or debating between all-day boob suckers or cherry lick-its. She didn't even want to think about the men's section which was packed with guys. She scanned the displays and saw that everything could be purchased through a website. She imagined Rafi made a fortune in Internet sales since most people preferred to buy their pornographic candy from home after their children had gone to bed.

The saleswoman had finished distributing the tray of nipples and was straightening a shelf of tit tarts when Dani approached her.

"Excuse me, but I was hoping to meet the owner, Rafaela Tores Verdes. Is she here?"

The girl shook her head slowly. "No, she doesn't come around much. Josh runs Purple and Madame Nougat runs Doces." She chuckled and added, "I wouldn't be surprised if Rafi sold this place off and moved to the south of France. She's probably suckin' up that fabulous French wine and some French pussy as we speak."

The salesclerk gave her an odd look and moved on to the next aisle. Dani resigned herself to checking out the men's area in search of Josh. She was overwhelmed by the multitude of displays worshipping male genitalia and tried to find an employee. She came upon a young gay boy organizing the Dicksicles who pointed to a tall, balding man working with one of the cashiers.

When he'd moved back out to the floor, she asked, "Excuse me. Are you Josh?"

He eyed her carefully. "Perhaps. Who wants to know?"

She noticed he wasn't dressed like the other employees. He could have been a customer and no one would have known. Another smart business strategy—management shouldn't stand out easily.

"My name is Dani O'Grady. I'm the CEO of O'Grady Candy, and I need to speak to Rafaela Tores Verdes."

Josh shook his head. "She's not here. She rarely visits."

She was tired of the stonewalling. She needed to get back to New York. She pulled out her business card and a pen. "I'm staying at the Fairbanks Inn until tomorrow morning." She wrote the name of the B and B on the back and handed it to him. "If you want to keep your job, you'll contact Ms. Tores Verdes and tell her that I was here and that if I don't speak to her soon I'm cutting off supply immediately."

She walked away, exiting through a side door that led to Commercial Street. She realized the Purple patrons wouldn't want to walk back through Doces carrying their chocolate penises and Clit Licks. She continued west past several of the shops she loved including Life is Good and the HRC store. She found a card shop and wandered inside. It hadn't been there four years ago, and she was impressed by their selection. She loved to collect cards and give them to people for no real reason. She had three drawers at her office filled with hundreds of cards that she'd purchased over the years. Any time she was in an airport or a mall she'd find the card stores and peruse the various assortments for as long as she could. The act of reading cards was therapeutic. For as often as she purchased one she sent one. She liked to remind people that they mattered. And e-mail just didn't seem to do the trick. No one felt special in an e-mail.

She trolled the racks, impressed by the many sentiments and pictures. It was obvious that a few artists had designed most of the inventory and none of it was typical Hallmark. Much of the calligraphy was intricately detailed and the paper was quality. She wasn't surprised that an hour had passed when she took her stack of twenty cards to the cashier, an older man in a Hawaiian shirt.

"You must have a lot of friends," he joked.

She nodded. "I know a lot of people. I'm very fortunate."

"And how many of them send *you* cards?"

She looked up and realized it wasn't the cashier who had

spoken but someone behind her. She turned to look and immediately cast her gaze downward to a woman who couldn't have
been more than five feet tall. She was wiry and muscular with
short jet-black hair and eyes the color of rich chocolate. She was
definitely Portuguese and appeared to be in her early thirties.
Dressed in men's cargo shorts and a plain gray T-shirt, she carried a white paper bag she handed to the cashier.

"Here you go, John."

"Thank you," he said, setting it behind the counter. "And
what do I owe?"

She smiled broadly, revealing perfect teeth as white as
marshmallows. "I'll put it on your tab."

Dani eyed her taut calves and attributed her physique to all
the exercise a delivery person would get running up and down
Commercial Street. The woman turned her smile toward Dani.

"You didn't answer me. Do you receive as many cards as you
get?"

"No," she said coyly. *Why do I feel embarrassed talking to her?*
"Most people just send e-mails or e-cards which are fine. I just
like these."

The woman reached for the stack in her hand and Dani felt
obligated to let the perfect stranger see her choices. She thumbed
through them, reading each cover and then laughing or nodding
after she read the words printed inside. She watched the brown
eyes scan the print feeling exposed and vulnerable and liking it.

She'd selected both humorous and serious cards for a variety
of occasions including death, illness and birthdays. There were
also several thinking-of-you cards and one all-occasion card with
a painting of a cobblestone street on the front. Tall buildings
lined the little road that seemed to go nowhere.

The woman studied the cover. "I really like this one. It reminds me of the streets in Venice. Have you been there?"

"Yes, twice actually."

"It's the most amazing city and so romantic." The woman
gazed at her for a beat and opened the card. "It's blank inside."
She sounded surprised and returned the stack, an enigmatic look

on her face. "I wonder what you'll write."

She breezed past Dani and headed out the door, repositioning her sunglasses before she walked away. There was something oddly familiar about her voice but Dani couldn't place it. She turned back to the cashier who'd given up waiting for her and had raided his white bag. He held up a yellow sphere and stuck it in his mouth, his face contorting with pleasure.

*Where have I seen that before?*

"These are *so* good," he murmured, quickly wiping his hands on his shorts and taking the cards from her.

"What were you just eating?"

"Oh, these are Lemon Balls. They are to die for, but everything at Doces is the best. Have you been there yet?"

She glanced at the white bag and saw the fancy scripted label in baby blue writing. She stepped to the bank of windows that lined the storefront and gazed up and down Commercial Street but the woman was gone.

"Who was that delivery person?"

"Delivery person," John snorted as he continued to ring up the cards. "That was Rafi, the owner of Doces and Purple."

# Chapter Eight

It was noon and after combing Commercial Street for Rafi with no luck, Dani decided to return to the Fairbanks Inn and check in with her office and Harry. She glanced toward the patio and noticed Cat had abandoned her sculpting leaving her tools and clay scattered over several tables. She wondered if she'd find her underneath the sheets in the Penthouse. She was tired from her adventure with Hope and realized she'd had enough sex—at least for the next few hours. She glanced back toward the Captain's House, wondering if Olivia was watching and waiting for her decision.

Fortunately her bed was empty. She flopped down and pulled out her BlackBerry to answer several texts and call Ray, who was handling all of her calls.

"Is your *business* concluded?" she asked sarcastically.

"It's really complicated," she said, massaging her temples. "I think the candy owner is playing games with me and the other issue is just . . . " Her voice faded away. There wasn't a way she could explain this.

"I see," Ray said, giving her standard answer when she really didn't care.

Phone conversations were not one of her strong points, and Dani had heard several complaints from clients who claimed she was rude which was probably true. She had trouble suffering fools.

"Harry called and wants you to call him immediately."

"Great," she sighed. "Anything else I should know about?"

"Liam called. He said he wanted to talk to you."

"Why didn't you forward the call?"

"I did," Ray said acidly, "but you must've turned off your cell."

She checked her volume and realized that right before she'd entered the bathroom for her little tryst with Hope, she'd silenced the ringer.

"Oh, sorry."

"Uh-huh," Ray added. "I told him where you were and he couldn't believe it, not after *the incident*. I assured him it was only for a few days at the most."

"Good," she said relieved. When she'd come home from P-town after that fateful weekend, she'd had to explain the damage to her Mercedes from Shaylalynn's ax, but she couldn't think of a good lie fast enough.

"Everything else is fine." Ray summarized and Dani could tell she was already on to her next task. She was all about completing her to-do list before the day ended. "We're all slaving over the quarterlies while you're off in the land of lesbians. But you'll be back soon."

It was a statement and not a question. She gave her Liam's hotel number before she hung up. Figuring her son was still more important than her company, she tried to call Liam before she dealt with Harry, but when she was sent to his voice mail she was grateful.

Harry picked up on the first ring. "Is your laptop on?"

"Uh, yes," Dani answered, opening her MacBook.

"We need to video conference right now," he said tersely.

After a few clicks of the mouse Harry appeared on her screen—next to Uncle Jimmy. He waved, and she realized they were sitting in his room at the care center.

"Hi Uncle Jimmy," she said, smiling.

"Hi honey," he said, and she could tell he was surprisingly lucid.

"I brought the fax over to Jimmy because I wanted to see if he recognized it."

The fax came into view and Jimmy peered at it.

"And?" she asked.

Harry nodded, wearing a painful look on his face. "Jimmy, why don't you tell Dani what this is."

"What is?" he asked.

Harry shook the papers and pointed. "Who wrote this?"

"Well, Dempsey, of course."

"Have you ever seen it before?"

"Is it lunchtime yet?"

Jimmy looked away toward the door, but Harry touched his shoulder and turned him back to the laptop. "Jimmy, this is very important to Dani. When did you see this? Tell Dani what you already told me."

His eyes flitted among the screen, the paper and Harry before he processed the request. "It's his will," he said simply. "He wrote it right before he died. Told me about it after he gave it to Olivia. Now, when's lunch?"

Dani sighed deeply and buried her head in her hands. She waited while Harry found an orderly to escort Uncle Jimmy to the dining room before he returned to the screen.

"Okay, so how do you want to fight this? There are several possible strategies—"

"But it's real, Harry."

"We may know that, but that doesn't mean Olivia Santos has to inherit half of O'Grady Candy. There are legal maneuvers to prevent that from ever happening."

"I understand, but our reputation could take a beating in the process. You haven't met this woman, Harry. She's a small business owner who's raised a child who wasn't even her own. Her story is every newspaper's dream. We'll look like monsters."

"PR can be controlled, Dani—"

"I can control a few things as well," she interrupted. "Don't do anything until I tell you to," she added before she signed off.

She grabbed her checkbook and hurried down the steps, frustrated that she'd wasted so much time when the quarterlies needed her attention.

If Cat were anyone else she'd have written the check and FedExed it to Olivia with no questions asked. Cat was jeopardizing O'Grady Candy. *But I'm too busy fucking her to see what I need to do. Maybe that was her intent all along—to distract me.*

She had no idea how she'd handle Rafi Tores Verdes, but this was a problem she could make go away immediately.

She was greeted by a wonderfully pungent smell and found them laughing together at the breakfast bar while Cat devoured a dish filled with something red and along with some bread.

"Join us," Olivia said warmly. "You must try my ragout. It's one of my specialties."

She placed a plate of what looked like tomato sauce in front of her along with warm bread. Taking her cue from Cat, she dipped the bread and savored the deliciously spicy yet refreshing sauce.

"What kind of bread is this?" she asked. "It's fantastic."

Olivia smiled, obviously pleased at the compliment. "It's called Broa. It's made with a fine white cornmeal. Cat loves it but Nathaniel actually moans when he eats it."

Dani glanced at Cat who ignored the mention of her intended. She continued to shovel food into her mouth as if she hadn't eaten in days.

It was time to get down to business. Dani took another bite, wiped her fingers on the napkin Olivia had provided and pulled her checkbook from her back pocket.

"Olivia, I've reconsidered our situation. I'm prepared to write you a check right now for an amount that will certainly exceed whatever you'll need. I'll also expect you to sign a document that my attorney will be preparing shortly. You will forfeit all rights to O'Grady Candy and make no future claims against my company. Do we have an agreement?"

She kept her eyes focused on Olivia who nodded pleasantly, but she could tell that Cat had stopped eating—possibly breathing—and she knew she was staring at her.

"That's quite acceptable, Dani," Olivia said. "Thank you. I never wanted to enforce the will. I feel as if I need to say that again. I'm actually hoping we can be . . . well, I don't know what we'll be, but I'd like to get to know you better."

She sighed and turned to Cat. "There you are, Catarina. Thanks to Dani our dreams will come true."

Dani met Cat's hard stare for a second and looked back at Olivia who continued to babble about their bright future. She tried not to wince every time Olivia said Nathaniel's name, but she couldn't look at Cat again who she was certain was dying inside.

She thought of a business trip to London when she'd wound up in coach squashed between a large man who had eaten onions for lunch and a teenager with an awful cold who constantly used the sleeve of his jacket to wipe his nose once his three tissues were completely soggy. She'd felt sick then and she felt sick now, particularly as she added several zeros to the amount.

She held the check out but as Olivia reached for it, Cat snatched it and made a fist.

"Catarina!" Olivia exclaimed. "What on earth?"

Olivia attempted to take the check but Cat jumped off the stool. She moved across the room toward the fireplace and gazed at the check. Dani imagined she was stunned by the amount as well. It was hefty, enough to satisfy Olivia permanently.

"Catarina, talk to me."

Dani heard the urgency in her voice. She was pleading with her, not just to give back the check but to step back in time away from this moment. Perhaps in the recesses of her mind Olivia always knew it would occur.

Cat stared at Dani as if she was a traitor and she felt like one.

Cat pulled out her lighter. She set the flame against the corner of the check and Olivia gasped. She rushed into the living room just as Cat threw the remains into the fireplace.

"What are you doing? Are you crazy? Don't you want to be happy?"

"Yes!" she screamed. "That's exactly what I want!"

Olivia took a step back wearing a worried expression. Her anger immediately dissolved into concern, and she reached out to Cat only to withdraw her hand when she flinched at the touch. No one said a word—the ticking of the old grandfather clock was the loudest sound in the room. Cat took two steps to the right and stopped. She put her hands in her pockets but quickly removed them. She turned away and turned back. Every movement telegraphed indecision and contradiction and she couldn't stand still. Her frustration eventually bubbled over, and she charged into the kitchen and found the tequila and a shot glass. After downing two shots she wiped her mouth and steadied herself against the counter.

"Do you remember that summer when I turned fifteen?"

Olivia sighed and rolled her eyes. "Ah, *com certeza*! You were out of your mind. All we did was fight. I'd ask you to do something to help, and it took three hours to get it done. You were completely unreliable and lazy."

"Yup," she agreed and drank another shot. "And do you remember that afternoon when you got so angry with me for being late to the afternoon tea party you'd planned for the other selectmen?"

Olivia's annoyance increased with the reminder. "That was so embarrassing. I gave you one simple task—deliver a pillow. Why would that take nearly an hour?" She stopped herself and looked confused. "But what does that have to do with anything?"

Cat took a deep breath and when she reached again for the bottle, Dani said, "No."

They exchanged a knowing glance and Cat sighed.

"I was late because I was really delivering a pillow—to an attractive woman who seduced me."

"What?"

"I lost my virginity to one of our guests, a *female* guest. She helped me realize who I was."

Olivia's face crumbled. "No, that can't be."

"It's true. And after that, well . . . " she chuckled and poured another drink. "After that it was just a lot of fun to live in a *bed-and-breakfast*." Olivia shook her head and stared at the floor. "I'm not making this up," she continued. "I'm bisexual, and while I sometimes enjoy the company of men I also like to date women. And I don't want to marry anyone right now. Nathaniel isn't the right guy for me."

She offered a furtive glance in Dani's direction that Olivia missed entirely. She was still staring at the floor and shaking her head, but Dani realized she was also muttering. *I think she's praying.*

"Olivia?" Cat pressed. "*Mom?* Are you listening?"

When she looked up she was laughing heartily. "Of course! It all makes sense."

She threw Dani an incredulous look. "What makes sense?"

"My love, you are so confused. I understand. It's very common in this day and age."

"Excuse me?"

She gave her a patronizing look. "My sweet Catarina, I've worked in Provincetown long enough to know. I've watched all the couples come through the inn. Do you remember Mr. and Mrs. Clay, the couple who met those nice lesbians at breakfast?"

"Yeah," she said slowly.

"Did you ever hear what happened *after* breakfast?"

"No."

She strode across the room obviously feeling much better. She leaned against the counter and looked at Dani. "Over mimosas, the lesbians convinced Mrs. Clay to have a three-way. Poor Mr. Clay was beside himself, but I assured him that it probably was nothing but curiosity. I'd seen it before," she added with a knowing tone.

"And what happened?" Dani asked.

"Oh, they had their three-way while I got Mr. Clay drunk on the patio. Two hours later Mrs. Clay emerged from their room and *cried* on her husband's shoulder. She felt so bad about the whole thing."

"Oh, Mom," Cat whined. "She didn't feel badly about sleeping with women. She felt badly about what she had to tell him."

"No, that's not what she told us," Olivia said adamantly.

Cat leaned against the counter and Dani was certain the effects of the tequila were taking hold of her. "I know she didn't regret sleeping with those women."

Olivia held out her hands clearly frustrated. "Ah, how do you know this?"

"Because I slept with her before she left."

Olivia's jaw dropped. "That can't be."

"It's true, Mom. Mrs. Clay isn't even her name anymore. They got divorced after their trip here. On her Facebook page, her name is Breakfast at Tiffany's because she always lets the women sleep over."

"I don't think we need to go into this, Cat," Dani said tersely. She figured Olivia needed to be spared some of the details. "You've told your mom who you are and that's all that matters."

"Well, I don't believe it," Olivia said.

"How can you not believe I'm bisexual?"

"You're not," she insisted. "It's a feeling that will pass."

"Like gas?" she deadpanned.

Olivia waved off her joke and went to the kitchen. She looked disapprovingly at her and replaced the tequila bottle in the cupboard.

"You will not convince me of this. It's just as possible that this is an experiment."

"Excuse me?" she scowled. "An *experiment?*" She laughed and clapped her hands. "If this is an experiment then it's more like a nine-year research project and the results are conclusive. Everyone in my life, everyone in P-town, knows I've dated women and I *like* women. In fact, I'm seeing someone right now."

Dani shot her a warning look and she closed her mouth.

"You're the only one still living in hetero fairy-tale land, thinking that I'm waiting for Prince Charming."

"That must be quite a list of women considering I remember you dating Seth, Dominick, Jorge, Isaiah and Tristan."

"Tristan?" Dani asked.

Her face turned red. "*He* turned out to be gay."

Olivia paused, staring at her and Dani grew wary. She looked like *a mother*.

"I'm the only one?" Olivia repeated.

"Yes, the only one."

"All our friends and neighbors know," she said smugly and Dani sensed a trap was being set.

Cat nodded. "They do. They've known since I was a teenager. Hell, I've slept with a ton of women you know." Olivia looked at her skeptically and she added, "I can prove it to you."

"How?"

"Let's go talk to some people," she said, her face brightening at the idea.

She glanced at Dani who wasn't at all sure about her plan. Years in business had taught her surprises were like the O'Grady Chocolate Tower, an amazing assortment of chocolate-covered treats stacked upon each other. Without the enclosed candy map, sweet lovers could be sorely disappointed if they bit into a Muddy Nutty and expected a Caramel Caress. She wondered if Cat really knew her neighbors the way that Olivia did.

Cat continued. "If I can prove to you I'm into women as much as men then you'll abandon this ridiculous idea of me marrying Nathaniel?"

"And what if you can't?"

"Frankly, I don't care. I'm *not* marrying Nathaniel."

Olivia slowly turned toward Dani, her expression stony. "Let's just wait and see."

Dani decided to accompany Olivia and Cat on their quest for bisexual confirmation. Her gut told her she needed to remain involved until Olivia accepted a check, signed the waiver and forfeited her claim to O'Grady Candy.

Cat led them up the street to Provincetown High School to visit her former guidance counselor Mrs. Bridgewater.

"Mrs. B was the first person I ever told," she said as they crossed the sprawling front lawn and climbed the front steps. She reached for the door handle and stared at her mother. "If *she* tells you, will you believe her?"

She pondered the question and finally said, "I always trusted Mrs. Bridgewater's judgment. As I recall she was the one who convinced you to finish school."

"That's true," she agreed as they entered the foyer and found the front office. "Not much has changed," she said, trying to be heard over the din of the ringing phones and chatting students waiting in the chairs outside the assistant principal's office. Since it was mid-June and the end of the school year Dani wasn't surprised that so many students were in trouble.

"Did you spend much time in there?" she whispered.

Cat smiled but said nothing. Dani glanced at three students relaxing in the cheap plastic chairs and realized they were staring at the art on her exposed arms and legs. A lanky boy whose long dark hair covered his eyes gave her tattoos a thumbs-up and she nodded. It was nice to know she was appreciated by the youth of America.

"Can I help you?" a young girl mumbled through her braces, her neon yellow gum tripping over her tongue as she spoke.

Dani saw that her nametag simply read *Student Assistant*, which translated to *Don't pick on me, I really don't work here and I'm just trying to get a grade.*

"We're looking for Mrs. Bridgewater," Olivia said with a smile.

The girl grimaced as if her morning Cinnamon Crunch hadn't agreed with her. "She's dead."

"What?" Cat gasped.

The girl shifted from one foot to another, obviously uncomfortable. "Um, like, she died a year ago. I mean, she was really old, like sixty-seven or something."

Dani resisted the urge to reach over the counter and throttle Gum Girl. Instead, she imagined the gum attacking the braces and forcing her mouth permanently closed.

"Oh, my, that's terrible." Olivia proclaimed. "As a selectman I should've known."

"Mom, you can't know everything," Cat said sympathetically and put her arm around her shoulder.

Gum Girl stared at *Birds of Freedom*. "Your tattoo is phat," she said. "I'm gonna get one when I'm old enough. I was thinking about a tiger or something."

"Great," Dani replied. "Is there another person who's been here a while?"

"Only Ms. Speaker, the AP."

Gum Girl threw a glance at the cheap wooden door that now stood open. A woman in a power suit was confronting the long-haired boy.

"Did you know her?" Dani asked Cat.

"Only too well," Olivia interjected. "Ms. Speaker had my number memorized. Let's get her opinion."

"No, no . . . " Cat said.

But Olivia had already waved at the assistant principal who only took a second to recognize her. Ms. Speaker quickly dismissed the boy, and he darted out of her office. She was probably in her early forties, her streaked blond hair falling loosely around her face. Dani imagined that at one point earlier in the day it had been styled but as the morning had withered away so had whatever product or hairspray she'd applied. She was slightly plump and her off-the-rack cotton suit and black flats triggered Dani's gaydar.

"Olivia," she cried as they embraced. "I haven't seen you since the town picnic last month. How are you? How's the inn?"

"I'm fine, the inn's fine. Life is good. I'm so sorry that I didn't know about Lucille."

"It was a tragedy. Such a loss."

The epitome of manners, she turned to Dani and smiled. "Nan, I'm sure you remember my daughter Catarina and this is Dani O'Grady. She's from New York."

Nan Speaker eyed her from head to toe in a nanosecond as she extended her hand. Dani knew when she was being checked out. It was a surreptitious lingering glance exchanged between gays in the presence of clueless straight people. More than a few times she'd offered the secret stare to business colleagues and new clients. It was a greeting that created an instant connection and often paved the way for a smooth transaction or an opportunity to hook up later.

"It's a pleasure," Nan said.

Nan and Olivia continued to chat with the familiarity of small-town residents who saw each other often, oblivious to Dani and Cat.

"We used to call her Speaker the Shrieker since yelling was the only way she could control us," Cat whispered.

Nan's gaze finally acknowledged her and she automatically frowned. "Catarina, are you staying out of trouble?"

"Yes, Ms. Speaker," she answered with a sing-song reply. "I'm in grad school."

Nan's poorly applied blue eye shadow arched as her eyes widened. "Really," she said, motioning for them to sit on a nearby loveseat. "I didn't think college would be your thing."

"I'm studying art."

"I see. And what do you plan to do with this degree?"

Dani saw that Nan's judgmental expression was matched by Olivia, who sat with her arms folded next to her, two interrogators picking at their suspect.

"I hope to work at the Met and perhaps sell my own sculptures as well," she said confidently.

Her condescending smile conveyed what she thought of Cat's plan. She clapped her hands together as if to signal the end of the pleasantries. "Well, what can I do for you both, and Ms. O'Grady," she quickly added, offering Dani a smile.

Olivia took charge and touched her arm. "Actually we came

to talk to Ms. B. I can't believe I missed her obituary," she said, shaking her head. "You'd think as a selectman I'd be on top of these things."

"Don't beat yourself up, Olivia. So what were you going to discuss with Lucille? Perhaps I can help."

"I doubt you can," Cat said sharply.

Olivia held up her hand to silence her and said, "Catarina says she's bisexual and most everyone knows it but me. Is that true? Did you know or ever suspect?"

Her jaw dropped and the cool exterior melted away like snow under an April sun. Her face turned pale, but no one seemed to notice except Dani. Nan nervously swept her hair out of her face and let out a slight gasp.

"I had no idea," she said.

Cat rolled her eyes. "Oh, please. You mean to tell me you didn't suspect after you suspended me for smoking in the bathroom?"

She shook her head automatically. "What does that have to do with this question?"

"You caught me and Jen Maroney sucking face *while* we were holding the cigarettes. I begged you not to tell my mom about that, remember? And you agreed?"

Her head continued to move from side to side in obvious denial. Dani took a deep breath and understood the entire situation immediately. The assistant principal was deep in the closet with her streaked hair and makeup, living in one of the gayest cities in America but still working as a public school administrator.

"C'mon, Ms. Speaker!" Cat protested. "You gotta remember that day. You were so mad at us for flushing the cigarettes down the toilet, or the *evidence* as you called it."

She held up her hands and shrugged. She looked at Olivia pathetically. "I can't recall. I've dealt with so many students over the years and frankly, Cat, you used to get into a lot of trouble. There were over one hundred disciplinary incidences in your file before you graduated."

Cat's eyes narrowed. "You can remember how many times

I got in trouble, but you can't recall the one time you caught me sucking face with another girl? I don't believe this. Why aren't you telling the truth?"

She leaned forward and Dani sensed she was going into administrator mode. "Young lady, I don't appreciate your tone and I'm certainly not lying. I have no idea what you're talking about."

"I think it's time for us to go," Olivia said as she stood up. "I'm sorry to have bothered you with this nonsense. I know you're very busy. You'll have to excuse Catarina. She's still struggling with her manners."

Cat offered a frustrated growl and bolted out of the room without a goodbye.

"It's all right, Olivia," Nan said, her voice still shaking slightly. She walked them to the door, and Olivia waved before heading out the front to find Cat.

Dani lingered behind and met Nan's piercing gaze.

"I know I'm a shit," Nan said.

"You are," she agreed.

Nan's hand grazed her bare arm and she flashed a wicked smile. "Are you as fine as I think you are?"

"Better. But you'll never know."

# Chapter Nine

They climbed the hilly side streets back to Commercial Street and headed toward the Post Office Café, a local hangout that Cat had frequented during high school with her girlfriends. Cat and Olivia continued to argue about the meeting with Nan Speaker while Dani searched for the mysterious Rafi Tores Verdes or a moving head of hair—Shaylalynn—among the multitude of pedestrians.

"I can't believe Ms. Speaker lied to you," Cat whined. "She's a principal! Isn't that like against the law?"

"Nan told me the truth as she remembered it," Olivia said diplomatically.

"Bullshit. After you picked me up that day she spent another half hour with Jen trying to convince her to stay away from me and talking to her about toning down her sexuality."

"Good advice," Olivia said. "I'm sorry she didn't give you the same speech."

She threw up her hands. "Unbelievable."

Several shop owners and employees acknowledged Olivia and sometimes Cat with a hello or a friendly wave and Dani saw how connected Olivia was to the community. One man outside a shop called the Pet Pamperer stopped her and inquired about a zoning vote that was apparently coming up in a month. He made it clear he wasn't in favor of it, and Olivia nodded politely and only responded after she was certain he'd run out of gas. She'd kept her body language neutral, and she didn't patronize him with her response. They'd walked away on good terms, although she hadn't promised him anything. *I'm impressed. She's quite the diplomat.*

As a Provincetown selectman she was a political figure engaging in the constant tug of war of pleasing her constituency and making unpopular decisions—like a CEO running a candy company. It startled her to think that Olivia had also inherited Dempsey O'Grady's power of persuasion.

Her discomfort grew as they walked west down Commercial Street, knowing that Shaylalynn's bar was a mile away and loyal locals with a long memory would quickly alert her to Dani's presence. She hadn't planned on being out on the street for so long. She'd assumed her meeting with Rafi Tores Verdes would consume a mere ten minutes and the rest of the day would have—should have—been spent enjoying a bottle of wine with Olivia and persuading her to give up the claim against O'Grady.

"I'm going to run into that shop for a sec," Dani said to Cat when they reached the café. "I'll catch up with you."

"Hurry," she pleaded.

She nodded and jogged across the street to a gift shop. Her red hair combined with her tattoos usually telegraphed her presence in most places, which was great when a friend was searching for her during intermission at a play, but now she needed to blend in. She quickly found a tacky assortment of tourist hats and clothing. She chose a nondescript blue baseball cap with Provincetown stitched across the front in white letters and a denim work shirt with long sleeves. After paying for the items and discarding the price tags, she tucked her hair inside the cap and threw the shirt on over her tank top.

Her cell rang as she waited to cross the street. She didn't recognize the number but saw a local area code.

"Hello?"

"Why did you cover up all of your amazing artwork?"

She whipped her head to the side. "What? How did you know . . . ?" She couldn't believe it. "Are you spying on me?"

"Dani, if I tell you that I'm watching you then I'm clearly not spying on you. That would be sneaky and imply subterfuge."

She studied the throngs of people floating up and down Commercial Street. Rafi could be anywhere, including inside one of the many shops with glass storefronts.

"Ms. Tores Verdes, where are you?"

She chuckled. "Obviously nearby. And please, call me Rafi."

"Well, Rafi, come out and let's talk. Let's meet."

"Not just yet. I'm not done watching you. You're not at all what I expected when I pictured the CEO of O'Grady Candy." Her tone conveyed a mocking superiority.

"And what exactly did you expect?"

"I figured I'd meet the stuffy woman in the Armani suit on your website, not a tattooed babe who looks hot in a tank top."

She turned in circles and scanned the people holding cell phones but none of them was Rafi. She was blushing and about to hang up when Rafi said, "Take it off."

She stopped turning. "What?"

"Take off that ridiculously ugly denim shirt. I don't like it."

"Go to hell," she blurted. She took a deep breath and controlled her anger. She wasn't used to losing her temper during a business conversation. "Look, I'm not up for games. I'm leaving tomorrow and if we haven't worked something out I'm cutting off your supply."

She smacked her phone shut and dropped it in her pocket. She closed her eyes for a moment unsure if hanging up was the right move to make. That was the problem. She couldn't plan her moves and Rafi was in complete control. She strolled across the street to a newsstand and bought a pack of cigarettes. Instead of immediately returning to the Post Office Café, she found a bench on the sidewalk and parked herself. The anxiety of being recognized was squashed at least for the moment since she looked like every other lesbian tourist.

The sidewalks choked on pedestrian traffic now that the bar-hoppers from the previous night had finally quelled their hangovers and were awake and moving again. Most everyone she saw was part of a couple, and she always found their interaction amusing. Local couples were easy to spot as they hurried along not paying attention to the sights. There was a purpose to their movement and they may or may not have an arm draped over their lover's shoulder depending on that particular moment. For them it was entirely about their mood, not the place. They lived under a dome of freedom and took for granted the diverse and tolerant atmosphere.

Tourists were a different story. Those couples were from somewhere else—usually somewhere much more homophobic—and they either sauntered down Commercial Street like Siamese twins, their lips and hands often engaged in a rated-R display of affection, or they walked side by side like two casual acquaintances who barely knew each other, unable to break their standard behavior that assured their safety in whatever town or city they lived.

A couple of the second type passed her, each with her hands stuffed in her own pockets while they discussed how wonderful it was to be in P-town. A pang of loneliness hit her as it always did when she was surrounded by couples.

But were they really together? Did they feel like they were together? Her relationship with Petra had turned her into a cynic as she realized that being together and sharing the same air space were two different things. Her first therapist was the one who helped her realize that she and Petra had spent most of their relationship like two spinning tops. For a short time they would be in perfect synchronicity, circling each other closely at the same speed. But eventually they'd collide and skitter apart.

That was a perfect summation of their relationship. Only for a short time had they been in harmony and truly in love—and *Kismet* was the result.

They had been together for nearly two years enjoying their Greenwich Village loft and a short interlude of a few summer months when Petra's roving eye took a respite, and Dani was the only woman in her life. They had passed the awkwardness of a new relationship and settled into a rhythmic understanding of each other's needs and vulnerabilities. She would later learn from Therapist Number Seven that Petra preyed on her vulnerabilities probably because she saw her as a powerful woman, which was true in the professional world but certainly not in her personal life. Petra had made no such distinction.

It was an easy period where everything had fallen into place. While they'd always had money and friends, for some reason it had finally been enough for Petra. She could never explain why, but for those few months they'd loved each other equally.

As they were sitting on the couch one afternoon reading magazines Petra had leaned over and kissed her neck. She'd pretended to be engrossed in her article titled "Powerful Influences on Corporate America" until Petra had flung her magazine onto the floor and crawled between her legs. She had laughed heartily as Petra's lips caressed her thighs and pulled off her shorts for what would become an hour of sheer delight.

As they huddled together in the afterglow, Petra suddenly asked, "Why do you think we're together?"

"Um, well I guess because we like each other."

"No, that's not it. I like a lot of people, as friends, and since I'm feeling honest, as lovers, too." She had checked Dani's expression and when she only gazed at her quizzically she said, "I'm with you because there's an extra layer beyond attraction and connection. Those are simplistic."

"I'm not sure I understand what you're talking about."

She had sat up and faced Dani, her mind clearly swirling in thought. "We choose someone as a friend because we have similar interests or temperaments. It's like the color blue, declaring fidelity and purity. And our attraction to others is red—"

"Not to be confused with fidelity," Dani said sarcastically.

Petra had chuckled and slapped her arm. "Seriously, honey, those are the obvious shades but what about relationships? Why am I *with* you? What color defines us?"

She'd opened her mouth to say, "Green, as in money," but Petra had jumped from the couch and headed toward her studio to answer her own question.

The result had been *Kismet* and when she saw the intersecting broad bands of color she understood what Petra had tried to explain. She'd instantly liked the painting and asked her to create a tattoo for her. It was the only time she ever had initiated an inking session.

The sound of an angry car horn drew her attention back to the chaos on Commercial Street. She stubbed out the cigarette under her sandal as a thin gay man swished by and their eyes met. While he didn't stop walking, he slowed and stared at her before picking up his pace again. *Was I just made?* She watched him travel away noticing that he'd pulled out his cell phone. *Shit.*

She rose from the bench and felt the tattoos hanging on her flesh. For the first time in a long time she wished them gone and made a mental note to call her friend Sammy who knew a great doctor who could do it. Maybe it was time. Perhaps if she permanently removed Petra from her body she could exorcise her from her heart.

She saw Cat and Olivia through the front window of the Post Office Café. They appeared to be engaged in a conversation with a waitress she didn't recognize. *Thank God there's so much turnover around here.* She had frequented the café a few times before she was banished, and she wondered if Zany Zooey still managed the place. *At least she liked me. She wouldn't tell Shaylalynn that I was here.*

She hadn't taken three steps inside when a voice said, "Stop right there. Can you read the sign? Do you see what it says?"

*Zooey.* Indeed there was a square sign that asked guests to *Please Wait to be Seated.* And coming from behind the counter was

Zooey, a woman who claimed to be half-black, half-white and a fourth Native American. And while her features were certainly unique Dani had never had the heart or the courage to explain to Zooey that her fractions didn't add up.

Every part of her face was wide and when she recognized Dani, the features expanded further and she wasn't sure if she was happy or really pissed off. She pointed a stubby finger and locked her in a bear hug, nearly breaking her ribs. Nothing about Zooey was small and she thought she might suffocate.

"What are you doin' here, girl?"

"I'm just here for a while to do some business and then I'm gone," she said seriously. She doubted Zooey would ever rat her out, but she didn't want to leave anything to chance. "I'm staying with Cat and Olivia for the night, then I'm back to New York tomorrow."

Zooey studied her sincerity and released her from the hug. "Good. It took us nearly two weeks to clean up the mess you made."

"I wasn't the only one responsible for the mess," she said. While she had no desire to discuss what had happened, she couldn't stop herself from defending her honor. All of the violence and mayhem had been Shaylalynn's fault. She'd just made her mad—really mad.

"Whatever," Zooey said. "Why are you here?"

She snorted. "It's good to see you too." When Zooey only scowled, she said, "I'm meeting with Rafi Tores Verdes. She sells some of our candy." She deliberately excluded the fact that Olivia was her half-sister, and totally avoided the reason for their visit to the Post Office Café.

"Rafi sells *your* stuff?" Zooey asked surprised. "Why?"

"Because it's quality candy."

"It's not as good as hers."

She couldn't believe it. O'Grady Candy had one of the best ratings in the entire country. *But I really thought that after-dinner nipple was sensational.* "How can you say that?"

"Truth hurts," Zooey concluded as she returned to the

counter and a customer waiting to pay. She pointed a finger at her and said, "By morning."

She nodded and decided not to join Cat and Olivia at the table. She perched on a nearby stool to watch the interrogation. The waitress sat across from them and seemed to be about Cat's age and of Portuguese descent. She twisted a napkin between her fingers and her nervous giggle was obvious. Olivia was doing all of the talking while Cat looked like she wanted to interject but couldn't find an opening. Olivia was like that. One sentence flowed into the other.

"Kimmie, I just can't imagine how hard it's been for you and your parents." Olivia patted her hand and she dabbed her eyes. "I know Kirk is your brother and you love him, but if he won't get clean then maybe some tough love is in order."

She nodded, wiping away the flowing tears. "I know. It's just hard to accept."

Olivia squeezed her hand and offered an empathetic look. "If there's anything I can do, you just tell me."

"Oh, no, Olivia, you've done so much already. Helping my mom find that support group and putting Kirk up all those times when Mom kicked him out. You've practically adopted my family. I can't ever repay you."

Her mascara streaked down her cheeks and Olivia handed her some napkins. Cat hunched in a corner of the booth, her arms crossed. She'd given up trying to interrupt their counseling session and just resigned herself to sitting quietly.

The conversation seemed to end naturally like a rolling ball that eventually stopped.

Olivia squeezed her hand. "I'm here because I need to ask you an important question." Cat immediately leaned forward as if coming out of a trance. Olivia glanced at her before continuing. "Kimmie, this might sound like a bizarre question, but does Catarina like women?"

She froze and her eyes widened. She finally blinked and stared at Cat whose expression was hard. It was obvious to Dani that Kimmie knew the truth and Cat expected her to share it.

She opened her mouth to do Cat's bidding, but her lips clamped together when she shifted her gaze back to Olivia. Whereas Cat appeared threatening Olivia wore a pleading look and swallowed hard. She bit her lip and Dani imagined a cartoon thought bubble over her head with an enormous question mark inside it. Who would she disappoint?

"Um, that's a really odd question," she said evasively. "I wasn't expecting it."

"Just be honest with me, sweetie."

"Yeah, Kimmie, you need to be honest," Cat echoed sharply.

"Shush, Catarina," Olivia said. "Cat told me when you were seniors you were her girlfriend. Is that true? You don't need to give me details. All I need is a yes or no."

Such a simple answer that was as heavy as a vat of dark chocolate and probably just as thick.

"I, well . . . "

She seemed to shrink in the booth under Olivia and Cat's searing interrogation. Dani pictured the imaginary question mark morphing into an arrow pointed at Olivia. After everything she'd done for her family there was no way she could side with Cat.

"No," she answered quickly and slid out of the booth. "My break's over, and I need to get back to work." As she walked away she held up her hands so only Cat could see and flashed a look that said, "*What did you expect me to do?*"

Dani slid into the seat Kimmie had just vacated as Cat dropped her head onto the table in defeat.

"I can't believe this. She just lied to you."

Olivia shook her head. "I'm surprised at you, Catarina. I can't believe you put your old friend in such a horrible position."

Her head shot up in disbelief. "Me? You're the one who can't accept the truth!"

"Keep your voice down," Olivia whispered. "We don't need the whole town knowing our business."

Cat rubbed her eyes and took a deep breath. "I know you

can read people's emotions. Couldn't you see that she was lying to you? That she was embarrassed?"

Olivia nodded. "Certainly I could see that she was embarrassed. And yes, it was obvious to me that she was quite uncomfortable discussing your past."

"And why do you think that is? Could it possibly be because I'm telling you the truth and Kimmie was my first girlfriend?"

"Do you know she has a steady boyfriend now? He's a sailor on one of the whale watching cruises."

She pushed her lips into a painful smile, obviously recognizing Kimmie's current situation didn't help her case. "That's great, Olivia. Maybe Kimmie's bisexual like me or maybe she was just experimenting, but—"

"Exactly," she proclaimed, poking her arm with a finger. "That's what we're talking about here, experimentation. It's so common when you're young." She threw an arm around her shoulder and pressed against her. "And you're still so young, Catarina. How can you know who you are or *what* you are when you're only twenty-four?"

"I just do," she said. "I'm sorry you can't accept that."

Zooey marched up to them with her hands on her hips. "You're done. It's time to go. I need the booth." She turned on a heel and headed back to the register, barking at a customer who'd ignored the little sign and was moving into a booth. "I did *not* tell you to sit there." She stood over him until he guiltily slid out of the booth and scuffled toward the table she indicated. *I certainly couldn't hire her to work in the candy business.* A palette of browns, blacks and grays filled her head as she watched Zooey. The candy industry was about yellows, pinks and bursting orange.

They wandered back out to the street. Cat slumped against the building entirely dejected. Dani could tell that she was beginning to realize what Dani already knew—people wouldn't cross Olivia. She'd invested herself entirely in Provincetown and the townspeople owed her. Saying or doing anything that would bring her pain was something they'd avoid at all cost even if it meant lying.

"Where should we go next?" Olivia asked.

"I'm not sure there's a point," Cat said. She pushed off the building and walked away. They watched her go, her casual saunter activating Dani's gaydar. How could Olivia be so blind?

"You'll lose her, you know," she said. Olivia shot her a worried glance. "This isn't about you. It's about her feelings."

"I just don't think—"

"She doesn't care what you think, at least not now. And if you're right she'll eventually come around to your way of thinking, and she'll meet some fine upstanding New York businessman, they'll have a huge wedding and she'll start popping out babies." Such an idea immediately made her think of Liam. "And if you're not so lucky, she'll start dating some two-bit loser who'll get her pregnant and treat her like crap."

She turned to go and felt Olivia's hand on her arm. "I don't know about you, but I could really use a drink. Join me?"


The Seafarer was only a block away, located at the edge of the main pier near Standish. It was a ramshackle wooden structure that had been built a century before. Long rectangular windows whose frames were in desperate need of a paint job allowed customers a marvelous view of the harbor or busy Commercial Street. The inside was a tribute to sailors and fishermen with nautical paraphernalia hung everywhere. Olivia waved at the bartender and they perched on the last two open stools. The place was full, and it was only the middle of the afternoon.

"How long has your family owned the restaurant?"

"For several generations, long before it became the Seafarer. Originally it was a fish saloon."

"A what?"

"Local fishermen would come in and rent a stall to use our equipment and gutting tables."

She sniffed dramatically. "That's what I'm smelling."

Olivia laughed heartily like someone who really appreciated a good joke. "You're about six decades too late. The Seafarer opened in the fifties and we've been serving the best clam chowder in Provincetown ever since."

She pointed to a sign over the bar that proclaimed the sentiment and several framed newspaper and magazine articles on the wall gave similar testimonial. And most of the customers were enjoying a steaming cup of chowder with their chosen beverage.

"You want the usual, Liv?" the bartender asked as he dropped two napkins in front of them.

"I do, Peck. And my sister will have . . . "

Her voice trailed off as she expected Dani to finish the sentence but she was dumbstruck at being called a *sister*. Fortunately Peck filled the gap.

"So you must be Dani. I'm Peck," he said, extending his hand with a warm smile.

She sensed he had a perfect personality for a bartender. He was definitely easy on the eyes and with the streaks of gray in his hair she guessed he was near fifty although his baby face telegraphed late thirties.

"What'll you have?"

"Martini—"

"No, no. You need to try a Portuguese Daisy," Olivia insisted.

She held up two fingers and Peck smiled before he turned away. Dani glanced at Olivia whose face was three shades of red.

She glared at her. "What?"

"Nothing."

There was obviously some romantic tension between them. *I don't want to know if my half-sister is doing the nasty with the hunky bartender. This is a business trip, not bonding time.*

"Not used to being called sister, huh?" Olivia observed.

"No, I . . . it's just . . . " She swallowed hard and shrugged.

Olivia averted her gaze and watched the patrons as if allowing her a moment of private space. "It's okay," she said. "I've had a long time to associate your face, which is plastered all over the Internet, with that word."

Peck set a Portuguese Daisy in front of each of them and Dani cracked a smile. It looked like a blond martini.

She lifted her glass and said, "To new relationships."

Dani saluted and took a tiny sip. Brandy and port. Two of her favorites.

"What do you think?" he asked expectantly.

She nodded and took a serious swig. "This is supreme."

Olivia grinned and drained her glass in three gulps. Peck, who hadn't yet moved, took it and went to work making her another.

"Just chug the first one," she advised. "The second one tastes even better."

She threw her head back, and the wonderful liquors trickled down her throat and coated her stomach. She loved brandy almost as much as chocolate. She held out her glass which Peck quickly retrieved.

Within a minute another Portuguese Daisy was in front of her and she sipped it slowly, well aware that she was already half drunk. Olivia seemed lost in her own thoughts as her gaze shifted from enjoying the happy expressions of the Seafarer patrons to studying Peck's fine physique as he cruised the length of the bar pouring shots, popping open beer bottles and rattling the metal shaker for various mixed drinks. She thought she heard her breath catch when he hefted a case of wine off the floor and his biceps bulged.

"Cat said you were married once."

"I was. I still might be in the eyes of law. I should probably check on the statute of limitations for marriage."

"What happened?"

"Killed at sea," Olivia said blandly. When she saw her surprised expression, she laughed her enormous laugh and took another sip of her drink before she said, "I'm just kidding. I *wish* that had happened, but the truth is much more predictable. He got tired of being married and wanted out. I wouldn't let him."

"Why not? If he doesn't want to be there why would you want him to stay?"

Her gaze dropped to the bar and she asked, "Have you ever been too stubborn to give up on something even if it wasn't right for you?"

She absently scratched her shoulder. "So maybe he was killed at sea," she said to change the subject.

Olivia grinned and lifted her glass. "I like the way you think, Dani O'Grady." She finished her second daisy and sighed. "What to do. What to do." She eyed her carefully. "Do *you* think Cat likes women?"

She almost spit out her drink but recovered before Olivia noticed. *Thank God she's a little tipsy.*

"Yes, I think she does. She doesn't have any reason to make this up."

"But you've just met her," she argued. "I believe that there are many people who are born gay, but there are many who are just experimenting, trying to be different for the sake of being different. That's my Catarina."

She leaned forward. "And why are you so sure? What if she finds a woman to spend her life with? Are you going to disown her?"

She turned away and stared at her hands. She didn't want to answer and Dani imagined the idea had crossed her mind. It would be her way or not at all.

"Nathaniel is a very good man. He'll be good to her."

"But she says she doesn't love him."

"She hardly knows him. She refuses to take the time to get to know him."

She bit her lip to stop a snarky comment from pouring forth. She looked over at Olivia with kind eyes. In her mind a square appeared with herself, Olivia, Cat and Liam at each corner. The situations were certainly similar.

"I'm just saying that love and marriage aren't within our control. We can't and *shouldn't* decide who our children marry. I certainly know about that."

Olivia raised an eyebrow. "Your child married someone you don't approve of?"

"Just last Saturday."

"Why would you let that happen?" she asked in total bewilderment. "He's your son, and I imagine he stands to inherit a lot."

"Money has nothing to do with love."

"I disagree."

Her eyes narrowed. "Apparently, or we wouldn't be having this conversation." Olivia winced and she held up a hand. "Look, all I know is that I love Liam, and I don't ever want him to resent me. These are his choices not mine. Even if they're the wrong ones."

Olivia took a deep breath and said, "At least your son won't have to worry about having the whole world judge his relationship."

She snorted and finished her drink. "He married an exstripper he got pregnant. I wouldn't be so sure."

"You don't sound as if you're really practicing what you're preaching here. Does *he* know how you feel about his wife?"

"Yes, I tried to talk him out of the marriage."

"Then who are you to judge? Don't I have the right to the same tact?"

She remained silent allowing her question to become rhetorical. It wasn't fair to compare Liam's specific circumstances with Cat's. An apple and an orange tree appeared in her mind with little Liam and Cat faces on the fruit. *That might be a really good idea for a candy commercial.*

"So you want to convince her that she's really not attracted to women? That this is a phase and she'll be happier with a man? Do you really think that's possible?"

Olivia stared at her with a frustrated look. "You need to understand my perspective. I've seen hundreds of guests at the inn and thousands more over the years when I managed the Seafarer. Provincetown has always attracted different people. But it wasn't until the last few decades that gay people claimed this place as their own. And it didn't happen right away. It took time for it to change and I saw a lot then. At one point there were as many

straights as there were gays but the gays wanted to take over."
Olivia held up her index finger to make a point. "They couldn't
share."

"Share what?"

"Provincetown. This used to be a quiet fishing village with a
slight flair for the dramatic, if you will. We've always had artists
and theater people but they kept to themselves. And then more
and more straight people started to change."

"Excuse me?" she asked with a laugh. She couldn't believe
what she was hearing. According to Olivia, a fairy crop duster
had flown over P-town and cast a spell over all the heteros.

"I know what you're thinking but you don't understand. I
watched people I knew—people in long-standing relationships
and marriages—throw it all away because they had a fling with a
gay. But they weren't gay. They were curious."

"There's no chance those people were bisexuals like Cat?"

Olivia grunted. "I don't believe it."

She turned and faced her unable to listen to her world view
anymore. "Frankly, you're full of shit, and I don't think you have
any idea what you're talking about when it comes to sexuality but
it's not my concern. I need to know what you expect of me and if
this has anything to do with the will."

Olivia stared at the bar and lifted her refreshed glass to her
lips. She said nothing until it was half gone. "You need to help
her see the light. Help her understand that she really doesn't like
women."

"I have no idea how to do that," she admitted, although dealing with unreasonable requests was something she understood.
She'd dealt with more than her share—a distributor who wanted
a ton of candy shipped to Bahrain in two days; a wealthy client
who wanted a ten-foot chocolate sculpture of his daughter for
her sixteenth birthday; and a Hollywood diva who had caused an
enormous scene at an O'Grady Candy commercial. She'd seen it
all, but she'd never been told to make someone straight.

Olivia's hard stare sent a shiver down her back. "Then you'd
better figure it out. If you want to keep your company to yourself

you should help me keep Catarina. It's only fair."

"That's not fair . . . " she started to say until her gaze drifted out the window—to a moving hairdo. It was like watching a cat flying through the air with a pile of fur swooping to the door.

She recognized Shaylalynn in an instant and flew off the stool toward the kitchen where she imagined there would be another exit. She darted out the delivery door before any of the puzzled servers or cooks could inquire and found herself on the pier. She circled back toward Commercial Street and heard a muffled scream. When she looked over her shoulder, Shaylalynn was inside and pounding on one of the windows. Dani could only imagine how loud her cries were in the restaurant.

She disappeared, and Dani guessed she was headed for an exit. If she continued around the building they'd inevitably meet, and there would be a fight worthy of newspaper coverage—maybe all the way to New York.

She double backed and continued down the shoreline behind the buildings on Commercial Street until she ran out of beach and was forced to return to the main thoroughfare.

She'd traveled several blocks into the West End and quickly crossed the street glancing over both shoulders for the mountainous hairdo. She tripped on the curb and realized the combination of brandy and natural adrenaline had dulled her motor skills. She leaned against the side of a building and caught her breath when her BlackBerry sounded. She scowled when she saw it was Rafi.

"What do you want? Are you enjoying this?"

"Where are you?" she asked in a clearly amused tone.

"Hiding," she said tersely. "Where are you?"

"I'm watching Shaylalynn make a complete ass of herself in front of the Chamber of Commerce. Olivia's trying to calm her down but it's not working."

She rolled her eyes and imagined that after Shaylalynn told Olivia about her banishment, she would find her things packed and sitting outside the Penthouse door when she returned to the Fairbanks Inn.

"Where are you?" she asked again.

She closed her eyes and focused on the soothing lilt of Rafi's voice. It still sounded strangely familiar, but she couldn't remember where she'd heard it before.

"Dani?"

She jumped at the sound of her name and looked around until she found a street sign. "I'm near Atlantic and Commercial."

"Wow, you really covered some ground. Stay there."

Before she could argue, Rafi disconnected. She dropped onto a bench no longer worried that Shaylalynn was nearby. The Chamber of Commerce was a quarter of a mile away, and she hoped Olivia could talk some sense into her.

As she scrolled through her e-mail, a pedi-cab pulled up beside her. "Are you Dani?" the dark, muscular driver asked.

"Yes."

"Hop in," he said with a smile.

# Chapter Ten

"How'd you get here so fast?" she asked skeptically, wondering if Rafi and Shaylalynn were conspiring against her.

He laughed and leaned against the handlebars. "Rafi's well connected."

She sighed and took a seat. They lurched forward and he headed for Bradford Street. She pondered their destination until her BlackBerry announced an incoming text. It was Liam. *Mom, I can't believe you're in P-town. Get out. Now. Can't talk but I'll see you soon. Love, Liam.*

When she looked up they were passing the Crown and Anchor Inn, the place where she'd first met Joelle at a Happy Hour. Perhaps it had been her charm or Joelle's promiscuity, but the subject of Shaylalynn had never come up—not while they were throwing back tequila shots, dirty dancing to the techno music or sucking face outside of her suite. She only learned that Joelle was with Shaylalynn when she showed up an hour later, staring through the blinds that Dani had forgotten to fully close before she left—the ones that faced the beautiful king-sized sleigh bed.

She wasn't sure how long Shaylalynn had been there, but by the time she started pounding on the window, Dani had coaxed Joelle out of her clothes and was busy pleasuring her toward ecstasy. At first, she hadn't heard her over the Melissa Ferrick CD and Joelle's hearty moans, but once the song ended and Joelle had climaxed, it sounded like a screaming thunderstorm.

Joelle had jumped from the bed and pulled the blinds open. Dani thought she was staring at Cousin It from the *Addams Family*. Joelle had started screaming and Shaylalynn was pounding—so hard that her hand came through the window. Glass shattered everywhere, and a naked Joelle had run outside to tend to her. Other guests emerged from their rooms and someone threw a towel over Joelle. Dani sat on the bed unable to believe what had happened. Eventually Joelle came inside and dressed, not saying a word to Dani who was on the phone with maintenance.

The evening had been colorful but in her world of lesbian life, it didn't hold a candle to the naked table dancing in Paris or the hashish trip and orgy she'd experienced in Amsterdam. Twenty minutes later she'd practically forgotten the whole thing until suddenly the hairdo had appeared in the doorway, cradling her bloody hand. It was then that she saw the face underneath the blond bouffant and she automatically cringed.

"You fuckin' bitch!" Shaylalynn had screamed.

There was much more swearing, lunging and gesturing, but Dani just cowered on the bed until some of the other guests led Shaylalynn away. Once the door had been closed and the glass cleaned up, she noticed the blood spattered on the rug, the bed and her clothes.

What she'd missed was the threat, one that was carried out the next night when Shaylalynn had appeared at the Lobster Pot where Dani had hooked up with a different woman, rationalizing that she didn't want her last night in P-town to be spent alone thinking about the crazy woman who'd vandalized her hotel suite.

She'd met a gorgeous, young redhead at Girl Power and offered to take her to dinner. She'd paid extra for a romantic table in a corner where she could commit serious public displays of affection without the entire restaurant watching as she caressed the redhead's fabulous thigh or whispered in her ear. By the time the main course arrived they'd already planned several scrumptious activities for the rest of the evening.

They were laughing and cracking lobsters when a shrill scream erupted and the entire restaurant went quiet. They had looked up at Shaylalynn across the room, her mouth open so far that it seemed her upper lip reached her huge mound of hair. She was crouched like an animal and her fists were clenched. When the scream had died, Shaylalynn's gaze settled on her, and she growled before she barreled across the room.

Realizing she didn't have a weapon, she'd grabbed a water glass from a busboy's tray and hurled it at Dani who quickly ducked and promptly bolted from her chair. Soon the redhead was screeching and, realizing she wasn't Shaylalynn's target, she'd cowered against the wall while Shaylalynn chased Dani between the tables, pelting any object she could grab in her direction, including a bowl of lobster bisque, a wine bottle and a live lobster. Only a basket of rolls had actually hit her before she barreled through the exit to Commercial Street. She'd heard weeks later that there was a permanent stain on the wall from the bisque and a woman had needed medical treatment after the thrown lobster landed in her lap and clawed at her breasts.

Shaylalynn had followed her outside, and more mayhem ensued as she pursued her down Commercial Street. By then Dani was hopping mad and looking to defend herself. She never got the whole story about what damage *she* had caused, but she did make restitution for a defaced statue in the town square, an overturned pedi-cab and a display of broken earthenware dishes. She'd safely reached her car and had sped out of town but not before Shaylalynn smashed her back window with an ax she'd grabbed from a display outside the Marine Supply. Dani considered herself lucky to have escaped without being beheaded.

She'd told Liam the story, and he'd been mortified when he saw the smashed back window of her Mercedes and was grateful when she was banished from P-town.

She could only imagine how worried he was about her now. It was what they did for each other. She quickly texted him back assuring him that she was fine.

They turned a corner and faced an enormous granite structure that loomed down the street, the Pilgrim's Monument. The pedi-cab driver pumped furiously up the winding road to the entrance while she looked for the short, wiry woman she'd met at the card store.

"Where is she?"

He pointed to the monument.

"You've got to be kidding," she said.

"Nope."

She went into the information office, paid her seven dollars and started up the ramps and steps that led to the top. It wasn't that it was a hard climb. She was just tired of the ridiculous gamesmanship. She glanced at the carved walls that celebrated the various cities in Massachusetts and only heard a few voices above her so she knew the monument wasn't crowded. No one passed her, and in a matter of ten minutes she'd spiraled to the top and stepped onto the balcony that overlooked all of Provincetown. It was an amazing sight, seeing the entire horn of Massachusetts and on a clear day, Boston.

She gazed out into the bay and sensed she was being watched but she didn't care. She continued to stare at Land's End, embracing the green landscape and the smell of the ocean. It was so different from New York.

"This is my favorite view."

She knew Rafi's voice already, and she looked over at the small woman leaning against the granite wall. She still wore the cargo shorts and T-shirt, but dark sunglasses covered her eyes. She approached Dani as the afternoon sun that rested behind her back cast an ethereal glow over her.

"It's almost like a topographical map but it's real. That's the incredible part."

When Dani looked at her profile, her gaze traveled the curve of her chin and stopped at two of the most luscious lips she'd ever seen. Always a woman who enjoyed kissing, she couldn't understand how she'd missed them the first time they met. *I was too busy looking into her eyes and studying her body.*

Rafi pulled out a square lollipop and handed it to her. Through the cellophane wrapper she guessed it was either cherry or strawberry but the color was unusually bright.

"What flavor is it?" she asked, removing the wrapper.

"Guess," Rafi teased.

"Strawberry," she said immediately, smelling the familiar scent as she popped it into her mouth.

"Just strawberry?"

It took a moment for her to realize this wasn't just plain strawberry and her taste buds worked diligently to identify a mysterious second taste, one that she knew but couldn't place.

"I don't know," she said frustrated.

"Yes, you do. Close your eyes."

She pulled it out of her mouth and forced her senses to work together. A vision of a bar came into her head, and she almost shoved it aside until she noticed the drink sitting by itself. "It's rum. You've made a strawberry daiquiri lollipop."

Her eyes fluttered open. Rafi was standing very close to her, wearing a broad smile of perfectly white teeth. "Exactly. What do you think?"

She stuck the sucker back in her mouth. Now that she knew what it was she was more astounded by the unique blend of flavors. *Oh, my God. This is as good as the daiquiris that Romeo makes at the Plaza.*

"This is excellent," she said, tempering her enthusiasm in front of the competition.

"I'm glad you like it. It's a prototype. I've got one that tastes like a piña colada and I'm working on the margarita," she added.

She glanced at her watch. "Well, I wish you the best, but we need to talk about the non-compete clause that you signed when you agreed to sell O'Grady candy."

Rafi's expression turned cool. She crossed her arms and stared out toward the bay. *I wish I could see her eyes to know what she's thinking.*

"I'm not competing. There's room for your candy and mine at Doces. And if you've checked your records, you know that. I sell out of your product every month."

"And you could sell more of it if you didn't sell your candy as well."

"Not likely," Rafi disagreed. "It's two different kinds of customers. My candy is bought primarily by locals who know me. Your candy is bought by tourists or people who have a personal favorite, like Marshmallow Creams, which is mine, by the way."

She smiled again, and Dani imagined Rafi Tores Verdes's smile was perhaps her most persuasive weapon. *Unless it's something else and I'm not going there.*

"Well, Marshmallow Creams are heavenly," she agreed, "but more locals would buy O'Grady if it was the only thing available."

"You can't assume that."

"And we'll never know if you don't follow the non-compete clause."

They stared at each other intently until Rafi said, "Then I guess we'll never know."

She blinked in surprise. She wasn't accustomed to such black-and-white decision making. "So you want to cancel your contract just like that?"

Rafi cocked her head to the side as if she was studying Dani. "You're upset. Were you assuming I'd just cave to the big corporation?"

"I'm not . . . " She started to argue and then realized a private jet had brought her to P-town. She swallowed hard and sighed. "I don't get you," she finally said, pointing the lollipop at her.

Rafi shrugged and plucked the lollipop from her fingers. "What's not to get? I'm a small business owner just trying to get by doing what I love, same as you."

Dani motioned to the bay. "Why are we here? I've done a lot of things up here but never business."

"Like what?"

Rafi buried the unfinished sucker between her own gorgeous lips while she rolled the stick between her fingers. Dani imagined her tongue busily caressing the red square and slowly dissolving the sugar to nothing.

*I'm starting to dissolve just watching her.*

It was sexual and a little obscene. Until she had stepped into Purple, she was naïve regarding the risqué or pornographic side of the candy business. O'Grady was strictly a family enterprise, and she had no experience with erotic confections.

Rafi popped the sucker out of her mouth and held it in front of her. "Want some more?"

She automatically nodded. Sharing used candy was unsanitary, but at least if she held the sucker she wouldn't have to watch Rafi make love to it. She might even be able to focus her thoughts which had plummeted over the side of the monument while she imagined Rafi stroking the sucker with her tongue.

"You still haven't told me what else you've done up here."

They were so close their shoes were touching, and Dani worried she'd swoon into her arms by accident. Dani tried to stay perfectly still as Rafi rubbed the candy along her lower lip, the sweet strawberry smell causing her olfactory organs to work overtime until she opened her mouth slightly and it slid inside.

Rafi chuckled and walked around the corner to the southern view of the monument, the heart of Provincetown. Dani remained alone with her fuzzy thoughts as she gazed out at the harbor and the Atlantic in the distance. She wished she could stay up here forever, above her problems and busy life. Her hand reached into her pocket as her BlackBerry vibrated, and she momentarily contemplated hurling the device over the side of the monument. Instead she read the text from Cat. *Where are you? Text me now.* She realized she was madly gnawing at the sucker which finally broke into pieces that she easily swallowed. *I'm probably imagining it, but I can taste her mouth.*

Rafi wandered around the corner from the north and saw her thumbs flying across the keyboard. "Is that business or pleasure?"

"It's my son," she lied. "He's on his honeymoon."

"And he's texting you?"

"He's worried about me," she hedged.

"Why would he worry about you?" She gazed out at Land's End and breathed deeply. "Except you've had Shaylalynn chase you through town and vandalize your car," she added.

She looked up. "You know about that?"

"Uh-huh. You're a legend, the only tourist who's been summarily banished from P-town."

"Did they ever get the stain off the wall at the Lobster Pot?"

She shook her head dejectedly. "Sadly, no. They tried to cover it with a picture of a man walking a dog, but the stain was so long that the picture didn't cover it and it looked like the dog was taking a shit."

They burst into laughter and Rafi suddenly said, "I've never kissed a redhead up here."

She stopped laughing immediately. "I don't believe that."

Rafi glanced at her shoes. "Okay, that's not entirely true but I'd like to kiss you."

She swallowed hard and knew her heart was pounding. She casually leaned against the monument and hoped her legs didn't give way underneath her.

"Why?"

Rafi moved very close and took her cheeks between her palms. She'd pushed her sunglasses over her forehead. "I don't know. I just do."

She was lost in the chocolate eyes. *I think it's amazing that her eyes match dark chocolate. How appropriate for a candymaker.* Rafi offered a tender kiss that felt as soft as marshmallow cream. Dani was surprised when she wouldn't let it end. So the kiss continued until they reached that natural moment when curiosity overtook lust and it was imperative to see each other's reaction to being kissed. And even when their lips parted their bodies remained entwined and their foreheads touched.

"My record remains intact," Rafi said.

"What?"

"Every woman I've ever brought into the monument I've kissed . . . or more."

Dani grinned. "Me too."

"Well, then I'm glad I could help you keep your record as well."

Her BlackBerry chimed and she grudgingly stepped away. "I'm sorry." Cat again. *COME BACK NOW!!!* She imagined things had escalated with Olivia.

"I've got to go," she said, heading for the stairs.

Rafi zig-zagged down the ramps and stairs with her. "And what are we going to do about your ultimatum?"

"I don't really like that word. It wasn't really an ultimatum."

"It wasn't?"

She groaned. "I don't have time right now. I've got a huge personal problem brewing. And I've got no clue how to solve it," she said.

Rafi grabbed her arm and stopped her. "I assume you're talking about Olivia, your half-sister?"

"You know about her too? Is there anything you don't know?"

Rafi grinned and stroked her cheek. "There are many things I don't understand, but I know much of what happens in P-town. When you own a store like Purple, people assume you'll keep their secrets. And I do."

She leaned into the sweet touch hoping Rafi would kiss her again—and again. She thought of her first parasailing ride and how she never wanted it to end. She wanted to soar. But Rafi refrained, and they just stared at each other on the dimly lit stairs until she realized the day was quickly evaporating. If she wanted to conclude her business in Provincetown today, she could use her help.

"Tell me what to do about Olivia. She just found out that Cat's bisexual and she's not taking it well. She thinks it's a phase."

Rafi couldn't contain her surprise. "Cat? There's no hope there. That girl came out with fireworks, and she's played for both teams ever since. I can't believe Olivia didn't know."

"She's clearly in denial. Is there anything you can do to help me?"

She met her gaze with a serious business stare. "If I help you with Olivia, will you tear up the non-compete clause?"

She eyed her shrewdly. "How well do you know Olivia?"

"Rather well, and I speak Portuguese so when she goes off on one of her rants I know what she's saying."

"Do you think you can get her to be reasonable?"

Rafi lowered her sunglasses as they headed out of the monument. "No idea."

"Then where's the incentive for me?" she argued. "Why would I agree to this arrangement?"

"Because you *want* me to keep selling your candy. It'll give you an excuse to see me."

Dani laughed. "You're rather sure of yourself, aren't you?"

Rafi pulled her close and kissed her hard. She only resisted for a second just on principle but she couldn't resist touching Rafi's defined shoulder blades and they wrestled for control of the kiss.

*I'm in charge here. This kiss will end when I say.*

And when she felt Rafi start to pull away she drew her tighter, unwilling to separate their lips and tongues at her command.

Her phone chimed again and she knew it was Cat. She pulled out of the kiss—almost violently—and Rafi bent over, gasping for air.

"Okay, you've made your point."

"Good," Dani said smugly.

She walked past Rafi who grabbed her arm and pulled her back into yet another embrace. "But I hope I've made mine as well."

They hustled back to the Fairbanks Inn which was only a few blocks from the monument and found Cat and Olivia engaged in another screaming match with Nathaniel stuck as the bystander. They stayed in the doorway and he acknowledged them with a slight nod of the head. He was near the kitchen and any other greeting would've required him to cross the kill zone and no one was about to do that.

The conversation volleyed between English and Portuguese and Dani guessed they switched to Portuguese whenever the topic pinpointed Cat's involvement with him, as evidenced by the automatic glance one or both of them continually made in his direction.

"Poor guy," Rafi whispered. "He's being trashed and he doesn't even know it."

"What are they saying?"

"She'd kill herself before she'd marry him."

"That's a little dramatic."

"She's twenty-four. What do you expect?"

She winced and couldn't look at her. *If she only knew the whole story* . . .

She focused on the conversation and realized that fighting was formulaic in any language and the climax was about to happen. Both women were gesturing frantically and had abandoned their respective corners for a face-off in front of the couch. Portuguese phrases poured from Cat's mouth as she approached Olivia—who slapped her across the face.

Dani gasped and took a step forward but Rafi grabbed her arm.

"Don't. It's not your place."

"But—"

"No."

The last few minutes had occurred with the speed of a lightning-fast roller coaster and now it seemed to suddenly stop. Neither Cat nor Olivia said anything and remained toe-to-toe with identical expressions of disdain on their faces. Rafi uttered a phrase in Portuguese and both turned their heads in her direction. Her voice was conciliatory, and she added a few more words quietly and the tension broke. Olivia reached out to Cat, but she recoiled and ran out the front door.

Olivia glanced in Dani's direction and immediately pointed a finger. "You! How could you do this to me? To your own *niece*?"

Dani realized that Cat had told Olivia about their affair. "Olivia—"

"Don't! Don't say a *word* to me." She stood so close to Dani that she could feel her breath. "You've helped corrupt her in my house! In my bed! I want you out now. Get out, you awful whore!"

She flinched at the slur but boiled over with anger immediately. "Fine by me! I'm going home."

She stormed out of the Captain's House and the last thing she heard was something about Olivia calling her attorney. She trudged up the steps to the Penthouse against a brutal wind that had picked up in the last hour.

"You and Cat? Really?"

Hearing Rafi say it slowed her pace. She'd embarrassed herself terribly, and she just wanted out of Provincetown.

"What about the non-compete clause?" Rafi shouted over the wind.

She shook her head and fished the room key from her pocket. "Do whatever you want. I'm going home."

After she'd secluded herself in the oddly shaped room, she went to the window and stared out at the street feeling as though from this height she was separated from all of her problems. *Too bad I can't stay. I really like this place.*

It wasn't the first time someone had called her a whore. She was rather certain Shaylalynn had uttered the term at least three dozen times as she'd chased her down Commercial Street. Somehow hearing it from her sister—someone related to her father—made it hurt and she wondered if it was true.

She repacked what few things she had while she called her

pilot about the departure time. She wanted out now and Cat was on her own. She'd lost half her company to a stranger, and it would be a long time before she forgave Olivia or her father.

As the airport tried to locate the pilot, she thought of the financial ramifications but recognized it was a looming iceberg, one that she could only understand and fear from a distance. It would take weeks of meetings with her team and Harry to sort through the legal jungle of a business partnership. A massive headache pressed against her temple, and she realized she hadn't had a decent meal all day.

The phone clicked and the airport operator said, "I'm sorry Ms. O'Grady, there's been a miscommunication. Your plane left Provincetown two hours ago."

# Chapter Eleven

"What the hell happened? Where's my plane?"

"The pilot received orders to return to New York."

Dani massaged her head. This couldn't be happening. "That's a company plane. Who authorized its return to New York?"

She heard papers shuffling. "According to our records, a Rayesha Ntoukam authorized the trip on your behalf."

She dropped onto the bed. Why would Ray send the plane back to New York without her? Ray was the one insisting that she hurry up and get home. It didn't make any sense. She hung up and dialed her, realizing that it was after five, and she might not pick up if she'd left the office. They didn't have a twenty-four-hour relationship where she could call her anytime about anything. It was one of her conditions of employment—Dani accepted it because of her incredible talent.

The phone went to voice mail, and she left a terse message before signing off. She tried to call Liam, but his voice mail also immediately picked up. *He says he really wants to talk to me, but he isn't answering the damn phone!*

There was nothing she could do at this point. She was stranded and also evicted, which was fine. She didn't want any more of the Santos drama. It was still early enough in the tourist season that she was certain if she wandered up Commercial Street she'd find a room in one of the many inns interspersed between the shops. She'd just have to be careful not to run into Shaylalynn again.

She grabbed her suitcase and peeked out the door. Not seeing Cat or Olivia, she hurried down the steps and was back on Bradford Street in a few seconds. There weren't any pedi-cabs in sight so she took a side street up to Commercial, already tasting the Scampi Alla Griglia that she planned to order at her favorite restaurant, Ciro and Sal's. She wanted a bath, a great dinner and a fine bottle of wine.

The Crown and Anchor Inn wasn't too far up the street and despite her last experience there, she decided that familiarity trumped bad memories. If she remembered correctly there were rooms with Jacuzzis that would be a wonderful complement to the wine. An image of swirling bubbles and a full glass of bordeaux hastened her pace.

She passed Doces again and noticed the crowd hadn't thinned. She decided that if she felt like it after dinner, she'd return to Purple and pick up some exotic treats to share with her staff. They'd all get a kick out of the porno candy—everyone except Ray who would remain stoic even if someone put a chocolate clitoris under her nose.

*But I won't want to walk all the way back. Once I eat I'm going to want my bed. It's how it goes in middle age.* She sighed and stopped. If she wanted the candy, she should get it now. Hopefully she wouldn't run into Rafi again.

*I can't seem to control myself around her. She's a worse temptation than an entire box of O'Grady Choco Delites. When we're together we argue and kiss.*

She crossed the street and threaded her way through the

Doces crowd. Madame Nougat's sing-song laugh made her crack a smile. She definitely could peddle candy.

It was late in the day, and the line for Purple was very short. She used the time to text Liam and let him know that she'd been trying to reach him when she felt a tap on her shoulder. She nearly jumped at the sight of Madame Nougat standing next to her with her glittery eye shadow and ruby pink cheeks. She looked closely and realized there was something familiar about Madame Nougat—the deep chocolate eyes and the rich lips. She never forgot a set of lips that she'd kissed. When Madame Nougat winked she was sure she was staring at Rafi. *That's why I recognized her voice.*

"You're so tall," was all she could think to say.

"Look down," she said quietly in a sultry voice that certainly didn't belong to Madame Nougat.

She noticed the enormous red and green platform shoes that added at least five inches to her height and allowing her to meet Dani's gaze at eye level.

"Great shoes," she said.

Rafi glanced over at the patrons, all of whom were waiting for Madame Nougat to return.

"Don't you have a few candies to sell?"

She smiled and Dani felt gooey inside. "I'm just passing time. I didn't think I'd see you again."

"I just thought I'd pick up some stuff to take back."

"Oh, sampling the competition, huh?"

She felt her cheeks turning red. "Well . . . "

She glanced at the suitcase. "Where are you staying?"

"I thought I'd just walk up to the Crown and Anchor."

She shook her head. "No." She motioned to a young man stocking a shelf and he quickly joined her. "Elvis, take Ms. O'Grady to my office, please." The chocolate eyes gazed at her intently. "I'll be over in just a minute. Don't run away again. I want to talk to you about something."

She returned to the crowd and Madame Nougat's extraordinary laugh filled Doces. Dani followed Elvis through Purple to a back door marked Emergency Exit. He flipped the latch and led her across a side street to a large two-story yellow structure that she imagined butted against Bradford Street. She couldn't believe how much property Rafi owned.

She followed him to a side door with an electronic keypad. He punched in a code from memory and when the door opened a smell she knew well invaded her senses—chocolate. This was Rafi's factory and despite the late hour at least ten workers dressed in hygienic scrubs scurried around the room checking the kettles of chocolate, filling sweets with cream centers and packaging the finished product.

She stopped and assessed the operation in a matter of seconds. It was incredibly well-organized, safe and clean. Any health inspector would be pleased. It was also too small. She could tell that Doces's popularity had outgrown its production facility. *Perhaps that's what she wants to talk to me about.*

"Right this way, ma'am," Elvis coaxed.

They climbed a winding staircase to an open loft the size of a small apartment.

"Would you like something to drink?"

"Water would be great," she said.

What she really wanted was dinner and wine, but having a chance to see Rafi's operation was worth the wait.

He handed her a bottle and left with a nod. She strolled around resisting the urge to snoop too much. An entire third of the loft served as her office complete with three desks and five computers of various sizes. Clearly she didn't work alone. Dani imagined keeping up with online orders could be a full-time job for someone. The large oak desk in the corner caught her attention as well as two pictures on the nearby credenza. The desk was cluttered with papers, invoices and phone messages. She smiled at her lack of organization. Hopefully she had a secretary as good as Ray.

Dani saw two photos and picked them up. One was definitely her and her mother at Rafi's high school graduation. The other photo was a black-and-white shot that showed her with a gorgeous African-American woman wearing large hoop earrings. She cradled Rafi in her arms and nuzzled her neck.

"That's Felicia."

Dani jumped and nearly dropped the picture. "You startled me. I didn't hear you come up." She smiled and held the pictures out to Madame Nougat. "Is she your girlfriend?"

"She *was* my girlfriend. I certainly wouldn't have been kissing you today if she was still here."

"I imagine not. She's absolutely beautiful."

Rafi leaned against the desk. "That's not what I meant. Felicia died three years ago. We were totally faithful to each other."

"I'm sorry. But how wonderful to have someone you loved that much."

She took the picture from her and stared at it. Dani watched her eyes, wondering if she would cry. Surprisingly she smiled and then laughed.

"She was only thirty. Contracted cervical cancer. She went quickly."

"Why are you laughing?"

"I didn't for a long time, but now all I remember are the wonderful memories. I taught myself to think about one amazing moment and focus on it whenever I look at this picture. And since we always had so much fun together I always find myself laughing."

"That's . . . fantastic," she said, realizing she couldn't relate to that feeling at all.

"Did you have that relationship with Petra?"

She offered a surprised look. Rafi had said nothing about Petra's canvas. She just shook her head mutely.

They stared at each other while she searched for a way to change the subject. Then she remembered the other photo. "Is this your mom?"

"Uh-huh. She lives here in the West End."

"Are you close?"

She didn't think it was possible, but Rafi's smile grew until it covered her face. "Very. She's my rock."

She replaced the pictures and led her to the window. They watched the workers who seemed to move in double time. There wasn't a slacker among them and Dani was impressed. They mixed, stirred, sorted, filled and chilled various Doces and Purple creations. A conveyor belt of after-dinner nipples caught her eye and she felt her cheeks flush.

*Those are so damn good.*

"So what do you think of my operation, Ms. CEO?"

Dani could tell by her tone that she'd offended her earlier. "I'm sorry if I sounded callous before. It's just business." Rafi nodded in understanding. She strolled the length of the window and assessed the entire facility. "Everything looks tight. Highly organized. Is this your only store?"

"Just here and the Internet, but online business is booming. Erotic candies are the new market. Have you ever thought about it?"

Dani blinked in surprise. "Oh, no. The O'Grady name could never appear on an after-dinner nipple, no matter how good they are."

"What if it was another name?" Rafi asked.

Their eyes met. "Are you suggesting we have a merger?"

Rafi seemed to wince at that word. "I don't know what I'm suggesting. I'm just a simple businesswoman. Maybe over dinner you can explain it to me since you're the one with the degree from the Wharton School. Are you hungry?"

She sighed and decided to ignore her smart ass comment. "Please. I've got to eat."

"Just give me a minute." She started toward the bathroom but turned around as if something had just occurred to her. "And for the record you're as beautiful as Felicia."


When Dani shared her desire to dine at Ciro and Sal's, Rafi agreed immediately, and they strolled further down Commercial Street to one of Provincetown's best restaurants. The original red brick and wooden windows gave the place a rustic appeal for the restaurant was housed in the cellar. Chianti bottles hung from the low ceilings and cheese graters covered the lights. And while the ambience was interesting the food was even better.

After greeting Rafi with a hug, the host led them to a table in the main dining room. Within minutes a bottle of Bordeaux was in front of them and Dani was savoring the fine wine and staring at Rafi who looked sexy in black jeans and a black shirt that clung to her in all the right places.

"What?" she asked after the waiter disappeared with their order.

"Nothing," Dani said. She grabbed a breadstick and chewed on it greedily. "I'm just starving. I haven't eaten all day."

"You were too busy running around Provincetown with Cat and Olivia."

"That's for sure." A thought occurred to her. "How did you know that? Were you spying on me the whole time?"

She swirled her wine and cracked a smile. "I saw you this morning when you came in the first time, or rather Madame Nougat noticed you."

"How often do you play that character?"

"As often as I can. I want to get out into the public and see them eating my candy—"

"You mean *our* candy?"

She nodded at the correction. "Of course. It makes me feel good and being Madame Nougat is a thrill because no one knows it's me."

"I certainly didn't recognize you. And the customers seem to love her."

"They do. And when Madame Nougat's around, sales increase. People buy more from a fictional character. Go figure."

"I understand what you mean. Back at my shop in New York I love giving tours to the schoolchildren and the tour groups. The personal touch is fun and profitable."

Rafi nodded in agreement and Dani heard Petra's voice. *Connection is blue. Friendship is blue.*

She reached for the bottle of wine. She was already on glass number two and feeling a little tipsy without any food in her stomach.

"So do you really want to go into business together?"

"Not really," Rafi said, picking out a breadstick. "I don't like the idea of anyone telling me how to operate."

"That's not how I work," Dani said somewhat defensively. "I'd like to think I'm a collaborator. I work with a team. I don't make major decisions in isolation."

"Huh."

Rafi's attitude grated on her. "So the only reason you'd consider asking for help is because there's no other way. You have limited production capability and all these great ideas like those suckers—"

"I call them Liquor Lollies," Rafi said in a neutral tone. "And what makes you think our production is limited?"

"Well, assuming that building is your only facility, the square footage is very small and affects how much and what kind of equipment you can house. I imagine there are actually candies that you want to make like the Liquor Lollies, but you can't because you either can't afford the equipment or you don't have a place for it. Not to mention the fact that the overhead is greater because of your limited production and that translates to less profit. I'm guessing you're netting less than two million a year when you could probably go up to six or seven with the right setup." She paused and glanced at Rafi who was leaning back in her chair studying her. "Am I on the right track here?"

"You got all that just from standing in my office for less than fifteen minutes?"

She shrugged and drained her glass. "Years of working in the business and that little degree from Wharton," she added with a smug smile.

Rafi laughed. "Touché. So what can I do, Ms. CEO?"

"First, you can stop calling me that. Do you have any other property or extra capital to use?"

"No."

"Have you maximized your space? Done a comprehensive study of your business?"

"Done and done."

"Then you're stuck. You can't make new candies unless you drop some of the others. Or you could join forces with a larger, more established company."

Rafi stared at the table for a while and when she looked up she wore an unreadable expression. "What else do you know?"

"What do you mean?"

She leaned forward over the table and rested her chin on her palm. "You've sized up my business faster than it takes me to write an e-mail—and you're right about almost everything—so I want to know what other talents you have."

*And attraction is red.* Rafi's brown eyes stared at her, but all Dani saw was *Kismet*. And for the first time she felt the tattoo burn.

"Seriously, Dani," she pressed, "what other talents do you possess?"

She had no idea how to answer that question. She ran a candy company and occasionally took a lover to bed. And she certainly wasn't going to list that as a talent. Fortunately the food arrived and amid the customary exchange with the waiter about grinding pepper, sprinkling parmesan on the entrees and ordering another bottle of wine, she escaped the question and steered the conversation back to the safe topic of business.

"Would you ever consider allowing O'Grady to market your candy?"

"I might," she said slowly, "but there would be several conditions. I would want to maintain control over the line. I've already acquired the trademark rights, which was a nightmare."

She offered an understanding look. If you didn't have a good attorney on your payroll, the legal aspects could be a headache. She knew how fortunate she was to have Harry around, but she knew it wouldn't be long before he retired his shingle for good.

"And I expect to oversee quality control. I make fine candies and confections, and I wouldn't want there to be any shortcuts as we moved to mass production."

"Not a problem," she said. "O'Grady doesn't believe in shortcuts."

Dani sipped her refreshed glass of wine and imagined the possibility of working with Rafi—and enjoying it. When she looked up, Rafi wore the look of an adversary.

"Did I say something wrong?"

"I have a problem mixing business with pleasure."

A slow smile spread across Dani's face. "If you agree to go into business with me, then the first benefit will be writing off this dinner as a business expense."

Rafi settled back into the chair. "What about the rest of the evening? Things might get complicated."

*I'm lost in those eyes. They're the richest, deepest, most beautiful eyes I've ever seen. For those eyes . . .*

"I think we're both old enough to handle complicated."

"I'll think about it."

"Which part?"

"All of it."

They changed topics and gushed over her delectable scampi and Rafi's tasty salmon, allowing her an opportunity to shift gears and control the conversation, a position she preferred immensely. She learned that Rafi's family, like Olivia's, had spent generations working on the docks of P-town and as laborers in the community.

"There are two Provincetowns," she explained. "The one that the tourists see is the engine that keeps us going, but it's not who we are. We're a diverse community with a fascinating history and we're very fortunate to have such commercial appeal. A lot of people might disagree with me, but I'm not sure we would still be on the map if it wasn't for the tourist trade. I think we could've slowly disintegrated into a ghost town if we hadn't continued to reinvent ourselves. Most people who live in Provincetown have two or three jobs, usually in the service industry. They can't make it on one income. It's truly a place of the haves and have-nots."

"And your family was part of the have-nots?"

"For a long time, yes. My father abandoned us a year after I was born. The only reason my mom didn't leave Provincetown was because of the community. It was important to her to remain around other Portuguese people like Cruz and Olivia Santos. Did you enjoy your little visit to the Seafarer?"

She noticed the sardonic grin on her face. "The Portuguese Daisies were fabulous, but I wasn't so hot on some of the clientele."

Rafi laughed and their eyes met briefly before returning to the heavenly meal.

She twirled a strand of her pasta and inhaled deeply. "I can't imagine anything being as good as this," she murmured. "So how did you get into the candy business?"

Rafi poured them each another glass and ignored the question. Dani felt an uncomfortable lag in the conversation and opened her mouth to fill it but Rafi pointed a finger at her.

"No more questions for now. Not until you're willing to answer some of mine."

She was stunned. Rafi was on to her. She continued to eat, the silence sitting between them and driving her crazy. She seemed entirely willing to allow the conversations of other patrons and the general din of restaurant noise to carry them to dessert.

When the plates were cleared and the waiter had brought them each an after-dinner brandy and an order each of tiramisu and cheesecake to share, Rafi speared the tip of the cheesecake and held it in front of her face.

"Make a wish," she said. Dani leaned forward and she pulled the fork back. "Uh-huh. You didn't wish."

She scowled. She didn't believe that blowing out candles or eating the tip of the cheesecake could ever make her luckier or solve her problems. *I've got too much to wish for. I want Liam to be happy. I want Olivia out of my life. I want Rafi to kiss me again. Why do I want that?*

Obviously sensing she'd made her wish, Rafi slipped the cheesecake into her mouth and she savored the unique sweetness of the decadent cream cheese and sugar. It gave her a rush as she closed her eyes and allowed her other senses to take over. The hum of the restaurant disappeared as she floated along a blue sky.

"It's really good, isn't it?" Rafi whispered into her ear.

She nodded slightly and her eyes fluttered open. She'd nearly fallen out of her chair and righted herself while Rafi giggled.

When the check came, Dani held it up. "Is this a business expense?"

"Still thinking," Rafi said.

Dani whipped out her American Express card. "I'll take my chances."

All of the shops were still open, and the June tourists were out in full force. The building lights were on, showering the pedestrians with a party atmosphere as twilight vanished. The heart of P-town was throbbing, and Dani smelled the profit in the delectable food being served on the outdoor patios, heard the hearty laughter of happily toasted pedestrians who'd frequented several happy hours and counted the shopping bags everyone clutched.

"It's almost high season," Rafi commented, obviously noticing her watchful gaze. "We'll make the money we need for the next year."

"What's it like living here in the winter?" she asked.

"It's selfish."

"What do you mean?"

She shrugged and said, "I'm not sure how to explain it to you."

They passed Doces and continued strolling toward the town hall. Street musicians vied for tips, their guitar and violin cases open like mouths waiting to be fed. Chatter and laughter as well as the loud rhythms of live bands seeped from the doorways of the various establishments. As they approached the Lobster Pot her pace faltered and Rafi took her hand.

"I guess living here year round is a well-kept secret if you like the snow and solitude, which I do. The tourist season is just enough for me, and then I get tired of so many people." She offered a little smile and added, "I guess I'd never survive in New York."

"You're definitely surrounded," she agreed, "but according to the *Times* there are millions of people who feel isolated and alone."

"That's different. I don't feel lonely or depressed. I just like being alone. Do you?"

She opened her mouth to say, *Oh, yeah. I love being alone.* And then she wasn't so sure anymore. "I guess I need to think about that question," she said, suddenly feeling off-balance. *What's wrong with me? Why don't I know? I love my job. I love New York.* She saw her confidence sliding down a storm drain like water after a rainstorm.

*I need to get out of this town.*

When she glanced up she realized they'd passed most of the businesses and had ventured into the east end art gallery district, which housed the Mews Café—one of her favorite haunts before the Shaylalynn incident—and Shaylalynn's club, Women's Work, whose wooden sign she could see in the distance under the glow of a nearby streetlight.

"I think we need to turn around," she said.

"No, we're only a few blocks from my condo."

Her eyes remained fixed on the club's sign, and she was certain Shaylalynn would suddenly appear and chug down the sidewalk, her hair bubbling on top of her head. Rafi had dropped her hand and circled her waist. It felt good. It felt safe.

"I think we should stop for a drink," she murmured into her ear. Dani laughed nervously in reply. "I'm serious."

"I'm not even supposed to *be* in P-town. Aren't you forgetting? I was the topic of a two-hour meeting four years ago. The selectmen decreed that I was banished. Technically I could be arrested for even setting foot across Route Six—"

Her litany of rationalizations died in her throat when Rafi seized her lips again, only this time the kiss was full of yearning, not curiosity. It wasn't a chocolate-covered wafer to be nibbled slowly but a tasty strawberry chewy that needed to be devoured all at once for full enjoyment. And in a few sizzling seconds it was over again.

"God, why do you do that to me?" she asked sharply.

Rafi's smug expression answered the question, and she pointed to the cobblestone path that led through a grove of trees to the well-secluded Women's Work lounge. She waited for Dani who shook her head.

"Are you sure? I'm sure I could smooth things over with Shaylalynn," she said confidently.

She laughed and grabbed her arm, pulling her further down the street. "I'm not in the mood."

The road bent toward the water, and she could smell the nearby sea. Rafi steered her to a sandy lane toward the bay and an old gray building that had been converted to condos.

"How old is this place?" she asked, instantly taken by its charm and location.

"It used to be a single home built by a fishing millionaire in the late eighteen hundreds, but eventually the heirs couldn't keep it. It sat empty for a few decades until a corporation bought it."

They trudged up the sand to a patio that faced the water. She leaned over the white wooden railing and gazed at the moonlight tip-toeing over the shimmering water. She closed her eyes and listened to the moan of the tide as it gobbled up the shore and felt the light breeze tickle her face.

*I can't do this in New York. I can't stand on a corner and just listen and feel. I'll be mugged or mowed over by frantic pedestrians.*

She pictured the ceiling fan in her bedroom and its whirring blades after she'd hit the off button—a blur of motion slowed as the revolutions grew longer until the blades finally stopped. Her heart rate decreased in the same manner, and she took a deep cleansing breath. She was completely calm for the first time in as long as she could remember.

She was alone and Rafi had left the patio door open. She went inside to a cozy living area complete with hardwood floors, a worn fabric sofa and a simple dinette set with a Formica top. Her suitcase was on the couch, and she imagined Rafi had more than a few people who did her bidding. The furniture was circa 1970, and the walls held only a single print in a cheap frame— Petra's *Kismet*.

She automatically walked toward the blues, reds, yellows and greens that fought for attention on the canvas and bled together in an intricate design.

After Petra's afternoon of color analysis, she had declared that yellow and green were the colors of relationships, the extra layers that explained their togetherness. When she'd asked why, Petra had stated that yellow was the strongest primary color and the one that could easily tint every other color by its presence, just as being in a relationship changed every other facet of a person's life. And she had noted a twinge of regret as Petra made this point. And when yellow joined forces with green, the color with the oxymoronic meaning of jealousy and growth, a relationship was defined—at least in Petra's way of thinking. All Dani knew was that she liked the painting.

Her shoulder started to burn as she remembered the long Saturday night when she'd insisted Petra ink her with her latest creation. Petra had been so excited since it was the one and only time Dani had initiated an inking session and one of the few times she hadn't been drunk. She was usually somewhat inebriated or she was at a moment of emotional instability and Petra capitalized upon it by cajoling her into sacrificing another section of flesh for her art.

Therapist Number Four had concluded that she loved *Kismet* because it was her idea. *I probably shouldn't have fired that woman. She may have known what she was talking about.*

"I love the way the colors blend together," Rafi said, returning to the living room balancing a bottle of port wine, two glasses and a small covered serving dish. "It's one of my favorite paintings of all time."

"Mine, too," she agreed.

They sat on the couch and sipped the wine. For the first

time Rafi really seemed to study her tattoos and she gazed intently at the shoulder covered by *Kismet*.

"I remember when I saw this in San Francisco," she said absently. "And I met Petra. I assume you broke up?"

"A long time ago. What did you think of her?"

She took a deep breath but didn't answer. Dani realized she wasn't prone to glib responses or sarcasm. Rafi was incredibly deep, and it made her uncomfortable.

"I thought she was . . . autobiographical."

"What?"

"After five minutes of speaking with her and being propositioned twice, I knew that her work was merely an extension of herself. Her creative nature derived only from her."

"I think that's true of most artists. Frida Kahlo said she painted her reality."

"That's not what I mean. Georgia O'Keeffe said art is not what you see but what you make others see. When I looked at Petra's work it was about *her* and *her reality*. I didn't get the impression she cared what anyone else saw."

She snorted. "Well, you're right there."

"What was it like being with her?"

"It was like eating a pound of peanut butter chocolate in one sitting. You love it while you're devouring it and hate the way you feel afterward."

She checked Rafi's thoughtful expression and couldn't tell what she was thinking. It had been like that all day. She plunged into long periods of silence wearing a stoic look on her face. She never felt the need for conversation and was entirely comfortable with silence. Dani liked her unpredictable nature.

Then Rafi kissed *Kismet* lovingly while Dani stared at the luscious lips caressing her flesh and suddenly the burning feeling was replaced by incredible warmth, like a soothing salve.

She automatically moaned and when Rafi gazed at her she said, "I . . . I don't why I did that."

"I enjoyed it," she replied, setting their glasses on the table and facing her. "So would you like to mix a little business with pleasure?"

Dani raised her eyebrow. "Would you?"

Rafi uncovered the lovely crystal dish and revealed five candies—two after-dinner nipples and three chocolates shaped liked clitorises with tiny cherries in the centers. She held out a nipple and Dani took it remembering how good they tasted.

"Let's try a little experiment and find out what else you like."

"So decadent," she declared as the rich chocolate filled her mouth.

Rafi handed her the glass of port and she took a sip, recognizing how much the wine complemented the chocolate.

"This is great."

Rafi raised her glass in salute. "Portuguese people know their port."

She set their glasses down and picked up one of the chocolate clitorises. Dani saw how intricate the detail was and she realized she was getting horny just looking at the candy.

"Now, I need to warn you that this candy is an aphrodisiac. If you eat it, we *will* wind up in bed together."

"You're sure?" she asked. *And what if she's right? I want her to be right. I want her.*

"Taste is the most erotic of the senses," Rafi lectured. "It controls everything else."

She placed the unusual candy on her own tongue. It started to melt, and Dani watched the cherry center bleed across the chocolate. She was completely mesmerized and unprepared for Rafi's mouth to meet her own. The dark chocolate was nothing like she had ever tasted. The feeling of their tongues savoring the wine and chocolate together served as the best foreplay she'd ever experienced.

Once the candy was gone, Rafi pulled the tank top over her head. She kissed her shoulders and Dani shivered.

"Close your eyes and lie down," she said.

Dani stretched across the couch like a human art show. Many lovers had kissed her tattoos, and most had ogled them during sex and she'd never felt anything except excluded. Whenever lovers touched her it was because they were curious about Petra and her art. She was always there, interfering and participating. She'd really never left.

She couldn't explain it but as Rafi's lips explored her body, it felt special. Perhaps it was because she continuously lingered and returned to the one patch of flesh Petra hadn't claimed, her right shoulder.

"More," Dani complained and turned over to face her.

Rafi straddled her and kissed *Loose Heart*. "Is your heart still broken? Does it still belong to her?"

She shook her head and managed a ragged "No."

Rafi slid her tongue across her chest and teased her right nipple. She closed her eyes, waiting for the image of the ice rink to overtake her but it wouldn't come. Even as Rafi lowered herself between her legs, all she felt, all she could see and all she could imagine was Rafi touching her. Her eyes flew open, suddenly not wanting to miss what was coming next. She touched her spiky hair and one chocolate eye glanced up for a moment, long enough to see the pleasure on her face before Rafi grinned and stripped off her shorts. She glanced at her wet underwear and smiled.

"Fabulous," she murmured, quickly discarding her own clothes until she was clad only in her thong.

Rafi snuggled against her and traced the outline of *Epiphany*. "Did Petra do all of your tattoos?"

"Yes, they're all her original artwork."

She sighed. "That's a lot of time and pain."

"I thought we were in love," she said quietly. "Wouldn't you do anything for someone you loved?"

"No," she admitted. "There's a whole *lot* I wouldn't do for a lover."

She fell back against the couch and stared at the ceiling feeling angry and ashamed. She knew Rafi was right like all of her therapists, but she didn't need to say it.

Obviously sensing the mood was slipping away Rafi kissed

her gently. "Sorry," she whispered. "I don't want to talk about the past."

They molded together perfectly, and she slipped her leg between Rafi's and found Rafi was already wet too. Rafi didn't seem to notice since her attention was focused on *Loose Heart*. She kissed it several times and looked up and said, "What if I could use my magical abilities and kiss all of these tattoos away. Would you want that?"

"I want to know where you got the magical abilities."

"Don't change the subject. What if I could?"

The question was unexpected, and she wasn't used to the unexpected which seemed to be the land where Rafi lived. When she opened her mouth and no sound came out, Rafi plucked another chocolate from the dish and placed it on her tongue before she kissed her deeply.

Lost in the taste of chocolate, the texture of her sinewy back muscles and the excitement of their breasts and pelvises colliding, she saw nothing else when she closed her eyes. No image replaced the moment when Rafi cried out and she quickly followed.

As they cuddled on the couch she realized that for the first time in her life she was completely present during lovemaking. It left her with an entirely different feeling like a sugar rush and not just from the physical satisfaction. Usually every nerve ending was a lit match that surrounded her heart and protected it from feeling any passion. But as she gazed at Rafi, tears streamed down her cheeks.

"Hey," Rafi cooed as she wiped away the tears. "Too much?"

She shook her head. "No, it's just . . . "

She didn't sound like herself and couldn't finish the sentence. It was too embarrassing. Normally she'd offer a lazy smile to a lover regardless of how much she liked it. An orgasm was an orgasm. But she couldn't smile now—wouldn't smile—at least not like that.

Rafi's unreadable expression returned and for a single

moment the rich, dark eyes liquefied. She blinked and quickly reached for a cherry clitoris. "So what do you think of my chocolate?"

She regained her composure. "Definitely an aphrodisiac," she said gratefully.

Rafi chuckled and hovered over her, her breasts teasing her mercilessly, the richness of her eyes returning. When Dani captured a nipple between her teeth, Rafi moaned in pleasure. They were ready to begin again.

# Chapter Twelve

A few hours later they awoke to someone pounding on Rafi's door.

"What the hell is that?" Dani asked groggily, barely lifting her head from the wonderful down pillow.

"I don't know."

She gasped when Rafi reached into her nightstand and withdrew a small caliber revolver. She checked the safety and headed toward the living room just as the pounding stopped. Dani followed her to the front door, still naked, and found her looking through the peephole.

"Whoever it was is gone," she said. She refastened the safety and glanced at her. "What?"

"Do you really know how to use that thing?"

"Damn straight. I'm a woman living alone. Don't tell me you've never fired a gun? And you live in New York?"

She leaned against the wall to slow her heartbeat. "I've never felt scared. I don't ride the subways at two in the morning, but any other time is perfectly safe."

Rafi raised an eyebrow and floated against her. "Really? You feel safe in a city with six million people?"

The heat intensified between them the minute she slipped her arm around her waist. Skin against skin just as it had been all night. She whispered kisses against her cheek and tossed the gun onto the couch. Dani didn't think they'd make it all the way back to the bedroom until a tap on the patio door interrupted their foreplay and both of them whirled toward the dining area. She froze at the sight of Liam standing on the patio.

"Mom?"

When she saw him she immediately pulled Rafi toward the floor and hid behind the couch. After a few more commands, one of which required him to face the bay for several minutes, she and Rafi greeted him after they'd dressed.

"What the hell are you doing here?" she asked in her most caring yet pissed off tone.

"I was worried," he said, his eyes never leaving Rafi.

She noticed he looked terrible. His hair was disheveled and he wore a wrinkled dress shirt and jeans. He hadn't shaved and she wondered when he'd last slept.

Before she could say anything he looked at Rafi and asked, "Hi, I'm Liam. And you are?"

She smiled warmly and extended her hand. "I'm Rafi. I sell your mother's candy."

She wore a silk kimono that hid very little of her gorgeous legs and Dani forced herself not to look south. Liam seemed to have the same difficulty.

"Would you like a glass of wine or something to drink?"

He raked a hand through his thick hair. "I'd love some vodka, please, if you have it."

She nodded and headed for the kitchen while Dani led him to the couch. Something was definitely wrong, and she cringed at the thought that his marriage had already gone south before the wedding bills were paid.

"She's a fraud," he proclaimed.

"Who? Rafi?" she asked suddenly.

He waved his hand and glanced toward the kitchen. "No, no. Not her. Cassidy. She couldn't even get through the honeymoon without coming on to four other guys. I caught her kissing the cabana boy last night."

"I'm so sorry," she said automatically. Even though she'd predicted Cassidy was a gold-digger she'd thought they'd at least make it through the honeymoon.

He started to cry, and she held him as she'd done throughout his life whenever the world had been unkind and unworthy to know someone as beautiful as him.

"And there's more," he said, the sobs choking his voice. "She had an abortion before the wedding."

She sat straight up and imagined Cassidy plummeting over a cliff. He stared at her, and she swallowed all of the angry diatribes, ridiculing comments and the obvious *I told you so.*

"Sweetheart, I'm so sorry."

He shook his head. "I should've known. I'm a psychologist, for God's sake. I'm paid to read people's emotions and tell when they're lying."

"But your wife isn't supposed to lie, honey. Your wife is supposed to be the one person who will love, honor and respect you. Isn't that what the priest said?" she joked sarcastically.

Rafi returned with a glass of Absolut and the bottle. She perched on the chair across from them like a bird watching a show from a telephone wire. She wore the same enigmatic expression that Dani had come to know.

"I'm sorry I took the plane," he said, gulping the vodka. "I just had to get out of there."

"Don't worry about it," she insisted. "None of this is your fault. You were deceived because all she wanted was your money."

He snorted. "I don't have any money."

She said nothing and waited until he understood. Then he shook his head.

"Unbelievable. I feel so stupid."

"Relationships do that, honey. They make you feel really stupid," she said absently, thinking of Petra.

She patted his knee. "We'll get back to New York tomorrow, and you'll get an annulment. You're the most important person in my life. You're all that matters."

When he finally raised his head and wiped his tears, he finished another drink before he glanced at Rafi. "I'm sorry for intruding on you. I barge into your home in the middle of night, drink your liquor and ruin your amorous evening with my mother."

She glanced at Dani and swallowed hard before she waved a hand of indifference. "Don't worry about it. It was just business."

He laughed, clearly assuming that she was joking, and she joined him. Caught up in the contagious moment of humor, Dani automatically smiled, but she was equally disarmed by the comment.

When the merriment subsided she asked simply, "Was it?"

At first it seemed Rafi assumed she was talking to Liam, but when their eyes met, she finally realized Dani was talking to her. "What?"

"You just told Liam that we slept together for business motives. And I want to know if that's what you really think, or as your laughter might suggest, you were joking."

The smile was still pasted on her face, revealing her incredibly white teeth against her bronze skin. Her spiky hair went everywhere and she looked absolutely adorable. Dani prayed it wasn't the truth.

She scratched her head and looked away, clearly embarrassed. "Dani, I thought . . . " She shrugged and the explanation died.

Dani glanced at Liam. She knew his moods and expressions. He'd dropped his personal problems off at the last rest stop and shifted into psychologist mode, studying Rafi with a trained eye. His lips turned downward into a frown, a face she knew well.

*I've been duped. This whole evening was a ruse. She's wanted my help all along, and she played me to get it.*

"Did you sleep with me because you want me to market your candy? You obviously know I'm an easy fuck, given my history in P-town."

Her gaze traveled between both of them. "Dani, C'mon. Don't talk about this in front of Liam."

She shrugged. "Why? He knows who I am." She glanced at her son and was unable to contain her pride. "He knows me better than I know myself. I should probably listen to his advice all of the time."

She reached over and kissed him on the forehead. It was one of their symbols of togetherness, comfort and care. When he squeezed her hand in return she realized everything was okay, and she saw the magnitude of what had happened in the last twenty-four hours. She pictured them above the clouds in a hot air balloon with no one else around. He'd dumped Cassidy and returned to her. That was all she needed. Whatever motives prompted Rafi didn't matter.

She pulled away and crossed her arms, forgetting that she was only wearing a terry cloth robe that Rafi had pulled from a hook in her bathroom. Her expression, mannerisms and posture were those of a business executive in a Dior suit. If this was business then she would treat it as such. Rafi would be sorry she'd tangled with Dani O'Grady.

"So, please answer my question. I want to know why I'm here."

Rafi wrapped herself in the kimono like a caterpillar folding itself as tight as it possibly could into a little ball. When she looked up, Dani couldn't tell if her eyes gleamed with tears or the fire of anger.

"We know who we are. We know what we want. We're mature, right? We know how to deal with *complicated*. We want to make a lot of money, and we want a good fuck."

Her words were a slap, and Dani rose from the sofa and retreated to the bedroom. She was a master at quick exits after so many one-night stands, and she was dressed in less than two minutes. When she turned, Rafi stood in the doorway.

"Are you leaving?"

"Yes," she said.

She grabbed her arm and pulled her close. Her chocolate eyes were full of pain. "Okay, here's the deal. I don't do hookups and you don't do girlfriends, right? So what's left? This had to be business, right?" When Dani didn't answer, she added, "Regardless, I'd like you to stay. This doesn't have to be defined."

Dani offered her most pleasant business smile, the one that soothed clients' fears and anxieties about profit and loss margins, the one that reassured distributors during hard times. It was a smile she'd perfected like a well-written recipe—one part sincerity, one part seriousness and two parts intelligence. Her father had told her a business smile was a key to success and she'd actually practiced it by staring in the mirror.

"Don't worry about the deal," she said, patting her arm. "I know a good opportunity to make money when I see it. And you didn't need to fuck me to open my eyes to it."

Rafi's arm fell away, obviously shocked. Dani passed her and motioned to Liam, who grabbed her suitcase and followed her out the door. She was relieved to see a Lincoln Town Car at the edge of the road, and once her bag was dropped into the trunk the urge for a cigarette was overwhelming. She finagled the keys from him, lit up and climbed into the driver's seat, ignoring his protests that he was sober enough to drive.

"Where are we going?" he asked as the engine purred to life.

She checked her watch and saw that it was nearly three o'clock in the morning. She didn't relish the idea of trolling the small towns that lined Route 6 between Provincetown and Hyannis, which she knew had great resorts, but none of them ran their establishments like a Motel Six. The light wasn't always on.

The idea of a sleazy motel disgusted her but she wasn't sure what to do. He was falling asleep against the window and needed a bed. She reached into her pocket for her phone and felt the teeth of a key—the Penthouse suite. In her haste to escape she'd forgotten to leave it on the bed.

"I know where we can stay," she said.

They fell onto the bed simultaneously having parked down the street and snuck up the creaky stairs. She had noticed a dim glow in number nine as they passed the landing and assumed that Cat was up. *She's probably got another lover in there right now.*

"Mom, what's going on? Why the hell are you in P-town?" he mumbled.

Even though he was exhausted he still took care of her. *That's how it's always been. He's always been there for me. I cried on his shoulder after Petra left. He was sixteen, and I treated him like one of my therapists. I'm pathetic.*

"Honey, there's too much to say. I wouldn't know where to start. Besides I'm supposed to be listening to you."

"I've told you everything so you get to have a turn. Just summarize."

"I'm here in P-town visiting my half-sister since your grandfather left half of the company to her in a handwritten will before he died. Her name is Olivia, by the way. She's more concerned about her foster daughter, Cat, a woman who has just declared to her that she's a bisexual. But Olivia doesn't believe that it's true, and if I don't get Cat to change her mind, she's enforcing the will and I'll lose half of the company. And the woman you met, Rafi, she's one of my distributors who needed to meet with me. It just got . . . complicated, I guess. I don't know how we wound up sleeping together. She's quite interesting. I know you didn't really get to meet her, but she's an extraordinary candymaker. Did you get all that?"

He coughed. "Half-sister, bisexual sort of daughter, losing the company and woman that you've fallen for. Got it."

She sat up on her elbow. "No, wait. That's not it. I have *not* fallen for Rafi. We don't even know each other. We just met today."

He managed to open one eye and stare at her. "So she was right."

"What?"

"It was business."

"Of course not. Maybe. I don't know."

When he opened the other eye and stared at her like a disapproving son she made some gurgling noises but realized there was no way to win.

She fell back against the pillows and he cuddled her. "I've got enough energy for a few more sentences so here goes. You're an amazing mom. You deserve to be happy and find someone. And you have a lot in common with another candymaker. Be glad you have a sister. And . . . and . . . I don't know what to do about *my* bisexual sister."

"She's not your sister. They're not even related." She wanted to protest, but he started to snore. It was so contagious that she fell asleep against him.


Again she awoke to odd sounds—loud laughter. For a moment she was disoriented until she saw the angular white walls and vintage furniture. They were squatting in the Penthouse suite of the Fairbanks Inn. She rolled around in the bed, and her arm swatted the other half of the queen-size bed, the place where Liam had literally dropped after walking through the door. But he wasn't there.

She pulled herself up and wiped a hand across her face to focus on the digital clock on the nightstand. It read ten thirty. *Jesus. I need to get out of here and back to New York.* She heard the laughter again, definitely females, but a third voice chimed in and she recognized his hearty, deep chuckle. Thoughts of Olivia Santos bursting through the door, her face as red as a candied apple, propelled her from the bed and toward the bathroom.

She stared into the mirror and felt old. And the lighting didn't help. All of her worry lines, crow's feet and wrinkles were highlighted against what used to be creamy skin, the face that

Petra first saw. She sighed in disgust. *How could I ever think that a woman like Rafi, who is at least ten years younger than me, would want me by choice? How could I not see her ulterior motives? I'm an idiot.*

She hung her head and took some deep breaths before retreating from the bathroom without another glance into the mirror. She got dressed and grabbed her bag. They needed to get out before Olivia found them, and whoever Liam was conversing with would need to be sworn to secrecy or bought off with a slick hundred.

She headed down the stairs determined to find him and escape quickly. He was telling a story from childhood where he'd managed to get lost in FAO Schwartz at Christmastime. He was only seven, and she'd been frantic to find him. She'd pushed her way through several crowds certain that he'd walk out the front door with a stranger who would promise him a Lionel train, the one gift he coveted that year. Instead, she'd found him with the store manager reporting *her* as a lost parent.

When she came upon them they were all sitting on the patio outside of room nine, laughing hysterically at the outcome of the story. He was drinking coffee, his legs stretched over the balcony railing. Next to him was Cat who sipped her coffee and wore a sweet smile. A white carafe and plates of breakfast goodies sat between them. The third person had her back to Dani, but when she turned her chair to the side Dani recognized her immediately—Hope from the Brew café.

"Hi, Mom."

Her knees went weak as Hope's grin widened. "Well, hi there. It's good to see you again."

"Hey," she said.

"Oh, so you know each other?" Cat asked pointedly. Dani also noticed her smile evaporated.

"Not formally," Hope said. "I just know her as *opportunity*."

Hope added a chuckle, and Dani felt her face turn red. She glanced at Liam who smiled pleasantly, ignorant of lesbian subterfuge, but Cat glared at her.

"Then let me introduce you formally," Cat said. "Dani O'Grady this is Hope Langley. I assume you've been to the Brew?"

She nodded with a forced smile.

"And did you become a member of the Brew's exclusive coffee club?"

"She sure did!" Hope said proudly before Dani could answer.

"Wow," Cat said sarcastically. She leaned back in her chair and crossed her arms.

"So what kind of club is this?" Liam asked. "Are the benefits good?"

Hope spewed coffee over the railing as Cat roared with laughter. Dani's gaze dropped to the landing as she imagined herself becoming skinny enough to slide through the tiny crevices between the planks.

"I mean, maybe I want to join," he added and they laughed harder.

She immediately went to his side to protect him from further embarrassment. "We need to go," she said, but he couldn't hear her.

When Hope finally caught her breath, she said, "Ah, honey, the benefits of joining Hope's Chest are too numerous to mention—if you're the right sex. And sweetie, as cute as you are, I'm a gold star."

"A what?" he asked.

"She's never been with a man," Cat clarified. "While I'm a bisexual, Hope is a grade-A lesbian. Just like your mom." She glanced up. Her face was bloated in jealousy. "In fact, your mother enjoys fucking many women, don't you, Dani? You're a bit of a tramp."

"Cat," she said sharply.

"Hey, don't talk about my mother like that!" he barked.

She patted his shoulder. "It's okay, honey. Cat's just upset."

Hope snorted. "Oh, this is rich. I get it now."

"Get what?" he shouted.

Cat leaned closer and touched his arm. "Liam, you're a psychologist so what do you make of a patient who sleeps with three different people in a twenty-four-hour period? Me, Hope and Rafi." She looked up at Dani. "Or are there others that I missed? Perhaps your good friend Joelle?"

He turned and faced her. "Mom, is this true?"

"Son—"

He shook his head in disgust and jumped from the chair. "Don't talk to me right now."

He stormed out the back gate. She couldn't imagine how embarrassed he was, and she turned her wrath on Cat.

"You are a conniving little bitch. I can't believe you just did that to him."

"Yeah, Cat," Hope added. "That was really cold. If I'd known you and Dani were an item I never would've screwed either of you."

"We're not an item," Dani answered. Her gaze was still on Cat's icy stare. "That's the point." She started back up the stairs and suddenly stopped. Cat was lighting a cigarette and seemed to care less. "I hope you and Nathaniel are quite happy together."

She couldn't be sure, but she thought Cat's hands shook as she brought the match to the cigarette.

She gathered her things and wondered how she could avoid seeing Cat and Hope again as she made her exit. *I could crawl out a window and swing into a nearby tree.* The problem fixed itself after she received a text from Liam stating that he was driving the rental back to the city, and she'd need to hire a taxi to take her to the airport.

From her third-story vantage point she watched Cat and Hope exit the inn and head down Bradford Street. She couldn't be sure, but it seemed as though Hope was comforting her. *And maybe that's just what I want to believe. That I hurt her as much as she hurt Liam.*

She headed slowly down the steep stairs with her bag to

wait out front for the car. It was still twenty minutes away but she wanted to be gone. She fumbled with the bag and when she looked up, Olivia stood at the bottom of the staircase.

She nearly lost her balance and prepared for her wrath. "I, I was just leaving. I'm sorry we came back—"

Olivia waved it off. "Please sit with me for a few minutes," she said and motioned to one of the patio tables.

While she retrieved a pitcher of mimosas, Dani relaxed on the patio and gazed at the magnificent foliage around her. She'd been initially impressed by the amount of plants, shrubbery and flowers that covered the inn's three acres, but she hadn't taken the time to notice that it was worthy of a photo shoot for a magazine like *Sunset*. Old-growth trees lined the edge of the property, their enormous canopies providing romantic privacy for the guests in the nearby Carriage House. Red brick pathways meandered between the three buildings, their formation dictated by the extensive gardens interspersed between. Since it was June, pink, purple and white flowers bloomed everywhere. At a table in the corner a few women captured the scene in oil paintings, confirming her belief that the setting was serene and peaceful. *I could sit here all day. I wish I wasn't banished.*

She closed her eyes and succumbed to the sounds of the birds singing and the painters chattering in the corner. She took a deep breath and the sea air filled her lungs. It was intoxicating, nothing like the smell of exhaust in Times Square or the smell of garbage at the mouth of every alley. She didn't hear Olivia approach until the tray clinked as she set it down.

"It's a beautiful place, isn't it?" Olivia commented.

She smiled and took the champagne flute Olivia offered. "It's perfect. I see why you'd never leave."

They both smiled slightly, and she realized it was the same smile—their father's smile. She noticed Olivia held a photo album under her arm that she set on the table.

"I'm sorry about yesterday," she said. "And I'm sorry for getting involved with Cat."

Olivia nodded. "Thank you."

She shifted in her seat and leaned across the table. "Olivia, at the risk of starting another fight, why does Cat need a man? You didn't need one. I didn't need one. We've both been single parents, and our kids turned out rather well."

She smiled faintly. "You always want more for your child. I know how hard it was for my mother and for me." She faced her and said sternly, "Two generations have lived with backbreaking work, poverty and loneliness. That's what I see. I don't want that for Cat."

She looked down. Her life had been privileged and while it was difficult at times with Liam, she had never struggled financially. "It's not right of me to compare my life with yours. I know that," she said slowly, "and I know you must resent that our father—"

"Don't," Olivia said sharply. "Don't go there. I've thought of it a thousand times and it doesn't help. It doesn't matter."

Dani glanced up and met her hard expression. She sensed she'd touched the core and quickly retreated. She bit her lip and kept drinking.

The wind softened to a breeze, quieting the trees and wind chimes that lined the patio, allowing Dani and Olivia to hear the muffled tones of the nearby painters. She lit a cigarette and busied herself with the act of smoking rather than talking.

She'd given up smoking with Petra. They'd gone on a health kick for six months eating a vegan diet and exercising. One day she'd come home early to the smell of smoke. For a brief moment she thought the condo was on fire until she'd heard laughter from the bedroom.

Expecting to find her in bed with another woman, she had been surprised to find a nude stranger posing on her bed—smoking—while a fully clothed Petra sat on her stool in front of a canvas, sketching the model, a cigarillo dangling from her mouth. Even more surprising was what had come next—her request for Dani to strip and join the model. It had taken coaxing via a bottle of tequila, but she'd crawled onto the bed for a twosome that eventually became a threesome. What she hadn't known at the time was that the model would be the one to replace her within a month after Petra inked *The Cleansing* on her back.

"What's your favorite memory of childhood?" Olivia asked suddenly.

That wasn't a question she could answer easily. *Favorite* implied there were many good memories to choose from, like an O'Grady sampler filled with some of the greatest candies O'Grady produced. She loved each and every one and apparently the rest of America did as well, for the sampler sales during the holidays were remarkable.

Her life had not been a sampler. While most people remembered moments of their lives and not calendar days, she was the opposite. She'd kept a journal throughout her childhood and bookmarked all of the days worth remembering. There were ten.

When she didn't answer her question immediately, Olivia said, "My favorite memories happened at the beach. I remember my mother holding my hand as we ventured out into the waves each summer. I was exhilarated at the sight of the ocean but not terrified because she had a tight grip on me. Sometimes I think I can still re-create that feeling when I sit by the shore." She glanced at Dani who stared intently at a luscious green bush. "Do you have any memories like that?"

"No."

Olivia surprised her when she said, "I didn't think so."

She picked up the photo album and flipped through the pages most of which were filled with snapshots of Cruz with Olivia and Cat at various ages, so Dani was taken aback when she showed her a five by seven of herself with her father and mother. It was one of their customary Christmas cards that they sent out each year, the large decorated tree serving as a backdrop. The picture had always been the same—the three of them standing next to the tree with holiday wishes printed at the bottom of the photo. Judging from her age, she guessed she was four or five when it was taken.

"Where did you get this?"

"My mother told me that she once asked your father for a

picture so she could create a mental image whenever he talked about you or your mother. He said this was the only one he had. I think it says a lot about your life."

"Why?"

"It's as cold and unfeeling as winter," she said in a soft, caring tone. "Your father has his arm on your shoulder and looks so proud of you, but your smile is painful. And if you look closely at your mother, she isn't really smiling at all."

She studied the picture and saw what Olivia saw. Her mother was a foot apart from her father and didn't bother to touch her. To anyone glancing at the card as they sifted through their holiday mail, her mother's expression would be dismissed as pleasant. But there was no warmth despite the roaring fireplace directly to the left of them. Her mother had always insisted they stand between the tree and the fireplace for balance.

And she remembered the annual drama that preceded the photographer's click of the shutter and what followed afterward. Her mother had nagged her father about his tie selection or haircut, and Dani had been told endlessly to stand up straight and quit pulling at her tights. The annual Christmas picture only brought distasteful memories.

"I hope you don't take this the wrong way," Olivia continued, "but whenever I felt badly about my life I looked at this picture. I'm sorry if that offends you."

She glanced at the array of other photos that surrounded the miserable Christmas memory. Each one showed Cruz, Olivia and others that she assumed were family and friends in various candid poses thoroughly enjoying life. It reminded her of the first seven photos albums that belonged to her father.

She looked up. "He belonged with your mother."

Olivia looked stunned. "I . . . I'm sorry. I never should've brought this out." She snatched the photo album and stood. "I hope you have a good flight back. I'll be in touch," she added as she hurried back inside.

• • •

As the plane roared into the sky she stared out the window as Provincetown disappeared beneath her. She felt heavy like a piece of fudge—her least favorite candy. She thought the name said it all. It was thick and often too sweet if it wasn't made well. It was the sugary version of heroin since it was an extreme candy, and most people couldn't handle more than a single square. And she hated the way it tasted in her mouth—gritty. Of course, her company made incredible fudge because it was an American favorite but she never ate it.

While she was dismayed about the encounter with Rafi, angrier with Cat than she'd ever been with anyone and worried about Liam, it was her conversation with Olivia that had left her terribly depressed—and not just because they were about to become business partners.

As she listened to her recount her favorite memory with Cruz, not only had she felt incredibly cheated by her own mother, but she realized her father had given her only one gift—the company. Yes there had been lavish birthday parties and a car when she turned sixteen, which she crashed into a tree when her French instructor couldn't keep her hands to herself one afternoon, but there weren't any moments of personal connection. She'd never talked to her mother about sex because she realized early on that her mother wouldn't want to talk about sex *with girls*. And her father had never read her a bedtime story because he was never home. An image of a hollow chocolate Easter bunny came into her mind.

"Get over it," she snarled and poured herself another Portuguese Daisy from the pitcher the steward had left beside her after takeoff.

She closed her eyes and snapshots of her liaison with Rafi took hold of her senses. She could still feel her back muscles tensing between her fingers as they rocked against each other and her exotic scent—a blend of a floral perfume and chocolate, a natural hazard from spending her days in a candy store. It had driven Dani wild and intensified her passion.

Best of all was the way Rafi had tasted. After the chocolate clitorises had melted against the action of their busy tongues, the rich cocoa lingered in their mouths while they made love over and over. *Taste is the most erotic of the senses.* All of her senses had been piqued, and she'd been uncannily aware of the bed creaking, the smoothness of her supple skin and the tickle of her spiky hair against her cheek. Only once during her relationship with Petra had she been so aware of her surroundings—the third time Petra had inked her and covered her arm with *Epiphany.*

They'd treated themselves to a romantic holiday in Venice and after a bottle of chianti and a ride in a gondola they'd returned to the hotel and made love. The night was balmy and afterward she'd thrown on a tank top and her panties and enjoyed the Italian sky from their private balcony. Petra had joined her and while she gazed at the full moon, Petra leaned against the railing and caressed her arm.

"What are you thinking about?" she had asked, already knowing that Petra had a vision.

"I've found the greatest way you can show your love for me."

She looked into the deep green eyes and lost her breath at the sight of her beauty in the moonlight. And she knew she'd agree to whatever request she made.

"I want to join myself with you," she'd said mysteriously, taking her by the hand and leading her to a chair in the sitting room.

She wasn't surprised when she pulled her tattooing kit from a duffel bag and prepared the black ink. Her anxiety grew when Petra swabbed her upper arm with alcohol. Even after two tattoos she wasn't used to the pain.

Obviously seeing the fear in her eyes, Petra kissed her and said, "This is an abstract. It won't be like the last time. It won't take long because I'm only using one color." She kissed her again and fondled her breasts through the sheer tank top. "And afterward we'll have some more fun."

She was already prepared for the incessant buzz of the tattoo machine and the burning sensation that increased each time she dragged the needle across her arm. But there was so much more. She'd never noticed that Petra liked to hum Neil Young songs while she worked, and she was certain that she could smell her flesh burning as the ink conquered the layer of dermis. In the end she'd actually *liked* the entire experience, and the final product—a self-portrait of Petra—was incredibly artistic.

Her eyes flew open and she fidgeted in her seat. She burrowed into her purse and found her cigarettes before checking the forty messages on her BlackBerry. She scrolled through the list of senders, recognizing that most were merely updates on projects that she could read later. An e-mail from someone named The Candy Lady caught her eye. She opened it and read the simple message.

*She's literally under your skin. You belong to her.*

# Chapter Thirteen

Rafi's words echoed in her head for the next week and she heard the beautiful lilting voice saying those two sentences repeatedly while the tattoos burned her flesh endlessly. She hadn't been able to eat or sleep, and she barely survived at work. Fortunately her staff, particularly Valerie, held everything together while her mental health took an insanity holiday.

She spent hours online researching tattoo removal and wished that YouTube had existed before she let Petra near her with her needle. But she had also realized that it wouldn't have mattered. No amount of pain would've prevented her from loving Petra—and this was the way she had wanted Dani to show her love. Some people desired expensive gifts, flowers or sappy notes. *I wish it had been that simple. She wanted to own me.*

At least that's what her new therapist thought. And after a month of biweekly sessions she'd contacted a premier plastic surgeon and asked for a consultation. He'd shown her several videos and convinced her that the reward of reclaiming her body would be worth the pain, the annoying sound from the laser's pulse, the cost and the dozens of cab rides to his office.

As she sat in the waiting room of the New York Physician's Group, it shamed her to think that she was the same woman that *Business Weekly* had called *a role model for all women in corporate America* just a few months before. They'd retract the article if they knew the truth.

"Ms. O'Grady?" a nurse called.

She followed her to a treatment room where she was given a smock and told to undress from the waist up. After the nurse left she stripped off her blouse and bra and stared at the mirror over the sink. Perhaps it was her newfound self-esteem or it was the mirror's glare against the fluorescent lighting, but when she stared at her reflection the tattoos seemed disproportionate to her body like stretched Silly Putty. She felt like a joke.

She turned away and threw on the smock just as the door opened and Dr. Hauser appeared. While he was the youngest and newest member of the Park Avenue practice, he was also a living testimonial for tattoo removal. When they'd first met he'd held out his arms which he said had been covered in tattoos during his military days. At first she hadn't believed him because she saw nothing and then he showed her some old pictures.

"Are you ready, Dani?" he asked pleasantly.

She nodded and hopped on the table. They'd agreed to start on the shoulders and back and see how much she could endure. Before she'd left work she'd applied an anesthetic cream on the areas she could reach. She'd thought about asking Ray to help her with her back, but she was too ashamed to tell anyone—even Liam—what she was doing. Of course, he was still barely speaking to her, but they were scheduled to have dinner later in the week. *I'll tell him then. I know he'll understand.*

Dr. Hauser prepared the instruments, and she put on the protective eye shields he handed to her.

"Here we go," he said as he activated the laser. Each pulse reminded her of the time she'd tried to cook bacon when she was six. The grease had splattered onto her hand and given her first-degree burns. This felt like five pounds of grease raining on her and the crackling sound from the laser added to the effect.

"How are you doing?" he whispered in her ear.

She nodded, urging him to continue. She wanted as much of it off as she could handle in one session. This definitely hurt more than the original inking. But perhaps she was getting old, and her threshold for pain was decreasing or she'd forgotten how much she'd really endured to keep Petra's love. Both possibilities disgusted her.

She tried not to think about the pain or the eighteen to twenty-four months Dr. Hauser estimated it would take to erase all of the tattoos.

"The good news," he'd said during the consultation, "is that your white Irish skin is a plus. The bad news is that some of this ink appears to be very deep and you've got every color in the rainbow all over your body."

He sensed her fidgeting and stopped to apply an ice pack. Then he helped her remove the protective eye shields and asked kindly, "Are we done for today?"

She didn't want to be through. She wanted it all gone immediately. She glanced at the mirror over the sink and groaned involuntarily. Hundreds of white blisters covered her upper arm, creating a perfect outline of what used to be *Birds of Freedom*. She twisted her body and saw blisters along her back.

"I told you these are common," Dr. Hauser said. "They'll disappear before you leave the office."

She sighed deeply and nodded again. She didn't understand why she was incapable of forming articulate responses, but she couldn't bring herself to speak. Perhaps it was the enormous ache creeping over her body. *Damn this hurts!*

"I know you wanted to hit all of them today but I'm thinking we should wait to tackle the front on the next visit."

She knew this was his nice way of saying *if you think this hurts, wait until I put this laser near your boob!*

She nodded again feeling like an imbecile—for not addressing her doctor properly, for looking like a circus act and for allowing a lover to do this to her. Again she heard Rafi's words. *There's a lot I wouldn't do for a lover.*

By the time she'd dressed, hailed a cab and ordered Ray to pick up the painkiller that Dr. Hauser had prescribed, she was angry at the world. She doubted she could function at work so she went home and took a shower. She knew it wasn't possible, but she imagined the water and soap washing Petra's canvas down the drain.

She rubbed the washcloth across the remains of the Arabic symbol, the first tattoo Petra had inked. They had been in the bathtub, and Petra was caressing every part of her body. She'd taken the sponge and dragged it across her shoulders causing her to glance at the new tattoo.

"Is it okay to wash it this soon? Will it come off?"

"It's fine, love," she'd said confidently. "I've removed the bandage and it's perfect. You'll have it forever."

The memory made her laugh. And when she stared into her beautifully lit bathroom mirror she was pleased. Already several of the tats were fading—except for the one she had decided to keep. *Kismet.* She'd loved it and so had Rafi.

The doorman delivered her prescription and within an hour she was floating on a lovely Percocet-induced cloud. As she lounged on her couch, she remembered he'd also brought her mail. She reached for the small stack and hurled all the junk and bills to the floor. She had no desire to lose her pleasant buzz over something ridiculous like the mortgage.

At the bottom of the stack was a small square envelope with no return address. She didn't recognize the artistic block letters that spelled her name and address, and she couldn't remember the last time she'd actually received personal mail. Unwilling to get up and go look for her letter opener, she hurriedly ripped the envelope and withdrew a familiar card—the screened image of a street that looked like Venice. It was the exact card she'd purchased in Provincetown, and her copy was still sitting in the top drawer of her desk, waiting for a worthy recipient.

She flipped over the envelope and noticed the postmark—Provincetown. She tried to stop the smile from creeping on her face but she couldn't. She opened the card and read the simple two lines that Rafi had composed. *Thinking of you. Still wondering what you'll write on* your *card.*

"We are not going to market a product called Taste No Evil," she said adamantly. "This is still a *family* business, and we're not going to tarnish our image."

"C'mon, Dani," Valerie argued. "Even Disney got over that. They didn't suffer after they started making PG movies. That's what we're doing here. Just a little adult fun. We've already said this candy isn't for the kids. It's for the adults who want a little treat for themselves."

"Yeah," Ivan Rocha added. As the PR director it was his job to protect the company as well as ensure that it made money. "Dani, it's an edgy name. We're certainly not marketing cherry clitorises here. I think it's a good choice."

She glared at the ten nodding heads staring at her from all angles of the conference table. She was the lone holdout regarding the name of their new upscale Halloween candy, a decadent combination of dark chocolate and chocolate mousse. It was their first foray into adult candy for adult parties and she imagined the inspiration came from Rafi's Purple line.

"Speaking of cherry clitorises," Helene from production asked Valerie, "How is the deal coming with Rafi?"

"It's going well. She's on board with everything, and I imagine we'll sign the final papers before the end of the year."

"You should see the eye-popping artwork we're doing," Ivan preened. "You've never seen so much purple in your life!" He turned to Dani and asked, "Have you checked out the boards? I need your final approval before we take it to Rafi."

She nodded and pretended to be studying a document in front of her. It was a common occurrence for their meetings to free flow into other topics or leapfrog around the agenda, such was the consequence at a laid-back company, but she'd removed herself from the Purple account for a reason.

"Can we please stay on track here? What are we going to do about this candy? I've got a real problem marketing the word *evil*—even to adults. As much as I might be inclined personally, O'Grady Candy can't afford to alienate the Christian right. They like candy just as much as anyone and some of our biggest markets are along the Bible Belt."

"What about Sinful?"

She looked up and realized the suggestion had come from Ray, whose main purpose at the meetings was to take notes.

"Go on," she said.

Ray glanced around the table. "I like what you said about the Christian right. They might not like the word evil but they're into sinning."

Everyone laughed—except Ray—and Valerie pointed at her. "She's got a point. Everyone sins and has vices. This would be a temptation, one you could enjoy without going to hell or even confession."

"I vote for Sinful," Ivan said, shooting his hand into the air.

All the others followed and she nodded her head. "Fine. Meeting adjourned."

Craving a cigarette, she bolted for the fire escape behind her desk. It was at these moments that she wished she had a real office with a door she could slam and curtains she could close.

Lately she'd spent much of her time out on the fire escape. It was a second office that afforded her privacy and allowed her to smoke freely, which she was doing often.

Olivia's attorney was conversing with Harry as they attempted to split the stocks for her share. Dani had accepted that she'd be working for the rest of her life as Olivia would inherit the portion that she'd allocated for her retirement. And she was okay with that. After meeting Olivia and seeing the photographic evidence of her father's happiness with Cruz, she couldn't deny Olivia her birthright. She'd realized that it was entirely possible O'Grady's success was partly due to the time he spent with Cruz.

And Olivia agreed to stay out of the daily operation of the business. She would just get the money. Dani didn't need any help picking out the candy wrapper colors or the names of the newest creations.

She gazed out at her city wondering if it was possible to move her desk onto the fire escape. She liked it out here. And right now it was cooler outside than indoors.

She fanned herself with a file folder and took a hefty swig of water. The air conditioning had died that morning at the peak of the hottest August in New York history. Everyone had changed into their workout clothes except for her. The professional environment of Dior suits and Armani blouses had given way to tank tops, shorts and a few sports bras in lieu of everyone going home, which they couldn't afford to do. It was nearly Labor Day weekend and Halloween was right around the corner.

As much as she desired to shed her silk blouse and dress pants, she couldn't, for it would create a distraction in the workplace and endless personal questions. Most of her employees had seen her tattoos over the years at various charity events or office parties. Some had asked her many questions, particularly about *Epiphany*.

While she believed removing them was the right decision, she couldn't look in the mirror anymore. She was ugly since much of the artwork was in various states of deconstruction. *Epiphany*, the self-portrait of Petra, looked especially disturbing since the left side of Petra's face had vanished, but the right side was resisting the treatment. Overall her upper body looked freakish, and she'd resigned herself to abstinence for the next two years. She couldn't imagine any lover being able to concentrate while staring at a human version of a messy artist's palette.

Eventually only *Kismet* would remain. And she wasn't sure if it was because *she* liked it or Rafi liked it. She'd read Rafi's text message a hundred times since that first visit to Dr. Hauser and rehashed her relationship with Petra endlessly. She wasn't anyone's canvas and by keeping the one tattoo she loved, she was affirming her individuality and her own choice.

She knew Rafi would approve, but she'd resisted contacting her. Rafi had called and texted a few times since she'd sent the card, but Dani had ignored all of the personal communications and vetted the business questions to Valerie.

She'd stayed out of the negotiations leaving Valerie to handle the account, most of which was done through e-mail and fax. Only once did Valerie and Ivan travel to Provincetown to see Rafi's setup and they returned gushing about the fabulous candies she made and praising Dani's amazing business acumen for landing such a huge account. *They just don't know how I got it. Even I didn't realize what I was doing to get it.*

No one had any idea that she and Rafi had mixed business with pleasure and she intended to keep it that way. She hopped back through the window and found Sanford sitting in her chair and wagging his tail. He gave a little bark when he saw her, and she knew that was his way of asking for help. He only appeared in her chair when Valerie was on a rant about something.

"What's wrong, boy? Is Valerie throwing things again?"

She scratched him behind his ears and went in search of her number two. She wasn't at her desk, but Dani quickly realized something was wrong since her entire collection of stress balls littered the floor. And a tin of Goofy Rocks, an O'Grady favorite with young boys who liked fizzy candy, had tipped over and tiny, multi-colored pebbles dotted the floor. Spike the Smiling Cat busily licked up as many as he could.

"Spike!" Dani called.

Hearing his name he looked up, and she saw that he was foaming at the mouth in multiple colors. He looked like he had rainbow rabies. He smiled at her and obediently sauntered away with Sanford trailing behind.

"She's downstairs with Gus," Ray said as she passed carrying a stack of folders. She glanced about Valerie's workspace and clucked her disapproval. "I really wish she wouldn't juggle when she's upset. She can't do it worth shit."

Ray continued back to her desk mentioning that she'd call maintenance while Dani surveyed the situation. Ray was right.

Valerie had studied juggling on YouTube when she heard it was a stress reliever, but her hand-eye coordination was subpar and almost always something broke whenever she attempted to throw more than two stress balls in the air at once. Her last victim had been the beautiful Tiffany clock Dani had given her for a Christmas present.

She descended the steps quickly knowing that time was crucial in helping Valerie regain her composure. She could hear Valerie and Gus shouting as she approached the door that led back into the candy factory. She found them arguing over some of the schematics for Rafi's candies. Gus was pointing at a large color photo of an after-dinner nipple.

"You really want to manufacture this? What kind of company are you running?"

"You're not going to make it. The plant out in New Jersey is doing it. What's your problem?" Valerie argued.

He noticed Dani standing nearby and waved the photo at her. "Your father never would've approved of this. We make candy for *kids*, not pornographers."

"It's a totally separate line, and it's not for pornographers," Dani said. "Normal people buy erotic stuff all of the time. Don't tell me you've never bought a *Playboy*."

"That's entirely different and has nothing to do with this conversation." He turned toward her with his hands on his hips. "You're taking this company in an entirely different direction, one that I don't approve of."

She took a deep breath and said softly, "I respect your opinion, you know I do. But this is about money and profit. If we don't jump at this chance someone else will. This is good candy, Gus. It tastes great."

He shook his head. "I'm disappointed in you, Dani. There's more to this business than money, principles like pride and tradition. This is smut!"

She looked him in the eye, not as the little girl he'd watched grow up or the good friend of the family, but as the CEO and his boss. "I disagree with you and as much as I love you, this isn't your decision to make."

The words came between them like a wall. He took off his apron and tossed it on a nearby counter before he walked out. She leaned against the counter and tried not to cry. He'd been a second father to her, and they'd never been at odds over the business.

She looked up at Valerie who understood. "It's a financial gold mine, Dani. Gus is stuck in the past. Everything changes."

She knew all of that but it still hurt. *Your father wouldn't approve.* And maybe he wouldn't. She yearned for a cigarette but they were upstairs.

"Is there anything else?"

Valerie nodded and she could tell it wasn't good news. "We have another problem. This issue with Gus wasn't even on my radar until five minutes ago."

"So this didn't have anything to do with the condition of your desk?"

She chuckled slightly. "No. He called right after I got off the phone with Rafi. She's changed her mind. She's backing out of the deal."

"What?"

"You might not have to worry about Gus," she explained. "Rafi says she won't sign the papers."

She couldn't believe what she was hearing. They had spent hundreds of hours and tens of thousands of dollars to create a subsidiary that would house Rafi's Purple candies and mass produce her mainstream confections such as Lemon Balls and the new Liquor Lollies. They'd invested heavily with only an oral contract holding the deal in place since she was so sure of Rafi's character and ability.

Now she really needed a cigarette. "Follow me," she said, barreling up the steps toward the fire escape. Only after she'd lit up and ignored Valerie's frown did she ask, "What happened?"

"She just said she had misgivings. She's decided that bigger isn't always better and that she needed to listen to her heart."

She shook her head, scowling. "She really used two clichés

in the same sentence? Those were her *exact* words?"

"Pretty much. We didn't speak for very long. She said she was sorry to cause so much trouble, and she hoped you understood. Something about clearing up a misunderstanding."

Her head snapped up. "She said we'd had a misunderstanding?"

"Yeah. Let me know what you want to do," she added, hopping back through the window.

Dani steadied herself against the railing and tried not to think of the financial ramifications. This would greatly affect her quarterly income and her bottom line. O'Grady wasn't a large company like some of the other powerful candymakers. To lose such an opportunity would hurt. The only question was *how much?*

Determined to find an answer, she stubbed out her butt and returned to her desk, summoning Ray to call finance and Valerie to bring Rafi's file while she called Harry to see what legal avenues were available.

"I hate to say it, Dani, but you really screwed this up," he said in his parental tone. "I told you to have her sign the contract first and why you agreed to wait until after so much time and energy was spent on the project, was the most foolish—"

"This is her baby, Harry. It's not even really a company. It's merely a *venture*. She's only done the minimal amount of paperwork and trademark protection to stay above water. She's a candymaker, not a businesswoman. I took that into consideration."

*And I really wanted to avoid her since we've slept together. Mixing business with pleasure. What was I thinking?*

He sighed heavily. "You did. And what color are her eyes?"

She stammered an answer that sounded like six different languages spoken at once.

"I thought so," he said.

She sighed. "Do I have any leverage here? What can I do?"

"Have you spoken with her?"

She bit her lip grateful that he couldn't see her cheeks reddening. "No, Valerie's handled the account."

"Well, I'd say it's time for you to step in. Take control and put aside whatever personal issues you had with this woman. I assume it ended poorly." She winced at his succinct assessment. "Then you should call her and if that doesn't work, get your ass on a plane and get up there. Beg her to do this or you'll have to live with the consequences. And promise your old Uncle Harry that until I drop dead and you hire a younger attorney with a better heart you'll keep your personal and professional lives separate."

He hung up before she could respond. She buried her head in her hands and stared at the desk. She flipped through the financial report and shuddered at the bolded six-figure number at the bottom of the page—the hit O'Grady would take if Purple disappeared.

She went outside for another cigarette with her BlackBerry in hand. She dialed without thinking, an image of their dinner and stroll down Commercial Street filling her head. Conversation was easy between them. It should be easy again.

She picked up on the first ring and said, "I was wondering when you'd call."

"Well, hello to you, too."

"I'm sorry it's not going to work out."

"Can you explain that to me?"

"Not really except that it's not what I envisioned."

"You don't like the PR campaign?"

"No, it's fine."

She grasped for possible explanations and suddenly regretted calling without a plan. The conversation slid down her throat like gravel.

"Are you worried about the production? We'll make sure the candy is the highest quality."

"No, I trust you."

"Rafi, please help me understand. Why can't we do business together?"

No quick, clipped answer followed her question, and Dani could hear noise in the background. She was obviously in her tiny candy making plant—the machines talked behind her in a language Dani understood perfectly.

"We just can't."

It was such a simplistic answer, but in the three words Dani understood that the lines between professional and personal relationships had blurred and she was choosing a side.

"Why did you tell Valerie that we'd had a misunderstanding?"

"Because we did and I can't stop thinking about it." She lowered her voice as if others might be listening. "I don't jump into bed with just anyone. I've only had one other lover since my girlfriend died so when we . . . when you *cried* . . . "

Dani flipped to that moment of vulnerability—the *only* moment she'd ever exposed herself to any lover except Petra, who'd seen nothing *but* her vulnerabilities. No wonder she was alone.

"Then you left and never called and handed me off to Valerie."

"Why wouldn't I? You told Liam that sex was a part of our business."

"That's not what I said," she argued.

"Yes, Rafi, it was."

She took a deep breath. "I was scared and confused, but I told you I wanted you to stay. Then later I realized you were right. We shouldn't mix business with pleasure—"

"And we'll never have sex again," Dani said tersely.

"It's not that simple, Dani, and you know it too. I can hear it in your voice and that's why you've avoided me."

Frustrated, she slammed her fist onto the desk and said nothing.

"Goodbye, Dani," Rafi said before the line went dead.

# Chapter Fourteen

When Dani thought of Christmas she always thought of an O'Grady Coconut Dream, a three-layered candy with a chocolate mousse center and a dark chocolate shell sprinkled with a coconut covering. It was one of those candies where she experienced one decadent flavor at a time, and the Christmas season—the most lucrative season—was a three-layered treat. She lived for the extra profit that kick-started the next calendar year, the positive PR the charitable donations gleaned and the general goodwill she experienced from the swell of school groups that filled the factory during the first two weeks of December.

But this year was different. She couldn't enjoy the Coconut Dream because she was surrounded by problems, most notably the year-end financials. Usually she savored the report which showed a nice five-digit profit margin that lowered her stress level, and O'Grady enjoyed a spike in positive reviews that always surfaced in the food columns just as people began their holiday shopping. And it didn't hurt that she had slept with a few of the more noted foodies. While the PR and the school groups continued to brighten the holiday season, the bottom line was sobering.

Thanks to Olivia's claim for half of the company and the loss of Rafi's contract, the gain for O'Grady was barely noticeable, and she would have to decide whether to forego Christmas bonuses, which would telegraph the company's problems to her employees, or she'd dig into her own pocket for the significant lump of cash that would ensure they all had a Merry Christmas and remained ignorant of O'Grady financial woes.

As she sat in the dark factory at two a.m. she'd already decided what she would do. She'd give them the bonuses, which is exactly what her father would've wanted. It was December 15, and they were expecting their extra checks in two days. It would be a larger hit to her savings but she didn't care. The company and Liam were all she had. Keeping her employees happy was the key to her happiness.

She enjoyed the plant at night. It was silent energy. Although it was painfully quiet she felt the pulse of the previous day—Gus's movements as he stirred the chocolate, baked the confections and sprinkled the toppings over the thousands of candies that snaked across the conveyor belts. She listened to the hum of the radiator and the noise of the street outside. Sitting in the dark was therapeutic. The moon's shadow outlined the important equipment that ensured her livelihood, and she breathed in the heady aroma of chocolate and sugar that was ever present.

She was proud of what she'd made and despite the poor showing on the financial statement, she knew she'd bounce back. Everything was incidental and nothing was forever. Not the bad financial. Not her company. Not Gus. Not Liam. Not her.

She bowed her head and thought of her father with Cruz. Olivia had spared her the pain of looking at any photos showing them together for Dani would have compared his familiar pleasant smile to whatever expression covered his face when he was with Cruz in Provincetown. She imagined it was exhilaration, joy—love. She wondered how often he thought of Cruz when he'd been with their family, wishing he was in Provincetown with her instead. She imagined breaking up with her had been devastating. Her father often looked distracted whenever he conversed with her mother, and Dani had always assumed he was preoccupied with work. What else could there have been?

She glanced around the darkness trying to feel his presence. She wished he were there because she desperately wanted to talk to him. She wanted to know what it was like to love someone. They'd never been close since he worked constantly and she was at boarding school, but there was a mutual respect that flooded their hugs and conversations whenever she came home for holidays or summers. She suspected that he knew she was gay but he never asked. She shook her head, angry with herself for missing an opportunity. *You could've helped me so much, Daddy.*

Her new therapist, whom she'd *nearly* fired during the third session, suggested that she was abused by Petra. She'd declared Dani a victim of domestic violence and wanted to document her story for a clinical paper but Dani had balked. She was not a victim. Yet even as she said the words she reflexively rubbed her upper arms and thought of the tattoos that grew more invisible with each visit to Dr. Hauser. The Arabic symbol, *Birds of Freedom* and even *Epiphany*, which had been so resistant to the laser, were nearly gone. She had to stare into the mirror to see their outlines, and a stranger wouldn't notice them at all.

It would still take several months and many more treatments for the colorful tats to be removed and *Loose Heart*, the purple and black brand over her breast, would be an ongoing reminder of how much she gave to Petra. She demanded that Dr. Hauser end each session by dragging the pulsing laser over what remained of the blue and black blob, which was still a lot. And it hurt like hell. She always needed a few minutes to compose herself before she left the office to ensure that the cabbie who drove her home or Ernie her doorman didn't inquire about her welfare each time they saw her red eyes.

Her hand touched her breast automatically and she flinched, thinking about the laser and her next treatment, which was scheduled for Christmas Eve. Afterward she'd decided to treat herself to a spa day. Then she'd spend Christmas with Liam who had assumed the role of backup therapist, constantly talking with her about the past, an agreement they'd made after the fight in Provincetown. He now knew far too much about her personal life, more than any child should know, but the revelations were a tradeoff for his understanding and continued presence in her life. And she was willing to pay the price. He'd started dating someone not long after the annulment, but all he would say was that it was too soon to tell. Yet he looked entirely smitten, and she couldn't pry the truth out of him.

She still didn't feel in control of her life and it sucked. That would be her next project with her therapist—what to do—if there was anything. *What if this is it? What if this is as good as it gets?*

"Then I should just shut the fuck up," she said out loud, thinking how blasphemous she sounded by swearing in a candy factory. "I own a company. I have a wonderful son. I just need to be happy. I just need to be happy."

She decided to say her new mantra fifty more times before she went home and tried to sleep.


"She's here again," Ray announced.

Dani looked up from her desk and saw Cat waiting at Ray's desk, simultaneously petting Sanford and Spike who grinned from ear to ear.

"Tell her I'm busy," she murmured.

"I've told her that the last three times she's come by. I sound like a broken record. Besides she can see you aren't *that* busy," Ray said. "That's what you get for having an office with no damn walls."

She motioned for Cat and left them alone. Cat plopped into one of the chairs and dangled her long legs over the side. She was beautiful in a red cable-knit sweater, black jeans and a beret. Her hair curled about her face and she could easily win a part in a shampoo commercial.

She smiled with no hint of jealousy in her eyes. "I'm sorry for behaving like a complete ass."

Dani nodded. "Apology accepted. You look different," she added.

"I do? How?"

"You don't look so . . . predatory."

Cat laughed. "That would be because I'm seeing someone special."

She offered a blithe smile. *God, to be this young again.* "I hope it works out."

"Me too. He's good for me."

"*He?*"

She swung around and planted her elbows on Dani's desk. "I'm dating Liam."

Dani nearly fell out of her chair. "What?"

She shrugged and looked embarrassed. "I felt really bad about what happened that morning and how I'd treated him. He'd told me he worked at the VA so I looked him up and took him to lunch. It lasted five hours. I guess that was a sign." She smiled and her brown eyes were the color of caramel. "So what do you think?"

"I'm not sure," she said honestly.

Cat nodded. "Given everything that happened between us, I think that's a fair answer." She sat up straight and added, "I've quit smoking."

She nodded her approval. "Good for you. I'll give it up again eventually." She wagged a finger at her. "It's your fault that I started after so many years."

Cat flicked a lint ball from her sweater and blushed. "I know and I'm sorry about that. It was a very confusing time."

"Excuse me? A confusing time?" She couldn't believe what she was hearing. When Cat looked away and played with her hair, she said, "Cat? Please don't tell me your mother was right."

"Fine, I won't tell you."

She moaned and put her head on her desk. "After all that?

You're not gay?"

"I was never gay," she corrected. "I always said that I was bisexual and I still am, I suppose. It's just that your son has a very distinct effect on me. He's surprised me. I've surprised myself. I didn't realize how much I could enjoy—"

"Do *not* extol my son's sexual prowess. I'll evaporate right here and now."

"It's not just about sex," she said.

"No, no. I didn't want to know you were *having* sex. I was imagining you holding hands and kissing each other on the cheek."

She laughed. "Fat chance. Not with Liam . . . " When Dani put her hands up like a wall, Cat stopped herself. "Sorry. Um, I should thank you for raising such a caring, smart and respectful man. He really makes me think—about everything. Are you sure he's only twenty-five?" she asked as an afterthought.

She smiled at her accurate assessment of him. "He's an old soul but you are too. Both of you have been through a lot, you actually more than him, but it's made you worldly. Maybe that's the attraction."

"Maybe."

They gazed at each other, and for the first time it didn't feel weird. She only saw a confident, attractive young woman before her, not a conquest. While she doubted she'd ever fantasize about her amazing body again, it was easy to picture Liam with her. And she was okay with it. Somehow she could separate their wildly passionate affair from the budding relationship between this young grad student and her son.

"So is this serious?" she asked.

Cat laughed again. "God, you sound like my mother."

"I am *his* mother."

She nodded reverently. "We'll see. We're going slowly. Between his annulment and my divided sexuality it seems wise to be cautious."

"Good choice," she said. She motioned to the fire escape. "So, will you come out and indulge me since you're responsible for my return to this terrible habit?"

They went out on the fire escape and Cat watched her smoke. She was jealous of youth. Everything was so easy, so malleable and susceptible to change. *Want to date a man instead of a woman? Go for it! Take up smoking? Do it! Give up smoking? No problem!*

Such unhinged flexibility was anathema to her profession. She counted on loyalty and consistency from her customers. Each time they stopped at the gas station or the grocery store she needed them to grab their favorite candy. Her sales and production departments depended on those faithful numbers.

"Olivia asked me to deliver a message," Cat said interrupting her thoughts.

At the mention of her half-sister she pictured a car running into a wall and flinched. "What would that be?"

"It's nothing bad. She wanted to know if you and Liam wanted to join us for Christmas."

Sensing this was a rhetorical request, she asked, "What does Liam want to do?"

She grinned. "He wants whatever you want. We're not trying to break up a tradition, but we had hoped to spend the holiday together. So this way you and I both get to spend it with him."

She appreciated the consideration. It was more than Cassidy ever would've given her. He was a prize to be won and her jiggling boobs and fictional bun in the oven easily trumped Dani's wishes. Fortunately, she'd been a liar and a snake, but Dani knew that sharing him was inevitable. At least if it was with Cat it would be equitable.

"That sounds very nice. Tell your mother we accept."

The plane ride to Provincetown this time was quite different from Cat and Dani's previous mile-high sexual encounter. While they all enjoyed Portuguese Daisies, which had become Dani's new favorite drink, the three of them spent the whole flight laughing at Cat's stories about people in her drawing class and Liam's characterizations of his most interesting patients.

She sat quietly and watched the exchange. *They genuinely care for each other. I feel like I'm watching a Lifetime movie. They'll probably think I'm an idiot if I start to cry.*

She balanced her emotions and thought of Rafi. She doubted she'd see her, and she felt relieved and disappointed all at once. During the business negotiations she'd always pictured a point in the future when they would meet again, maybe at the grand unveiling of the Purple line. Even though she'd handed Valerie the account, she'd always assumed there would be another moment when she'd gaze into those rich chocolate eyes and at least fantasize about kissing those luscious lips that were a candy all their own. And by then the tattoos would be gone. Perhaps that was what she'd been waiting for—to be free of Petra.

Her session that day with Dr. Hauser had gone longer at her request. The bright colors of *The Cleansing* were now muted hues and Petra's name was almost completely erased from her belly as was the rest of *The Flowering*. Even *Loose Heart* was starting to look more like an oversized mole than a tattoo. Her next lover wouldn't ask about Petra or point and stare. She smiled at the thought of being in control.

The early afternoon landing into Provincetown was smooth and she could already feel the cold, clean New England air. She ignored Liam and Cat's lovey-dovey cooing and gazed out the window as their car traveled to the B and B. She'd never been to Provincetown in the winter. The fresh snow blanketed the earth in perfect white just like an O'Grady cream. It was divine, and she never thought of winter in the city that way. If she was stuck traipsing up Fifth Avenue the sooty snow was something to endure, not enjoy. But as the car meandered along the highway between the rows of beautiful trees, she thought each mile could be a snapshot for a different Christmas card.

Cat insisted they travel down Commercial Street to see the festive decorations on display. Many of the shops were closed for winter, but there seemed to be just as many that were open. She especially enjoyed the huge Christmas tree in front of the Lobster

Pot, which was covered in lobsters and pots. They turned off toward the inn a block before they passed Doces, but she noticed the glowing neon sign against the dark storefront. She craned her neck as they made the turn remembering Madame Nougat and her enormous laugh.

"We need to go to Purple tomorrow," Cat said to Liam.

"What's Purple?" he asked.

"Do *not* answer that question in my presence," she said tersely.

They whispered and giggled like teenagers while she gazed out the window until they arrived at the B and B.

Olivia greeted them with great warmth and hospitality, reserving her longest hug for Dani.

"I'm glad to see you," she said, and Dani knew she meant it.

They spent the next hour chatting and imbibing Portuguese Daisies. Her brain was fully lubricated after her fifth Daisy and regardless of how many times she glanced at the beautiful portrait of Cruz Santos, she felt nothing but a peacefulness that she attributed to good liquor and the contagious happiness of the holiday. Then her BlackBerry vibrated, and she excused herself to the patio. It was Harry.

"Merry Christmas, Harry."

"I won't keep you," he said immediately, obviously hearing the impatience in her voice. She was actually enjoying her alcohol and the company, which was a pleasant surprise.

"You're in Provincetown with Olivia, right?" he asked.

"Uh-huh. We've had a significant development. Liam is dating Olivia's adoptive daughter Cat. So yes, we're here."

He paused, obviously pondering the situation. "Hmm. Very interesting. Well, since you're there you might want to ask her why in the hell she still hasn't signed the papers. I've got a lot of work to do to put this together correctly and she's holding everything up. Have her sign and bring them back to New York, okay? At least save us the postage."

She agreed and stumbled back inside. *These Daisies are good!*

Eventually they moved to dinner, a combination of American and Portuguese favorites. She hadn't even noticed the formal dining room on her previous visit, and Olivia readily admitted that she didn't use it for clients, only her personal friends.

"You've set a beautiful table," Dani commented, noting the lovely crystal and china settings. It looked like something out of Martha Stewart's magazine.

Olivia beamed with pride and nodded as they took their seats and passed the variety of bowls filled with readily identifiable foods such as green beans and mashed potatoes and those Dani couldn't name but happily earned a place on her plate. She knew she'd be in trouble if she forgot to deliver Harry's message and since Cat and Liam were engaged in their own private conversation, she turned to Olivia.

"My attorney wants to know why you haven't signed the documents. He needs to put everything in order. Is there a problem?"

Olivia passed the green beans to Liam and smiled. "You know, I've heard from others that having a little sister is a general pain in the ass. They take your stuff, they make ridiculous demands and they get you in trouble with Mom and Dad. Have you ever heard that?"

She had no idea where the conversation was headed, but she found her use of metaphor amusing. "Yes, some of my friends have definitely struggled with their siblings."

"I think I'm making up for lost time."

"What do you mean?"

"I'm not signing the papers. I don't want half the company."

"What? But I thought—"

She set down her fork and wiped her mouth. "It's not right. First, you actually kept your end of the deal. It took a little longer than I expected, and it certainly hasn't turned out how I expected but look at them."

They both glanced at Cat and Liam who were sharing a little kiss between courses.

She was stunned. She'd resigned herself to having a sister and a partner. She'd met with Harry and her financial planner, who'd retooled her entire portfolio based on the loss. Now she was learning it was a total waste of time. In her life, time was an expensive truffle that couldn't be squandered or spit into the trash.

"Shit, Olivia, what are you saying?" Her voice caught Liam and Cat's attention.

"I'm saying that I've reconsidered."

Liam clearly sensed her irritation and took her hand. "Mom, isn't it wonderful that Olivia's being so generous?"

She slowly looked from him to Cat, who wore a knowing smile. When she leaned over and kissed him on the cheek, Dani knew it was for her benefit. Cat had made her choice. She'd picked him over any other man *or* woman, and Olivia would never again put her in such a ridiculous position. The least she could do was be gracious.

"Thank you, Olivia."

"I really am sorry for creating such a mess. But I do have one favor. I'd like to live in the Florida condo for half of the year. I'm tired of the winters here. Would you be okay with that?"

*How can I say no?* "Of course."

After dinner they drank brandy, and Dani hardly noticed when the doorbell rang as she was laughing hysterically at something Cat was saying. *I'm drunk. I just know it.*

When she glanced toward the hallway all she saw was the hair and she instantly flew out of her seat and headed for the French doors, spilling her brandy in the process.

Since it wasn't tourist season, the sunroom wasn't in use. The deadbolt was engaged and pulling on the knob did nothing. She turned around expecting to go through the tiny panes with Shaylalynn's body on top of her, but that would be impossible for Olivia stood between Shaylalynn and Joelle, their arms entwined. Shaylalynn's expression was fluid and her eyes watery. *I think she's been drinking too.*

It was Olivia who spoke first. "Dani, I invited Shayla and

Joelle over for dessert. We had a nice chat last week about forgiveness and making amends. I think she's ready to let the past go, aren't you, Shayla?"

Shaylalynn remained mute, her expression hard until Joelle reached around Olivia and poked her shoulder. "Uh, yeah. I'm ready."

"What about you, Dani. Are you ready to let this go?"

She nodded. "Absolutely. Shaylalynn, I'm sorry for hooking up with Joelle four years ago. We were drunk and not making good decisions."

Joelle's face was beet red, and Dani decided not to include a few details from that evening—such as Joelle pretending she was single and flashing her boobs at Dani on the dance floor. She stuck her hand out and Olivia released Shaylalynn's right arm so she could meet the handshake. Dani had a momentary vision of her breaking her forearm in half, but her handshake was limp.

"This is just wonderful," Olivia observed in her most effusive voice. Then she put her arms around them. In a voice that conveyed her power as a selectman and reminded Dani of her own CEO voice, she said, "Ladies, this matter is concluded. There will be no further scenes, outburst or vandalism. Am I clear?"

Shaylalynn glared at Dani and Olivia caught it. "I mean it, Shayla. I'll close your bar and don't think I can't."

Shayla's eyes widened and she nodded.

Olivia sighed. "I'm so grateful that we could resolve this on Christmas. Now let's have some dessert."


Dani was stuffed from the fine dinner and dessert, and coupled with the Portuguese Daisies, wine and brandy she was definitely drunk. She would soon fall asleep in front of everyone—probably on Shayla's shoulder if she was unlucky. Shaylalynn had insisted she call her Shayla now that they were past *the incident*. In fact, Shayla had invited her to the New Year's Eve party at Women's Work and promised her some exceptional action.

Feeling Liam's eyes on her she politely declined.

"I'm going to take a little walk," she announced as she put on her coat.

Liam extricated himself from Cat's embrace and started to stand. "Do you want some company?"

She waved him down and Cat smiled appreciatively. "Stay with your girlfriend," she said.

She stood on the stoop and let the crisp air purify her lungs, invade her nostrils and chill every inch of her face. She closed her eyes and listened to the silence. Bradford Street was empty, many of the inns closed for the winter, their owners vacationing in warmer climates as Olivia desired. She saw the amber glow of a few lights, but it was six o'clock on Christmas and darkness was settling over Provincetown.

They were staying the night and Dani had prepared a bag. Due to her inebriated state and the coming darkness she was happy to oblige. *I never thought I'd get another night at the Fairbanks Inn.* She chuckled as she hustled down Gosnold and emerged on Commercial, which was much busier than Bradford.

The restaurants accommodated those who wanted to make merry without the hassle of cooking or dirty dishes. A few stores like Adams' stayed open to make a quick buck on the couple who needed batteries for their new vibrator or forgot coffee to go with the dessert. She trudged through the snow enjoying the prickly cold and thinking about candy and profits.

It was the one candy sensation she'd never tried—frozen confections. She'd always wanted to make O'Grady chocolate bars or O'Grady pops, combining the company's trademark flavors with ice. There was something wonderful about cold treats particularly in the summer. But she'd never tried it mainly because it created extra costs and anything that could melt was a risky business proposition. *Maybe next year I'll go for it. Now that Olivia is stepping aside.*

The Doces light illuminated much of the block. She peered through the dark windows comforted by the beautiful arrays of candies. She withdrew the envelope from her pocket and stared at it.

Before Dani had left New York she'd written a note to Rafi on the blank greeting card with the cover that looked like a street in Venice. She'd praised her candy making skills and added that despite the collapse of their business plans, meeting her was a *treat*. She had cringed when she reread that sentence and almost threw the note into the trash but thought better of it. It was an old industry joke as well as a cliché.

Now she hesitated, remembering a summer during childhood when a box of cherry popsicles was left out on the counter for over an hour. She'd come upon them and was crushed to find her tasty treat seeping through the seams of the box. She tried to put them back in the freezer but it was too late. They were past the point of no return. Perhaps she and Rafi were as well, but Dani hated leaving a mess.

She didn't mind dealing with problems and headaches, but there needed to be favorable resolutions whenever possible. Her father had taught her the old adage about burned bridges was true and until a business rival died, he or she could potentially be an ally years later. *And now I actually have a connection to P-town, possibly two if Cat and Liam stay together.*

She slipped the note through the mail slot and watched it tumble to the floor before heading back toward the inn, focusing on undoing Olivia's involvement in the company. It wasn't as simple as merely rewinding all of the steps, but fortunately Harry would know what to do.

She heard laughter when she stepped inside the foyer and was relieved to see that Shayla and Joelle had departed while she was gone. Only Liam, Cat and Olivia were curled up in front of the fire drinking hot toddies.

"Did you see Rafi?" Cat asked expectantly.

"No," she said simply, taking off her coat and hanging it on the hook.

She joined them for a drink and was consumed by the warmth of the fire and the potent alcohol. It suddenly occurred to her that she hadn't had a cigarette since their arrival nor did she crave one now. She was content listening to her gregarious son while his girlfriend and her pseudo-mother laughed in all the appropriate places at his stories. She was the first to excuse herself but not before each of them embraced her tightly. And she noticed Olivia's hug was the longest and both of them were almost tearful.

Once she'd locked herself in the lovely Room Two of the Captain's house, she took off her clothes and stared into the full-length mirror. While her gaze was automatically drawn to the vibrant colors of *Kismet*, the flattering bedroom light dulled the lingering shadows of the other tattoos. It was as if her skin was as pure as the day she met Petra. She turned slowly and caressed her arms and belly so unused to seeing *her flesh*. Only *Loose Heart* looked the same in the feeble light because Petra had meant for it to be permanent. According to Dr. Hauser it was extremely deep and difficult but he promised her it could be removed in time. *I have time. I'll wait.*

Her phone chimed announcing a text message. It was from The Candy Lady. She smiled as she read the message. *Thank you for the card. I enjoyed meeting you and I hope you had a good Christmas with Olivia. Treat—funny. LOL.*

She closed her phone, wondering if Rafi had watched her deliver the note from the building across the street. The idea pleased her and she smiled. *Another bridge salvaged. Dad would be pleased.*

# Chapter Fifteen

As Dani sat in the front pew of the Meeting House in Provincetown, she couldn't help but compare Liam's first wedding disaster to the lovely ceremony she witnessed now. She'd never been inside the Unitarian Meeting House until last night's rehearsal, but she felt uplifted by the beautiful white woodwork and long windows that caught the morning sun. It was a setting that mirrored the brilliance and joy of the occasion. While Trinity Cathedral was certainly majestic, the dark wood, stained glass and sobering visual historic reminders of early Christian history weren't conducive to happiness, at least not for her.

And his marriage to Cat was about their mutual happiness. Although they'd moved in together three months after that fateful Christmas where Dani and Shayla had reconciled, he'd waited another year to propose. *And I really like May weddings. It's not too hot and not too cold.*

She smiled as they exchanged vows, and she glanced at Olivia sitting on the other side of the aisle, dabbing her eyes with a tissue. Peck, her bartender and newly proclaimed boyfriend squeezed her shoulder.

Ray nudged her. "You're paying attention, right?" she asked. "This is just so damn beautiful," she sniffled. "Nothing like that circus last time."

Dani almost chuckled remembering how sick to her stomach she'd felt at Liam's last wedding. The wretched image of the broken Tilt-A-Whirl was replaced by a much more domestic scene, one that she'd actually stumbled upon a few weeks before—the two of them snuggling in a hammock in the small backyard of their Park Slope house, each reading a magazine related to their chosen profession. It had reminded her of the afternoon with Petra that inspired *Kismet*.

When the ceremony concluded and they'd greeted the guests in the receiving line, the wedding party took pictures and headed back to the Fairbanks Inn for the reception Olivia had organized. Shayla and Joelle gave her a huge hug with their gushing congratulations. All of the anger and memories of *the incident* were completely forgotten as evidenced by Shayla's constant e-mails and invitations to visit—all of which Dani had politely avoided.

As she passed through the Meeting House gates, she threw a glance up Commercial Street at the fire engine red building, wondering if Madame Nougat was entertaining.

Rafi had declined the invitation to the wedding, and Dani had felt a stab of disappointment. She'd spent the last year *in* therapy and *out* of strange beds. She hadn't taken a lover since Rafi and she was okay with that, particularly since she'd been terribly self-conscious of her body until Dr. Hauser had finished the removal. And she smiled when she thought of that morning, when Cat had embraced her as she admired her *sleeveless* dress.

"You look wonderful," Cat had said. Dani had anticipated a sarcastic comment regarding their behavior at Liam's last wedding but Cat only kissed her cheek and added, "I'm glad you're my mother-in-law," before rushing off to help a bridesmaid.

Olivia had employed all of her hospitality skills and created a lovely reception outside on the patio and in the garden. Cat and

Liam had insisted there would be none of the usual reception silliness. There wasn't even a toast, only wonderful conversation, dancing and laughter. Harry came by and gave her a kiss on the cheek.

"This is my kind of wedding. And judging by the gift you gave them, you obviously approve."

Dani smiled as they watched Liam twirl Cat across the makeshift dance floor. The Park Slope house had been her gift.

Once the party had crested she sat down next to Olivia and patted her arm. Both of them had been drinking significantly and their conversation quickly devolved into laughter. Their relationship had been like the first day on a cruise. It had taken time to get their "sea legs" but once they'd found a comfortable space, visiting and e-mailing was enjoyable. Dani realized Olivia possessed many of the fine qualities she admired in her father and once in a while she fantasized about his relationship with Cruz.

Lost in her thoughts she didn't noticed the young man standing in front of her wearing shorts and a Polo shirt.

"Excuse me, are you Dani O'Grady?" he asked politely.

"I am," she said dramatically and they both laughed again. "Please tell me you're not a process server."

They all laughed and he replied, "No, ma'am. I'm a pedi-cab driver. Could you come with me?"

She looked at him warily. The last time she'd gotten into a pedi-cab . . . *Rafi*. She shook her head. "I don't think so. This is my son's wedding reception."

He coughed and handed her a paper. She unfolded it and saw that it was a Doces bag. On it was written a single word—*Please*.

Olivia read over her shoulder. "You should go. Every time I see her she always asks about you."

She shrugged. She really didn't want to carry the past around with her. She said as much to Olivia who scoffed. "You were here for a *day*. How much history can you have? Go." Then she whispered, "Today is definitely the day to see an old flame. You look great, and I've already given your number out to a dozen lesbians."

She scowled as Olivia pushed her out of the chair. She followed the driver who helped her into the pedi-cab since her dress clung tightly to her curves, all of which had been greatly improved by her fascist trainer. Olivia was right. She'd never felt better in her whole life.

Instead of heading to Doces the driver ascended Bradford Street toward Rafi's factory. He dropped her outside the familiar door with the keypad and sped away. The door was locked so she stood there alone wondering if she was the victim of a cruel joke. A minute passed and she was about to walk away when it clicked opened and Rafi appeared, probing her body with her eyes.

"Wow," she said. "Wow."

A golf ball stuck in her throat as their eyes met. Rafi wore her standard attire of cargo shorts and an old yellow T-shirt. Her hair was still spiky short.

Dani offered a tentative smile. "Hi."

"Please come in."

She held the door open and led her through the plant to a sweet little kitchen that Dani hadn't seen before. While the appliances were state-of-the-art, the furnishings were circa 1950, and she admired the Formica dinette set with red vinyl chairs and black and white checkered tile. A small copper pot sat in the center of the table.

Rafi reached for a wooden spoon and stirred the contents which Dani easily identified as a sweet chocolate. When Rafi glanced at her she wore a mysterious smile.

"I invited you here for a test and your honest opinion."

"What are you making?"

"Chocolate," Rafi said sarcastically. "What else?"

She laughed and stared into the pot. Like a sommelier evaluating a wine, she could tell a lot about chocolate by using all of her senses to enjoy it.

"This smells divine and looks incredibly rich." She took the spoon from Rafi and stirred, surprised that it was actually quite thin.

"Is this a coating?" she asked.

Rafi grinned. "Sort of." Dani raised an eyebrow and she continued. "It's my own chocolate body paint."

"What?"

"It really came about because of public demand. Many of my Purple clients have asked why I don't carry my own line. They often complain about a lot of the other brands. The paint is too thick or it tastes terrible against the skin. So I decided to create one myself. And I wanted your opinion."

Dani stirred and tried to ignore the intoxicating smell coming from the pot and Rafi's nearness. Although they weren't touching, she sensed Rafi all around her and felt her hand around her waist. *Or am I just remembering the past?* She didn't dare look over her shoulder to see if Rafi really was embracing her. *Would I be shocked or elated?*

"So will you be my guinea pig?"

She flashed her gleaming teeth that reminded Dani of little marshmallows. "Sure," she managed to say, bringing the spoon to her lips. "It's delicious. Is that caramel?"

She nodded proudly. "I'm mixing several flavors together. You can eat your lover as your dessert. What do you think?"

"I think it's marvelous," she said, handing her the spoon and wondering if she was having a hot flash.

Rafi took the spoon to the sink and pulled an object from a drawer. She tapped it in her hand with a wicked grin. It was long and looked like a chopstick—a paintbrush. She swallowed hard.

"I'm glad you like the taste but that's not the real test with body paint."

"It's not? I wouldn't know," she said weakly.

Her hands seemed to be glued to the Formica and her feet were sunk in a vat of marshmallow cream. Rafi dipped the brush into the chocolate and painted the inside of her own forearm with a single stroke.

"The real test is the taste on the skin when the chocolate mixes with a person's natural flavor and, of course, sometimes sweat. Will you lick it off, please?"

Rafi's luscious lips and deep chocolate eyes were more

beautiful than Dani remembered. She was helpless. Starting at Rafi's elbow she lazily ran her tongue along the chocolate streak noting that the caramel flavor overwhelmed the natural saltiness of the skin which was exactly what a candy-addicted, erotic lover would want to taste as she devoured her partner.

Once Dani licked all of the paint away her taste buds fully enjoyed the experience as if she was savoring a Choco Caramel Delite. She suddenly blinked.

"Is this *your* chocolate or *my* chocolate?"

Rafi offered a slow smile. "It's a little bit of yours and a little bit of mine. It's us coming together," she whispered. She dipped the brush again and held it up. "May I?"

Dani nodded, too stunned to utter anything intelligible. Rafi slid the paintbrush down the side of her neck and into her exposed cleavage. She closed her eyes and lolled her head to the side when Rafi's tongue flicked against her collarbone and worked its way up. She played dirty and eventually nibbled on her earlobe.

"What are you doing?" Dani mumbled.

Instead of answering her question, Rafi's lips wandered between her breasts. She hadn't realized how much she'd missed a woman's touch—Rafi's touch—until this moment. She leaned back on the table and Rafi sighed in gratitude.

"I promise I won't get any chocolate on this beautiful dress," she said between licks.

Her lips remained in Dani's cleavage long after the body paint was gone. When she felt her zipper descend she laughed.

"You are so smooth," she purred. "But we should talk, don't you think?" Dani pushed her away gently, and they sat up and faced each other. "I don't understand why I'm here."

Rafi's gaze remained downcast. "I didn't mean for this to happen. I was trying to find just the right consistency and it wasn't working with my chocolate. I'm not sure why I thought to try an O'Grady Traditional but I did. And it was perfect."

When their eyes met Dani saw confusion and hopefulness. She wondered if Rafi realized that she felt the same. And as quickly as the feeling came it apparently passed. Rafi offered a businesslike expression and sat up straight.

"You still haven't told me why I'm here," Dani said again. "What do you want from me?"

"I don't know."

She felt her heart sinking toward disappointment. "Permission to use my chocolate in your paint? You have it. I'll have my attorney draw up a usage fee agreement, but I'd appreciate it if you didn't tell anyone that O'Grady was involved. As you know we're not in the market for adult candy, and I have some employees who'd like to keep it that way." She turned her back to Rafi. "Could you zip me up, please?"

She stared at the opposite wall waiting until she heard the slow ascent of the zipper. Rafi said nothing, and Dani worked hard to temper all of the conflicting emotions that hit her at once. She worried that at any moment she might yell, cry, laugh or cackle as she pulled Rafi into a burning kiss. But her acute business sense pummeled her emotions, and she easily slid away from the table and collected her purse from a nearby chair. She adjusted her dress and pulled the combs from her hair since Rafi had dislodged them significantly with all of her fondling and kissing.

With no mirror she asked the obvious question. "Do I look presentable?"

Rafi nodded, busying herself with the copper pot. Dani lingered a while longer, fumbling with her purse, but it became apparent there was no way they could bridge their professional and personal lives.

An image of Liam on the log ride at Disney World came to mind. Almost the entire ride was spent inside a log as it languidly twisted and turned in the flume while "Zippity Doo Dah" played at full blast, and little forest animals sang and danced. As a seven-year-old, he had been mesmerized by the creatures and started to bop in the log. There was no indication that anything remotely surprising would happen—except for the puddle of water at Dani's feet. Of course, he never noticed. He was far too busy pointing and laughing at the mechanical animals.

Then they reached the top and as the music swelled, the log jutted through an opening at the top of the mountain. And at that moment he realized a cruel joke had been played on him. He looked down and saw he was no longer at the *bottom* of the mountain. Hundreds of bystanders lingered below, their cameras ready for the inevitable. And when his shriek echoed inside the mountain, she realized she'd made a terrible mistake subjecting him to such an unpredictable twist of fate—something she would never do again—and they plunged.

She felt she was plunging into the water now. Just as he had never wanted to return to Disney World she had no desire to set foot in Provincetown again. Rafi was too cruel. By summoning her, Rafi had revived her hope that a connection could exist between them, seducing her with kisses and body paint only to push her away suddenly—was unbearable. It was like denying the children who visited the factory a chocolate sample after their other senses had been teased mercilessly.

She focused on the door and moved swiftly.

"Dani, wait!"

Rafi's voice was commanding and desperate. She automatically turned—just as the entire pot of warm chocolate spilled over her head.

She gasped as dark tendrils oozed into her mouth and onto her dress. *Holy shit! My dress! I paid three thousand dollars for this dress!*

Rafi laughed like Madame Nougat. Dani sputtered an angry protest, but the chocolate coating tormented her tongue and prevented an intelligent comment.

She could hardly see anything through the chocolate veil but Rafi moved against her, joining their bodies, their lips, and she welcomed the wet and sticky embrace.

# Chapter Sixteen

The Lincoln Town Car rolled to a stop at Rafi's back door, and Dani grabbed her overnight bag before waving goodbye to her driver. She pulled her coat around her to stave off the December wind and punched in the key code too fast and had to repeat it.

"C'mon," she murmured already feeling the cold.

The lock clicked and the door popped open an inch. She hurried inside and climbed the steps to Rafi's office. Elvis sat at a desk processing online orders for Purple. When he saw her he jumped up and gave her a hug and a kiss.

"Hey, darlin'. Rafi's over at Purple but she said to tell you she'd be back in just a few minutes. That body paint is selling like crazy," he said wide-eyed. "We're making a fortune."

"I like fortunes," she replied.

He returned to his work, and she curled up on the couch with her BlackBerry to answer her e-mails while she waited. She laughed at the picture Olivia had sent—her on the beach sipping a Mai Tai and wearing shorts and a T-shirt. She replied quickly and hurried through the business issues that needed her attention, many of which focused on her most important business transaction—making Doces and Purple subsidiaries of O'Grady.

Despite Gus's objections and Rafi's initial concern, she convinced both of them that it was a sound and lucrative venture. It didn't hurt that she also gave Gus a sizeable bonus that allowed him to purchase a retirement home in Arizona, where he and his wife intended to go at the end of the year. She secretly hoped Rafi would take his place as the top candymaker, but she knew it would be difficult to persuade her to move from quaint Provincetown to chaotic New York.

Twenty minutes later Elvis excused himself and soon she heard Rafi's footsteps on the stairs. She stood and fluffed her hair. When Rafi saw her, they fell into each other's arms.

"God, I've missed you," Rafi said between kisses.

She moaned her agreement as Rafi's lips explored along her collarbone while she stroked her buttocks and back. *I love her back. It's so sexy.* They continued for several minutes with their reunion ritual, the term she'd coined after her third trip up to P-town. They'd learned that talking, walking and eating—any activity—couldn't occur until they'd satisfied the lust that built up between visits. Their ritual satiated their appetites long enough for them to conduct business or visit other people like Rafi's mother, Shayla or Olivia until they could finally retreat to Rafi's bed.

The kissing and fondling eventually slowed to a tight embrace. "I have wonderful news," Dani announced. "Cat's pregnant!"

Rafi grinned. "Congratulations, sweetheart. Can I call you Grandma?"

She narrowed her eyes. "You better not. I'm not even fifty. Now show me the figures. Elvis says we're doing great."

"We are," she said as they moved into business mode.

They spent another hour analyzing profit margins,

production costs and the details of the upcoming merger. Rafi bored quickly with the business minutiae. She was all about the candy.

They had a wonderful dinner at the Mews Café before braving the cold for the walk back to her condo. They huddled together, smiling and laughing as they shared the little details of their lives since their last Skype conversation the day before.

Dani had realized that their original twice-a-week conversations now occurred daily. *I can't live without her.*

She stopped walking and turned to her. "Kiss me." Rafi obliged, and she melted at their connection. "I've missed you terribly, more than ever."

And it was true. Skype and e-mail wasn't the same. *I see her, I listen to her, but I want to touch her, smell her and best of all, I want to taste her.*

Even the beautiful notes they regularly exchanged through snail mail weren't enough. Only the tenderness of Rafi's embrace satisfied her. It was like eating a Peanut Cluster when she really wanted a Choco Delite. And Rafi was an entire O'Grady Chocolate Tower.

"I want more," she said suddenly through the gusting wind. "Move to New York."

Rafi didn't look surprised. She didn't flinch or scowl. She stared with her trademark enigmatic expression that Dani still couldn't read.

"Please?" she added.

"I'm thinking about it," she said. "Long-distance relationships suck."

"I'd teach you how to like New York."

"Maybe I could practice by standing in a small closet for an hour with six people," she said wryly. She glanced at the sky. "We need to hurry back to the condo. The weather's getting worse. And I have a surprise for you."

They walked the last tenth of a mile motivated by the increasingly harsh weather and the promise of great sex. She made a fire while Rafi poured port and prepared a tray of chocolates, their favorite form of foreplay.

When their bodies were warmed by the fire and their passion ablaze from the kisses, Rafi pulled off her T-shirt and Dani stared at the heart drawn with strawberry shortcake body paint that covered her chest. In the middle were the words *I love you*.

"Now that's my kind of tattoo," she said.

In seconds they had retreated to her bed. As was her usual custom, she kissed *Kismet* first, believing that Dani had kept the tattoo as much for her as for herself. They held each other until Dani's tongue slipped between her breasts and enjoyed the taste of strawberry and her soft moans. Determined to take charge, Rafi flipped her on her back wearing a huge smile. At first only their lips touched and she thought she'd go mad, but eventually Rafi lowered herself until all their parts fit together perfectly.

Rafi savored her lovely morsels with an expertise and care possessed exclusively by wine connoisseurs, gourmands and candymakers, people for whom taste is the most acute and appreciated of the senses.

"You're mine," she whispered.

Dani froze and Rafi looked into her eyes, bewildered and hurt.

"What?"

"I'm not yours," Dani said emphatically. "I don't belong to anyone but me."

BLIND BET by Tracey Richardson. The stakes are high when Ellen Turcotte and Courtney Langford meet at the blackjack tables. Lady Luck has been smiling on Courtney but Ellen is a wild card she may not be able to handle.
978-1-59493-211-3    $14.95

JUKEBOX by Gina Daggett. Debutantes in love. With each other. Two young women chafe at the constraints of parents and society with a friendship that could be more, if they can break free. Gina Daggett is best known as "Lipstick" of the columnist duo Lipstick & Dipstick.    978-1-59493-212-0    $14.95

SHADOW POINT by Amy Briant. Madison McPeake has just been not-quite fired, told her brother is dead and discovered she has to pick up a five-year-old niece she's never met. After she makes it to Shadow Point it seems like someone—or something—doesn't want her to leave. Romance sizzles in this ghost story from Amy Briant.    978-1-59493-216-8    $14.95

DEVIL'S ROCK by Gerri Hill. Deputy Andrea Sullivan and Agent Cameron Ross vow to bring a killer to justice. The killer has other plans. Gerri Hill pens another intriguing blend of mystery and romance in this page-turning thriller.
978-1-59493-218-2    $14.95

SOMETHING TO BELIEVE by Robbi McCoy. When Lauren and Cassie meet on a once-in-a-lifetime river journey through China their feelings are innocent...at first. Ten years later, nothing—and everything—has changed. From Golden Crown winner Robbi McCoy.    978-1-59493-214-4    $14.95

LEAVING L.A. by Kate Christie. Eleanor Chapin is on the way to the rest of her life when Tessa Flanagan offers her a lucrative summer job caring for Tessa's daughter Laya. It's only temporary and everyone expects Eleanor to be leaving L.A . . .    978-1-59493-221-2    $14.95

WILDFIRE by Lynn James. From the moment botanist Devon McKinney meets ranger Elaine Thomas the chemistry is undeniable. Sharing—and protecting—a mountain for the length of their short assignments leads to unexpected passion in this sizzling romance by newcomer Lynn James.
978-1-59493-191-8     $14.95

WEDDING BELL BLUES by Julia Watts. She'll do anything to save what's left of her family. Anything. It didn't seem like a bad plan . . . at first. Hailed by readers as Lammy-winner Julia Watts' funniest novel.
978-1-59493-199-4     $14.95

WHISPERS IN THE WIND by Frankie J. Jones. It began as a camping trip, then a simple hike. Dixon Hayes and Elizabeth Colter uncover an intriguing cave on their hike, changing their world, perhaps irrevocably.
978-1-59493-037-9     $14.95

ELENA UNDONE by Nicole Conn. The risks. The passion. The devastating choices. The ultimate rewards. Nicole Conn rocked the lesbian cinema world with *Claire of the Moon* and has rocked it again with *Elena Undone*. This is the book that tells it all . . .     978-1-59493-254-0     $14.95

FAÇADES by Alex Marcoux. Everything Anastasia ever wanted—she has it. Sidney is the woman who helped her get it. But keeping it will require a price— the unnamed passion that simmers between them.
978-1-59493-239-7     $14.95

HUNTING THE WITCH by Ellen Hart. The woman she loves—used to love—offers her help, and Jane Lawless finds it hard to say no. She needs TLC for recent injuries and who better than a doctor? But Julia's jittery demeanor awakens Jane's curiosity. And Jane has never been able to resist a mystery. Number 9 in series and Lammy-winner.     978-1-59493-206-9     $14.95

2ND FIDDLE by Kate Calloway. Cassidy James's first case left her with a broken heart. At least this new case is fighting the good fight, and she can throw all her passion and energy into it.     978-1-59493-200-7     $14.95

MAKING UP FOR LOST TIME by Karin Kallmaker. Take one Next Home Network Star and add one Little White Lie to equal mayhem in little Mendocino and a recipe for sizzling romance. This lighthearted, steamy story is a feast for the senses in a kitchen that is way too hot.
978-1-931513-61-6     $14.95

SUBSTITUTE FOR LOVE by Karin Kallmaker. No substitutes, ever again! But then Holly's heart, body and soul are captured by Reyna . . . Reyna with no last name and a secret life that hides a terrible bargain, one written in family blood.     978-1-931513-62-3     $14.95

DEADLY INTERSECTIONS by Ann Roberts. Everyone is lying, including her own father and her girlfriend. Leaving matters to the professionals is supposed to be easier! Third in series with PAID IN FULL and WHITE OFFERINGS.                                978-1-59493-224-3    $14.95

WHEN AN ECHO RETURNS by Linda Kay Silva. The bayou where Echo Branson found her sanity has been swept clean by a hurricane—or at least they thought. Then an evil washed up by the storm comes looking for them all, one-by-one. Second in series.                    978-1-59493-225-0    $14.95

LESSONS IN MURDER by Claire McNab. There's a corpse in the school with a neat hole in the head and a Black & Decker drill alongside. Which teacher should Inspector Carol Ashton suspect? Unfortunately, the alluring Sybil Quade is at the top of the list. First in this highly lauded series.
                                                 978-1-931513-65-4    $14.95

THE WILD ONE by Lyn Denison. Rachel Weston is busy keeping home and head together after the death of her husband. Her kids need her and what she doesn't need is the confusion that Quinn Farrelly creates in her body and heart.                                    978-0-9677753-4-0    $14.95

CALM BEFORE THE STORM by Peggy J. Herring. Colonel Marcel Robicheaux doesn't tell and so far no one official has asked, but the amorous pursuit by Jordan McGowen has her worried for both her career and her honor.                                    978-0-9677753-1-9    $14.95

THE GRASS WIDOW by Nanci Little. Aidan Blackstone is nineteen, unmarried and pregnant, and has no reason to think that the year 1876 won't be her last. Joss Bodett has lost her family but desperately clings to their land. A richly told story of frontier survival that picks up with the generation of women where Patience and Sarah left off.        978-1-59493-189-5    $12.95

SMOKEY O by Celia Cohen. Insult "Mac" MacDonnell and insult the entire Delaware Blue Diamond team. Smokey O'Neill has just insulted Mac, and then finds she's been traded to Delaware. The games are not limited to the baseball field!                                    978-1-59493-198-7    $12.95

WICKED GAMES by Ellen Hart. Never have mysteries and secrets been closer to home in this eighth installment of this award-winning lesbian mystery series. Jane Lawless's neighbors bring puzzles and peril—and that's just the beginning.                                978-1-59493-185-7    $14.95

NOT EVERY RIVER by Robbi McCoy. It's the hottest city in the U.S., and it's not just the weather that's heating up. For Kim and Randi are forced to question everything they thought they knew about themselves before they can risk their fiery hearts on the biggest gamble of all.

978-1-59493-182-6    $14.95

HOUSE OF CARDS by Nat Burns. Cards are played, but the game is gossip. Kaylen Strauder has never wanted it to be about her. But the time is fast-approaching when she must decide which she needs more: her community or Eda Byrne.    978-1-59493-203-8    $14.95

RETURN TO ISIS by Jean Stewart. The award-winning Isis sci-fi series features Jean Stewart's vision of a committed colony of women dedicated to preserving their way of life, even after the apocalypse. Mysteries have been forgotten, but survival depends on remembering. Book one in series.

978-1-59493-193-2    $12.95

1ST IMPRESSIONS by Kate Calloway. Rookie PI Cassidy James has her first case. Her investigation into the murder of Erica Trinidad's uncle isn't welcomed by the local sheriff, especially since the delicious, seductive Erica is their prime suspect. First in series. Author's augmented and expanded edition.

978-1-59493-192-5    $12.95

BEACON OF LOVE by Ann Roberts. Twenty-five years after their families put an end to a relationship that hadn't even begun, Stephanie returns to Oregon to find many things have changed . . . except her feelings for Paula.

978-1-59493-180-2    $14.95

ABOVE TEMPTATION by Karin Kallmaker. It's supposed to be like any other case, except this time they're chasing one of their own. As fraud investigators Tamara Sterling and Kip Barrett try to catch a thief, they realize they can have anything they want—except each other.    978-1-59493-179-6    $14.95

AN EMERGENCE OF GREEN by Katherine V. Forrest. Carolyn had no idea her new neighbor jumped the fence to enjoy her swimming pool. The discovery leads to choices she never anticipated in an intense, sensual story of discovery and risk, consequences and triumph. Originally released in 1986.

978-1-59493-217-5    $14.95

CRAZY FOR LOVING by Jaye Maiman. Officially hanging out her shingle as a private investigator, Robin Miller is getting her life on track. Just as Robin discovers it's hard to follow a dead man, she walks in. KT Bellflower, sultry and devastating . . . Lammy winner and second in series.

978-1-59493-195-6    $14.95

LOVE WAITS by Gerri Hill. The All-American girl and the love she left behind—it's been twenty years since Ashleigh and Gina parted, and now they're back to the place where nothing was simple and love didn't wait.
978-1-59493-186-4    $14.95

HANNAH FREE: THE BOOK by Claudia Allen. Based on the film festival hit movie starring Sharon Gless. Hannah's story is funny, scathing and witty as she navigates life with aplomb—but always comes home to Rachel. Thirty-two pages of color photographs plus bonus behind-the-scenes movie information.
978-1-59493-172-7    $19.95

END OF THE ROPE by Jackie Calhoun. Meg Klein has two enduring loves—horses and Nicky Hennessey. Nicky is there for her when she most needs help, but then an attractive vet throws Meg's carefully balanced world out of kilter.
978-1-59493-176-5    $14.95

THE LONG TRAIL by Penny Hayes. When schoolteacher Blanche Bartholomew and dance hall girl Teresa Stark meet their feelings are powerful—and completely forbidden—in Starcross Texas. In search of a safe future, they flee, daring to take a covered wagon across the forbidding prairie.
978-1-59493-196-3    $12.95

UP UP AND AWAY by Catherine Ennis. Sarah and Margaret have a video. The mob wants it. Flying for their lives, two women discover more than secrets.    978-1-59493-215-1    $12.95

CITY OF STRANGERS by Diana Rivers. A captive in a gilded cage, young Solene plots her escape, but the rulers of Hernorium have other plans for Solene—and her people. Breathless lesbian fantasy story also perfect for teen readers.    978-1-59493-183-3    $14.95

ROBBER'S WINE by Ellen Hart. Belle Dumont is the first dead of summer. Jane Lawless, Belle's old friend, suspects coldhearted murder. Lammy-winning seventh novel in critically acclaimed mystery series.
978-1-59493-184-0    $14.95

APPARITION ALLEY by Katherine V. Forrest. Kate Delafield has solved hundreds of cases, but the one that baffles her most is her own shooting. Book six in series.    978-1-883523-65-7    $14.95

STERLING ROAD BLUES by Ruth Perkinson. It was a simple declaration of love. But the entire state of Virginia wants to weigh in, leaving teachers Carrie Tomlinson and Audra Malone caught in the crossfire—and with love troubles of their own.    978-1-59493-187-1    $14.95

LILY OF THE TOWER by Elizabeth Hart. Agnes Headey, taking refuge from a storm at the Netherfield estate, stumbles into dark family secrets and something more... Meticulously researched historical romance.

978-1-59493-177-2 $14.95

LETTING GO by Ann O'Leary. Kelly has decided that luscious, successful Laura should be hers. For now. Laura might even be agreeable. But where does that leave Kate? 978-1-59493-194-9 $12.95

MURDER TAKES TO THE HILLS by Jessica Thomas. Renovations, shady business deals, a stalker—and it's not even tourist season yet for PI Alex Peres and her best four-legged pal Fargo. Sixth in this Provincetown-based series.

978-1-59493-178-9 $14.95

SOLSTICE by Kate Christie. It's Emily Mackenzie's last college summer and meeting her soccer idol Sam Delaney seems like a dream come true. But Sam's passion seems reserved for the field of play...

978-1-59493-175-8 $14.95

FORTY LOVE by Diana Simmonds. Lush, romantic story of love and tennis with two women playing to win the ultimate prize. Revised and updated author's edition. 978-1-59493-190-1 $14.95

I LEFT MY HEART by Jaye Maiman. The only women she ever loved is dead, and sleuth Robin Miller goes looking for answers. First book in Lammy-winning series. 978-1-59493-188-8 $14.95

TWO WEEKS IN AUGUST by Nat Burns. Her return to Chincoteague Island is a delight to Nina Christie until she gets her dose of Hazy Duncan's renown ill-humor. She's not going to let it bother her, though...

978-1-59493-173-4 $14.95